MIRROR
WAKES

By Catherine Webb

Mirror Dreams
Mirror Wakes

Coming soon . . .

Waywalkers

MIRROR WAKES

Catherine Webb

www.atombooks.co.uk

An *Atom* Book

First published in Great Britain by Atom 2003

A CIP catalogue record for this book
is available from the British Library.

ISBN 1 904233 09 0

Typeset in Cochin by M Rules
Printed and bound in Great Britain by
Bookmarque Ltd, Croydon, Surrey

Atom Books
An imprint of
Time Warner Books UK
Brettenham House
Lancaster Place
London WC2E 7EN

Contents

INTRODUCTION

Shadows and Sunlight

There is a place, just the other side of shadow, but you cannot see it, you cannot hear it, you cannot touch it. The harder you look, the less it is there. Only when you are not looking, when you lie asleep, does the shadow burn away and you can cross from your world into mine. Only then.

For those whose sleep is dreamless, there is the Void. Huge, eternal, silent, it is the empty space created by millions of humans on Earth dreaming of nothing. And from the Void, with a bit of luck and a lot of magic, a clever mage can draw forth whatever he can imagine, for the Void is made of pure possibility and there are no rules to it.

But for those who dream, there are the kingdoms of the Void. For the woman in Africa who dreams of flying, there is the huge kingdom of Skypoint. For the man in Asia who dreams of thunder and lightning, there is my own little kingdom of Stormpoint. For the man in Europe who dreams of his dead dog alive again, some-where, in some corner of the Void, that dog will indeed live. For it is by dreaming that humans change the physical shape of our world. If they dream it, so it exists.

Someone dreamt of me once, but she is gone and I cannot find her. Unlike most dreamers, ghostly as they drift through the Void, she found her dream and didn't wake up.

Unfortunately, there are a large number of people who have nightmares. And absolutely *whatever* you dream will come to pass in the Void. So I sit in Stormpoint, my kingdom of stable reality shaped from the Void by the will of my mind, with the Key – the power to control everything within its borders – safely inside me, and I watch. I watch while Haven, City of Dreams, glowers at Nightkeep, City of Nightmares, and I twiddle my thumbs and hope that one day, someone will come out of the Void running from nightmare, and in that process find a dream. For a dreamer, a human asleep, his mind detached from the mortal demands of flesh, is practically a God. It's the rules – dreamers can change the physical landscape of the Void simply by wishing it, for the Void responds to them. They travel at the speed of thought, and thought isn't above going from A to C without calling at B. But it is rare, rare indeed, for dreamers to find their dream, their paradise, within the Void – because dreamers are weak. They wake, they forget what they have seen, and it is all for nothing.

We don't forget, when we dream. As dreamers of the Void, so I dream of Earth, and I remember what I see. And I remember something else too, something that makes the never-ending battle between Haven and Nightkeep suddenly far more important. If by dreaming of nightmare a man's mind is filled with darkness and despair, and if by dreaming bright warm dreams a woman's mind is filled with light and joy, then the Void, and we, its inhabitants, affect the minds of Earth while they are asleep, and can cross the borders between worlds.

Dreamers affect the physical form of our world, we affect the mental shape of theirs. Who now the greater power holds?

ONE

Welcome, Dear Dreamer . . .

It began that morning when Lisana barged in on me uninvited. 'Kite,' she demanded, 'how would you like a job?'

It was early, and I'd just begun the slow journey from unconscious bliss to full awareness. She'd swept into the room in a trail of white dress and yanked the curtains back, letting in a blast of light that dispelled my mental fog with savage suddenness. In the royal city of Haven, capital of dreams, it seems decreed that the sunlight is always bright whether you wish it or not. During the few weeks I'd been there, for the coronation and the endless partying that went with it, the weather had started to make me homesick. More and more I missed my own, lesser realm of Stormpoint, the dream of storms, where as Warden I usually arrange for the day to lighten late and darken early.

'A job?!' I exclaimed, then remembered to add, 'your majesty.'

You may wonder why even a newly crowned queen – and, believe me, they don't come queenlier than Lisana – would enter anyone's room just like that. When the queen of dreams seeks an interview with Laenan Kite, mage of legend, you're entitled to expect a bit of flummery. For a start, you'd think we'd be in a throne room.

But Lisana is a woman of contradictions – not least because she never changes in wanting to impose her will. The only difference is how. Being abrupt with me, who'd made her queen in the first place, was her way of pretending to both of us that I'd do whatever she said. Besides, if you want to catch a guy off guard, not much beats barging in first thing when he's still dozing in his pyjamas. Lisana likes me best when I'm off guard.

'Why, yes! That's what I'm offering you,' she replied, as if I'd no right to be surprised. As if, indeed, in her time as a royal mistress jockeying for position at court, she hadn't had me fitted up on a treason charge. No wonder even she couldn't meet my eyes right now.

'Let me get this straight, ma'am. *You* are offering *me* a job?'

'Are you always like this first thing in the morning?' she demanded, with her usual tact and compassion.

With you, always, your majesty. 'What kind of job are we talking about?' I was tempted to drag out the discussion, just to watch her squirm.

But then she smiled, which wasn't good. Lisana has a whole range of smiles. There are the bright, sunny ones she uses on courtiers who are really pissing her off; the shy, sincere ones she uses to lure a stranger to her bed; the slow, calculating ones that spread across her face when she's seen a chink in an enemy's armour. This smile was pure evil. 'It's right down your road.'

I confess, I still dislike Lisana. Having risen all the way to the throne in several easy bounds, she's generally considered a 'good' queen, in the way that a triumphant warlord is regarded as a 'bringer of peace' instead of a victor of war. She's tall, blonde, wears white a lot and possesses such a blend of natural grace and stern resolve that most beholders' knees bend involuntarily.

But I know the real Lisana – the woman who shed not a tear over her royal lover's death, and who'd stick to any plan though the heavens themselves threaten their wrath. She's ruthless, cunning, ambitious – and, dreams above, a bloody good queen. It's a sad fact that the kind, gentle people of this world just aren't up to such responsibility, and those least deserving of rank and privilege, caring solely for their own status, will often use it most efficiently.

Yet Lisana was offering *me* a job!

I named my price.

'A salary?' she exclaimed, as if the idea had never crossed her mind. 'Surely you'll be honoured at the chance to do it for dreams, goodness and light!'

'No,' I told her. 'For money. And because the job sounds necessary and I don't have anything better to do.'

She'd sighed, and said, 'Oh, very well.'

So that's how I was to acquire the title of Liaison to the Silverhand Consortium and Associated Bodies, though most people just called me Silvereye. It was a remarkable role, half spymaster to the queen herself, and half Silverhand, as a member of the spy ring of that name, allied to the people of dreams and serving an ideal roughly similar to what you dreamers term 'communism'. Not surprisingly, the Consortium – that body of spies and thieves making up the major weapon of dreams that thankfully no one really noticed – and the crown had always kept separate, with the king scarcely aware of the Silverhands' existence. The two working together, however distantly, was a new idea.

Meanwhile I asked Lisana, 'So why do you want me to do this?'

'Try to be more specific,' she snapped. 'Why do I want you personally? Or why do I want you to liaise with the Consortium?'

'Both.'

She shifted uncomfortably. 'When Haven was invaded and you and the Consortium organized the revolt that freed it, the Consortium could easily have taken control of Haven for itself. But it didn't. So I can't deny that the Consortium's loyalty is proven. Yet from my point of view, it's not safe that such a powerful body should exist, with no idea of who leads it or what, at any given moment, he plans to do. The Consortium are guardians of dreams, it's true. But sometimes it becomes necessary for some person or persons to guard the guardians.'

'Me?'

'Yes.'

I thought about this. 'Lisana?'

'Yes?'

'Who shall guard the guardian of the guardians?'

She smiled at me, brightly. 'Kite, the Consortium respects you. That's why you're ideal for this job. And I – I can watch you from dawn to dusk and beyond, and never tire nor lose you. You guard the guardians and I, the person I trust more than anyone, will guard you.'

Against all odds, it proved ideal. Good working hours – I only had to report into Haven and Silverpoint, the Consortium headquarters, for one week in every month, and any other information came by courier straight to Stormpoint. Good salary too, kinda. And good relations. At one time I even rose to lead the Consortium, where I'd become popular with the Silverhands for devising such things as the magical network of elementals – beings summoned into existence directly from the Void – and a canteen for resting spies in Silverpoint. It also helped that the Consortium's present head, a man called T'omar, owed me several favours.

'You damn well gave me this hellish job,' he said when I went to Silverpoint with the news of my appointment by Lisana. 'So don't blame me if I do it properly and keep the queen at arm's length.'

T'omar, who'd been a soldier, at less than a hundred years old was one of the youngest men ever to take up the post of Consortium leader. He was of the traditional Silverhand school that believed all royalty were idiots and needed *someone* to watch their backs. Nevertheless he and Lisana recognised in each other a similar mindset, being both ruthless and determined.

'Lisana can deal with presentation and suchlike big stuff,' he'd said. 'We'll just find the plots.'

'T'omar can do that,' she'd replied in due course, 'so long as he *tells* me about them. There's been too much of the Consortium hanging around in the shadows and not explaining what they're doing.'

'That's the whole point,' I'd said. 'Spies don't like to publicise themselves. Besides, it's not our favoured policy to tell kings what they don't care to hear.'

She'd laughed, the bitter sound of a woman who already knew more than she wanted to. 'That's why you alone can be my personal spymaster. You're the only one in the whole Void who'd be fool enough to tell me the truth.' I kept my face empty while she looked shrewdly at me out of the corner of her eye. 'Or,' she added, 'to keep information from me but still do the right thing.'

'Is that a compliment?'

'From me, my dear Kite?'

'Doesn't seem likely, does it?'

The work of the Consortium was still the people before the crown, but I was responsible firstly for the welfare of Lisana. The first months of her reign were fraught with stress as Consortium and crown were forced to unite in order to prevent the Warden of some subordinate realm or other from declaring himself king in her place. It smacked of totalitarianism, but when the first assassination attempt was not only discovered but prevented, all doubts were put aside by the feeling of righteous victory that filled Lisana, her guard, the Consortium and me. Even in dreams, T'omar said, there has to be someone to shovel the shit. It was, in short, a job I'd been designed for. The Kite of legend could go on slaying kings and necromancers to the bards' content – in reality my calling would almost always be to the dirtier tasks.

Sometimes though, I did have to call on the legend. An incident occurred only a few months into my new job where as Laenan Kite I ceased to be a silent observer, and was forced to become the mage in white again.

I had been trying to get it right for several hours. But either the glass was too thin, my spells were too complicated or I had too little skill with the kind of illusion I sought. The shape half formed inside the bottle was still vague, and mounds of shattered glass swept into a corner offered proof of just how delicate was the task I'd undertaken.

Any fool can do illusions. But even now the art evades me of creating illusions that can expand to ten times their ordinary size at the most mundane of actions – opening a glass bottle, for example.

There came a hammering on the door, and I nearly dropped the finely woven spell. I juggled for several painful seconds to keep it stable, in which time the knock came again. Someone yelled, 'Kite! Warden Kite!'

'Sod off,' I muttered under my breath, frantically working to ease the spell into a different bottle. It shimmered dangerously, ready to break free of my grasp at any second.

The noise outside mounted to a commotion, and then someone shoved the door open. I turned round, mouth opening to form an objection, and stared into T'omar's glowering face.

The illusion around my fingers faded, a good spell undone. But I was not about to complain that T'omar had broken into my work.

He'd come from Silverpoint to oversee the investigation of a chamberlain suspected of stealing funds. The money was thought to finance a mercenary bandit group who'd been terrorising caravans in the Void. It was bad enough that the chamberlain saw his part in this as a nice little investment. But worse was the mercenaries' likely connection to the potentially rogue desert kingdom of Sunpoint. It was a connection that my instincts as a native of that realm only served to confirm.

The Consortium had informed the queen that they were already investigating this same chamberlain. I was pretending meanwhile that I'd come to the city only out of 'courtly duty'. Unfortunately, to keep that cover unblown I had to indulge in some such duty for real – tedious nights of dances and aching smiles in ballroom after ballroom, watching courtiers go about their point-less lives even as I groaned with curiosity to know how the operation was doing.

'We've found the link.'

I gawked openly at T'omar. 'The one who takes the bandits their money?'

'So the fools in Silverpoint tell me. And I want *you* to make him admit it.'

'*Me?* Why?'

He ticked the points off on his fingers. 'One. This guy's a mage and would see through anyone else like *that*. Two. He's a bit of a romantic and in awe of anyone who's done something even remotely dramatic. Three. You're the only figure whose word the court will respect when we bust him to hell. Four. If there's a connection with Sunpoint, you come from there, you know their ways. Five. It's your sodding job, you work with Lisana and the Consortium, and this is a joint operation, there-fore your territory. Six.' He hesitated. 'Look, I'm overworked, okay? If you can do this it'll save so much effort. Do it for old times' sake.'

I wrinkled my nose with distaste. 'The court wouldn't trust me an inch.'

'They trust you more than some anonymous tip-off. And you must have made a *few* friends at all those fancy dinners and dances.'

Lisana summoned a chamber for the purpose, with partitions between the walls into which a Silverhand listener might squeeze. It was a pleasant room, with high windows open to a cool breeze. Ever since Lisana had acquired the Key to Haven and with it the power to change the city and palace at whim, she'd been inflicting her Zen-minimalist taste with a vengeance. Cool stone floors, bright stabs of sunlight, wooden furniture of achingly simple design, open cloisters and discreet golden pools. Nothing too extravagant. But ... sometimes I just longed for a nice fat padded sofa.

This room was no exception: blue marble walls, a soundproof door, a table and a couple of matching chairs. The one incongruous thing was a bookcase heaving with papers and scrolls of all kinds. A reliable source had told me that in recent months they'd been sorted into some sort of order. I had to take his word for it.

T'omar had promised that the man to be interviewed wouldn't recognise me for Laenan Kite, but I'd still tied back my impossibly unruly hair for the occasion and put on a clerk's uniform. At something over five hundred years old, by the reckoning of my peers I'm still in my prime, and have blue eyes and black hair. It's useful that I look nothing like most people's idea of a mage. Mages, they say, should be grey-bearded old guys with pointy

hats and long staffs. While I can appreciate the occasional benefit of a well-charged staff, the pointy hat
business is completely out and *no* man springs fully
formed into grey-beardness unless the subject of an
especially savage curse. On the other hand I've had my
share of romance, but 'handsome' is *not* how people
describe me. By the time you've killed two kings the
word they mostly use is 'legend'. That too doesn't really
apply, for the Kite celebrated by the legends is this well-
muscled guy with high principles and white robes, and
the only thing I share with him is the same name.

It's a strange fact that if you have ballads sung about
you, it only means fewer people recognise you for who
you are. How many legends feature a little guy with a
strange, bony face who isn't much over five feet tall? On
Earth I've learned from something called television, a
form of 'technology' I still don't understand, that, sadly,
to be accounted a legend you must look the part as well
as do the deed. In that world hundreds of unsung heroes,
who may have saved thousands of lives, are ousted from
the fame due to them by undeserving gits with classic
looks and a daily workout.

Here too in the kingdoms of the Void, there are dif-
ferences between the legend and the real man – at least,
in my case. When the forces of the realm of nightmare
invaded Haven, it was the Kite of legend who was supposed to have vanquished them – a wise mage who sees
all and has always served goodness and dreams. No
doubt the legend struck a heroic pose too, as the king of
nightmare fell to his death.

The real Laenan Kite, to speak frankly, did nothing of
the sort, but stood trembling before that same king,

almost frozen with fear. When he fought the king, he struck back on reflex alone. The battle had nothing to do with honour, just two bloodied figures hitting each other with every last shred of physical and mental strength. The real Kite cared nothing at that moment for dreams or goodness or the smile of a loved one – when he struck a blow it was so that the enemy couldn't strike back.

Yet the fact remains that the legend and I have both killed kings of nightmare and survived. There at least our paths unite . . .

When our suspect, one Dislas Barilor, entered, I saw a beefy young man who looked like he'd rather have been a soldier (and with his little, little magic, soldiering might have suited him better). He was wearing mage's robes and taking in the room with the nervous little glances of a guilty man.

'Oh, do come in!' I said. 'It's . . .' I consulted my hastily drawn-up list, extending the penpusher routine to the limit '. . . Dislas, isn't it?'

'Yes,' he said doubtfully. 'What's going on?'

The sure sign of a guilty man, I thought with an inward smile. 'What's going on?' is not what you say if nothing's happening that should affect you. It was a fool's reply.

'Oh, we're just doing a few check-ups, and I wondered if you could help me?'

'Sure. What with?'

I gestured towards the other chair and he sat as I made a show of fumbling through some papers.

'Ah yes, here it is. Now, our queen is only just getting into her new role, as you know, and has ordered a whole re-organisation of the files. Oh dear, it is *such* hard work, you would not believe it. And I'm already understaffed and I *asked* if she'd summon a few more people to help me, but when she did they were just mindless abacuses, no use at *all*!' I looked at him with an appeal for understanding on my face. 'Don't you find these Key-bound creatures irritating? They only know as much as the Warden – and how many Wardens can tell the difference between a 3B report and a 3A? None, that's how many!'

'How can I help you?' he demanded, eager to get out of the room.

'Well, it's just a minor thing, but I've got a problem with some of the accounts. A series of payments were made from the treasury, but the files can't tell me to whom or why. I thought perhaps you could help me?'

'Why me?' His voice had risen slightly, and his face was turning a faint pink. Dislas was, in short, one of the worst spies I'd ever seen – no wonder the Silverhand Consortium had missed his activities for so long. Even as errand boy he must have been about the least likely suspect.

'Well, the money was extracted from the vaults in large bags. The vaults are of course sealed with magic and guarded by some of the queen's creatures. However, even when the money disappeared with the wards left intact it seems these creatures felt no need to raise the alarm. I thought you, as a skilled court mage, might know how a thief could've managed it.'

He contrived to look thoughtful. 'Difficult.'

'Of course, if a thief *didn't* do it, we are led into more unpleasant lines of thought.'

'Quite,' he said, a man remaining cool under pressure.

'I believe you are responsible for monitoring the treasury side of things,' I continued. 'Illusionary money, false

gifts, gifts with curses, the warding – the list is endless.
You must be terribly overworked.'

'The queen has summoned a lot of creatures to aid me,'
he replied carefully.

'Oh quite! But we know what *they're* like – just useless
for practical tasks!' I leaned forward with a sombre look.
'Now, this is something I really must ask you rather than
your superiors, because they themselves are suspect.
You're still a junior mage, loyal and with not an enemy in
the world. Some of your seniors may have . . . shall we
say, longer histories? That's why I'm consulting you first.

'Who do you think might *possibly* have any motive for
stealing from the vaults? There are so many people with
access to them that I really don't know where to start. I
need a *personal* opinion. Everyone who takes money is
obliged to fill out the details of why, when and who. Is
there anyone you've seen not doing this? Anyone at all
whom you even *suspect* of not doing the paperwork?'

'I . . . don't know,' he stammered.

I sat back, drawing the pile of papers to me like a personal friend. 'It's surprisingly easy to mess up the
records, you know. Take a sum, write that you're taking
less in the records, thus taking out quite considerable
amounts of cash in dribs and drabs. While never suspecting, of course, that an inventory of accounts would
be done because, frankly, what with all the recent chaos
of war and a new queen, who'd have *time*?'

'Quite,' he repeated – he seemed to take a lot of
comfort from that word, as if it somehow put him on the
same level as his interrogator.

'But anyone, *anyone*?' I repeated. 'Do any of your col-
leagues have debts, perhaps? Is it just a mistake in

accounting? The chamberlain of treasuries assures us that a mistake is most likely, but then *his* accounts are less than accurate. I mean . . .' here I paused, and gave a bewildered look, 'he's paid a not inconsiderable sum for his services, yet he owns a mansion far above his status! Even with this mansion, he never seems to be in it! It's bizarre.'

'Perhaps the chamberlain is to blame,' he blurted, fazed by this range of suggestions.

I feigned surprise. 'Do you think that's possible? But he **seems** such a loyal man? And why? What possible use **could he h**ave for the money taken from the accounts **unless . . .**' I let my voice trail off. 'Oh my. What if he's plotting something? But . . . no! Not the chamberlain. Consider the work involved. You'd need a motive, for one, and the chamberlain is such a sweet man, with not a complaint in the world. And then he'd have to get someone to run errands for him, assuming anyone would! I mean, a man of his rank couldn't organise . . . well, *anything* without somebody noticing; he'd have to get a junior to do it. Otherwise the problems facing him would be immense.'

Dislas said nothing, and I didn't blame him. If by that point he hadn't worked out just how deep in he was, the realization was close to dawning.

'I've got an idea!' I exclaimed, as if I'd only just thought of it. 'If the chamberlain is indeed contriving some ill, and taking treasury funds to do so, perhaps we could check the accounts from the date when the anomaly first started. If the amount lost coincides with when *he* took money from the treasury, then we'll know he's playing something dirty! But then why? And what could he possibly be doing with it? And who's the middleman, since there'd have to be one?' I sighed. 'Well, whoever it is, he'll be in trouble soon enough. Let it not be said that Laenan Kite lets any traitor go unpunished.'

His eyes flashed up from their study of the tabletop and met mine. 'Laenan Kite?'

'Yes?'

'You are Kite?' 828,321 YA

'Oh dear, don't let it get you down,' I said companionably. 'People always get it wrong – they think I'm supposed to be grey-haired and sitting in a library somewhere. I really don't know why I've got this job – it's not my thing at all, pre-empting traitors by hunting them down and killing them. I always imagined myself as a musician of some kind, but it never worked . . .

'And as for the paperwork, oh dear! There's the warrants for the arrest, then the special "interrogation" warrants, as they like to call them, so that you can use magic on them to get the truth, and *then*, if one thing leads to another, death warrants and all! And have you tried mind-reading a mage when he's squirming and yowling in your grasp? It takes hours just to peel down the shields, and then you leave the guy gibbering and trashed even before the information's out of him.'

'I didn't think you could mind-read a mage.'

'Oh, it's hard, and usually leaves the victim in agony, but sometimes these things have to be done. For queen and dreams. I guess that's why they think it worth calling in someone like me to do the dirty work.'

He swallowed. 'The . . . chamberlain. If he is guilty, what will you do to him?'

'Oh, probably execute him and all of his. After the

amount of work expended in catching the group, they'd deserve nothing less. And by the time I do catch the one stealing all this cash I *will* be in a bad mood.'

'Execute them all?'

'Well, unless someone stepped forward and confessed. A loyal, honourable man in an evil plot is always valued by us, even if he was originally misguided. After all,' I said with a little laugh, 'what is mercy for?'

He met my eyes, I met his. We didn't need magic to read each other's face. Weariness was already etching itself in him, and before my eyes he'd acquired the submissive slouch of the prisoner.

I stood up, shuffled my papers into a neat bundle and tucked my chair under the table. 'Thank you for your help, Master Barilor.'

The door opened. A pair of palace guards moved into the room, followed by their captain and a mage. Dislas' eyes followed me to the door, where I nodded to the captain and slipped into the corridor without another word.

It was the legend, that day, who broke Dislas. In his subsequent confession he named the chamberlain, two treasury guards, and all the mercenaries involved, furnishing magical images of their appearances, and descriptions of their habits. He also identified as a fellow conspirator the Warden of a minor kingdom in dreams, recently fined by Lisana for breach of conduct.

At the end of the line, too, there was Sunpoint. But that part of the affair was expediently glossed over. The balance of power – of mutual convenience at least – between Haven and the neutral kingdom of my birth seemed to make this a good idea. For their own part

Sunpoint, finding their plot so easily blown, thought it best to offer Haven a very large gift. I'm not sure of what, but it seemed to do the job.

How self-satisfied we all were that day – and I, how overruled by outright pride. Yes, by pride in a job well done. But also by reluctance to look further. At the time all I thought, as we closed the case officially, was that if I hadn't used the name of Laenan Kite, the breaking of *that* conspiracy would have been a lot messier. And I never could stand mess.

TWO

In a Time of Peace

Then there was my little Stormpoint, the kingdom reshaped entirely from my own imagination. Within the Void, the two great empires of dreams and nightmare contain hundreds of realms, each embodying an aspect of dreamers' minds on Earth. As Stormpoint is the dream of storms, so Skypoint is the dream of flying, and Nightkeep is the city of nightmare just as Haven is the city of dreams.

Here in Stormpoint at various times I had led an easeful life of exile, and fashioned the fantastical creatures who lived and played in this place; here too I'd recovered from the injuries sustained when fighting for Haven. I had developed spells that were uniquely mine, and perfected the landscape so that wherever I looked, a smile would come to my face. Every night thunder would roar on the horizon, and heavy rain refresh the grass, afterwards leaving its strong clean smell hanging in the air. In the enchanted forest elves studied the latest fashions and perfected their make-up, in the river water-sprites frolicked like otters, and in the sky phoenixes indulged in mating rituals that didn't really bear describing.

Stormpoint had had its share of unlikely times. Before I killed the previous Warden, a mage angled towards the kingdoms of nightmare, it used to be the dream of thorns. A bleak, bleak place, only tolerated here in dreams because it had been thought too small to bother conquering. Later, when nightmare had overrun the city of Haven, Stormpoint had housed thousands of refugees led there by my sister, Saenia Kite. Saenia, and I admit this freely, has always been better with magic than I have – and I was the man who played a not inconsiderable role in freeing Haven from nightmare in the first place. It's a long story involving high magic, swords, sewers and a lot of rather stupid fire elementals, but suffice it to say that if I can sit here and be given the name 'great archmage' by idiots from Haven who know no better, then Saenia is off the scale.

On one particularly fine evening Saenia and I were sitting and arguing over the sunset. We'd just spent ten minutes tweaking the colours in the sky to get just the right bloom of pink, streaked in well-judged places with gold and orange and given texture by the play of light against a pattern of clouds. As a result of our tinkering, sunset was several minutes overdue and the night-sprites, all ready to come and play in the darkness, were whispering impatiently at the base of our tower. We felt our efforts could have used a more appreciative audience as we sat in a window and chatted idly of this and that.

'I saw a pair of dreamers here today,' Saenia remarked.

'Really? There've been more dreamers lately, dreaming of friendlier kingdoms.'

'They may shape the very Void, but we affect their minds,' she said, playing absently with the cat who was now her constant companion. In the aftermath of Haven's reconquest Saenia's far-too-young lover, a man I'd disliked on sight, had left to rule his own small kingdom after his father was killed by nightmare. My sister – delicate, fragile, but powerful Saenia – had come to live at Stormpoint.

I used to think I was unique in my spell-skills – who was it, after all, who created the spells protecting me from the sight of other Wardens, though their kingdom itself tried to tell them where I was? But she is something beyond even my magic, and certainly knows more than she ever lets on.

'We affect dreamers' minds,' she continued, 'and since things are good now, so they are happy.' She sighed and stretched before asking – too casually, I thought, 'And your job?'

'There've been no rumours of plots lately, and Lisana doesn't want anything from the Consortium – or vice versa. I feel almost redundant.'

'And the court? You're still on good terms?'

'Why do you ask?'

She smiled. 'You have a knack for upsetting people.'

'Thanks.'

My sister made a face and said nothing. Mostly she didn't need to talk, and just being with her was enough to know what was in her mind. Since we were mages as well as joined through blood, I could sense most of her feelings, and share them too. What poured off her now was contentment.

Nonetheless she said, 'It won't last, you know.'

'What won't?'

'This,' she said, indicating the sunset. 'It's always the same with you, Laenan. You come home, get all relaxed and just as you're ready to get the harvest in something bad turns up and you're sent running all over the Void saving people's lives and getting shot at.'

'I don't get in a harvest.'

'You know what I mean. You're a magnet for trouble, and this Silvereye job will only make things worse. The court will never like you.'

'Thanks.'

'It's true. You come from too low a background and have too much power.'

Whatever Saenia said about trouble, for several weeks I'd found I was restless. If nothing else, it was time to put in some work on designing and perfecting the spell of the moment. So, lurking in my workroom and glowing a mutinous purple, was one of my more twisted ideas.

Saenia had come in after supper to examine it. 'So what do you want it to do?'

It was at that early stage when it embarrassed me to try and explain. 'Well, it's kind of like . . . you know.'

'No, I don't.'

'It's to do with the job. You know how it is when you have an assassin . . .'

She looked at me steadily.

'. . . and you dunno who sent him. And you kind of want to find out?'

But she'd turned to examine the spell with her mage's senses, which always were and always will be more acute than mine.

'It's a scry,' she said finally. 'But it's also a standard probe. You're trying to scent hostile intent, but— Aha! Here it is! You've left one end untied – right? – so that you can attach the spell to your assassin and it can follow him home?'

'Only it doesn't work. I tried it out under controlled circumstances, and it tied down to the assassin just fine. And the scry activated okay, and found all connected people with hostile intent . . .'

'But it still went wrong?'

'It only works on a living assassin, and then just for a second or so. And the point of assassins is that if *they're* living, then you won't be for much longer. Also it only followed the assassin's thoughts, rather than his memory. So all I got were pictures of knives and bodies, with not one image of who'd sent him.'

'"Controlled circumstances"?' she echoed. 'I won't ask.'

'Oh, it was fine, honest!'

'You'll end up one day in such trouble, little brother. Just—'

'—you wait,' she was about to add. But it was at that moment that my holiday came to an end. Saenia's prophecy had, as always, come true.

I had felt the first stirrings of a contact. Immediately Saenia caught on. 'Call-signature?' she murmured.

I nodded, reaching out to answer the mind who'd drawn the symbol opening a path to my own consciousness.

She rose, with a look of *I won't say I told you so.* 'I'll be downstairs.'

Again I nodded and felt, then answered, the mind that was calling me. <T'omar! What's up?>

<Kite, you would not believe how overworked I am.>

<You need me to know that?>

<Kite, I am up against it!>

<And?>

<Just come to Haven, okay?>

<What, now?>

<Yes, now! This very second, for preference.>

<Who as?> I asked cautiously. We both knew that, coming from me, it was a good question.

<Everyone! Be the Silverhand, be the Silvereye, be the great mage, but above all be a cunning schemer!>

<It's serious, then?>

<You could say that,> he replied. <And Kite?>

<Still here.>

<Be braced for cloak-and-dagger work of the worst kind. If you stop off at Silverpoint, I'll explain it all.>

Which was how, at an insanely early hour next day, I was slinging a fully packed bag over my shoulder and standing before Saenia.

'Tell me what happens,' she said, then laughed uneasily at her own words. 'Or shall I just look out for fire in the Void and the fall of kings?'

Then it was time to turn my mental eyes inward, even as outwardly I still heard myself saying, 'And while I'm gone I don't want you doing anything arty to *my* kingdom.' Shooing it from its nestling place inside me, I brought out the Key of Stormpoint. A little sphere of

magic, destined to control the kingdom from its beginning to its unseen end. Silence descended as I held it in
my hand, then passed it to Saenia. 'Keep my kingdom
safe.'

Wordlessly she took it, stared at it for a few seconds
and then pulled it into her with a gesture. It sunk in as if
she were no more substantial than a vapour. 'My
kingdom now,' she said. With a humourless smile, she
added, 'Be careful, Laenan.'

'Hey! I'm the most careful man alive!'

She cocked her head. 'No, you're just not the heroic
type.'

I stepped out of the familiarity and comfort of Stormpoint,
into the silent, temperatureless fog of the Void. The
swirling colours danced around me in silence and would
have been beautiful but for the emptiness of it all.

Come this very second, T'omar had said. I'd already
waited an evening. Besides, it's a lonely walk through the
Void, and the sooner I got where there was something to
see, smell or hear, the better. I shifted the weight of my
bag and picked up my pace.

By noon I reached the kingdom of Healpoint. It's
famous for flowers, niceness in everything and an almost
sickeningly friendly population. The first person I met,
passing down the shade-splotched road between breezy
meadows, was a priestess who offered me some bread
with the merry greeting, 'Welcome to Healpoint, trav-
eller.' It was hard to thank her without squirming at the
earnestness of the place. But part of me remembered
how it felt to need compassion, and I accepted the bread
with a fair reply.

I knew I'd better go on without stopping. Luckily the Warden didn't notice me among the many visitors to his kingdom, and I was grateful to Saenia for taking my Key – that *would* have drawn unwelcome attention. If the Warden had found out who I was he'd certainly have tried to help me – partly because this *was* deeply concerned Healpoint, but also because of my standing with Lisana. It was well known at court that I was one of the few to whom the queen listened, even if she did answer every other comment with a disbelieving, 'Do I need to be told that?' or a cool, 'This is hardly the time.'

The rolling green hills of Healpoint dropped away behind me at the return of the Void, and the shrill sound of birdsong abruptly faded. At this hour there were a fair number of people about – mostly sick pilgrims travelling to Healpoint in search of a cure. Here and there a sedan chair was borne sombrely along by the ailing passenger's relatives, who were hoping to prolong his life for whatever reason, be it basic human compassion or some family necessity that only a suspicious mind like mine would consider.

I remembered another journey, very like this one. Then, I'd been headed for another coronation and, had I known it, a battle to the death for the deliverance of Haven. Another thing I'd not anticipated, as I trudged through the Void that time, was my first meeting with Renna, the most powerful dreamer of them all.

The fearless Renna, with her serene brow and lively glance. A coma victim, trapped in a state of dreaming from which she couldn't break free. As her body slowly died on Earth, so her mind endured here in the real world. It was she who got our armies into the besieged city of Haven, enabling us to travel at the speed of thought. If I fought there for anyone apart from myself, it was Renna. She vanished shortly after that final battle was won, never to be seen again. I do not fear for her safety, for she is now beyond anyone's reach, being a thing immortal. The Void is full of possibility, and she will fit in perfectly.

As intended, I reached Starpoint just as its Warden brought a long sunset to its close. Starpoint nights are beautiful in endless ways. Sometimes only half the sky will be dark, the better to be shown up by a slow sunrise that turns in a heartbeat to sunset. At other times the whole sky is swept with silver and purple and blue and yellow fire, supplying as much light as though the sun itself were risen. Stately planets and moons whirl through the heavens until you believe that a God up there is making them dance for your sake alone.

The inn where I'd decided to stop was by a lake, near one of the roads, forever silvery under a Starpoint heaven, that threaded one end of the kingdom to the other.

I ate alone at a table outside the inn, and watched travellers of all sorts as they came and went. The inn was filling up and I moved over to make space for two loutish men. They talked at first as though I didn't exist, for which I was grateful. Both spoke as people who believed utterly in their own nothings, which they'd be ready to defend with more than something.

I listened only with half an ear, so failed to notice when they got drunk enough to want a larger audience. It came as a surprise when one of them said, 'Where you from, friend?'

'Friend' was meaningless enough to have me worried. 'Stormpoint,' I replied to the purple-nosed man who'd spoken.

'Never heard of that one.'

'It's not far from here.'

'You lived there all your life, then?'

'I was born in Sunpoint.'

This seemed to make one exclaim, and the other choke on his beer. 'Sunpoint?' echoed the first one. 'Then you know all about *them*.'

'Depends who "they" are.'

He waved a wobbly hand. 'You know. The Warden. Going through here only a few days ago. Amazing kid. Wore white, acted polite – he *looked* like a king. Between you and me, now – seriously – I think your Sunpoint men are all right. If you ask me – if you ask me, mind – it won't be long before they're officially part of dreams.'

This was not how I remembered my original home. In the past the squalid desert kingdom of Sunpoint had been an object of scorn elsewhere in the Void. Though it had been my home throughout childhood, I had left with the full intention of never going back. Since when, I wondered, did any prince from Sunpoint, a neutral realm, ride through Starpoint – and not roaring drunk or ranting like a tyrant but actually looking like a king? And since when were the people of dreams willing to toast a neutral kingdom?

Since when was Sunpoint looked on with admiration, for that matter? Last I heard they were stealing funds to employ mercenaries against the greater glory of dreams . . . *Oh, wait. You don't know about that, do you Kite? Since such is the diplomatic power of a well-placed gift.*

It took time to shake off my illustrious companions, whose talk had been getting more emphatic by the minute. But once in my room I found sleep reluctant to come. I went back outside in shirt and trousers – not even a jacket or a pair of shoes – and sat by the lake that dominated the middle of the kingdom. The reflection of the stars quivered in its waters, and I savoured the coolness, the wind, the smell of cooking from the inn and the distant melded sounds of the locals enjoying themselves. After the silence of the Void I wanted to see, hear and feel something solid, and sensation of any kind was welcome.

Then something stirred within me. A mage's senses are a law unto themselves, and I was immediately curious. I looked deeper at myself, wondering what it could be that was so alarmed, and felt a warning flare up. On principle I always keep up some sort of ward, as a primary means of detecting danger. Uncertain what this nearby peril could be, I rose to my feet and peered through the darkness.

Nothing. Or – nothing I could see or feel. If anything, that was more unsettling than if a whole army had burst upon me. I raised my shield, feeling slightly safer, if not much, within my bubble of protective magic. Something tickled my ear, and I spun round.

No one was there. As often happens when you become fearful, imagined dangers feel real.

'Come out, come out . . .' I whispered.

'Wherever you are.'

I turned again, raising my hands defensively to ward off whatever danger was about to spring on me. And froze.

Renna. Looking nervous, but as solid and mortal as the day I'd first set eyes on her. She was pale, and trembling from the night-time cold as much as I was, even though I knew she had no body to be affected by such feelings. Only if she wished it would she experience such sensations as cold or warmth.

I exclaimed her name in an astonished whisper and she smiled a shaky smile. Her eyes were wide and her arms were wrapped about her slim frame, as if by desperately clasping herself she could hold together her very being.

'I have to equal them,' she whispered. 'Promise me, though, that you won't hurt the girl.'

'You're making as much sense as . . . an oracle,' I replied, unsettled by her urgency. Oracles, dear dreamer, are famous for making no sense at all. It's the only way they keep in business.

She raised one trembling hand. 'Palm to palm is holy palmer's kiss.'

'Palms? You've . . . been in a desert?' I suggested hopefully.

'Shakespeare.'

'Wasn't he a playwright guy on Earth?'

'Yes. You've dreamed of him?'

'Not recently.'

She took a deep breath, and from that seemed to draw strength. Reaching down, *through* my shield which I'd forgotten to lower, she caught my right hand and with a savage strength pressed it against her own. Palm to palm. Her skin tingled and though I could barely begin to sense it, something like magic filled her from top to toe.

'You must understand. The girl thinks the man is real.

She is still in both worlds, but on Earth all that remains now is for her to die. When she does I can take her but until then I need you, Kite. I *need* your mortality.'

'What do you want me to do?' I asked.

She smiled. 'Nothing. It will come to you, and when it does, we will fight and win together.'

Too late I saw her move, her free hand slicing upwards. As she drew a dagger across my wrist, it was mostly surprise that gashed a line of pain across it. That, and knowing that the wound from such a small neat movement could be fatal.

I croaked her name, half in outrage, half in disbelief.

She cast the dagger aside and laid her hand over the wound, my blood running red through her fingers. And then – this even I, the mage of legend, had never seen – it began soaking *into* her flesh, as if she were made of linen. Her fingers brushed my skin, sunk into skin, became one with my blood. Something like liquid ice passed through my veins, and suddenly I couldn't see, couldn't hear, couldn't do anything but shriek aloud at the betrayal of it.

'Who *are* you?!' I screamed.

<You,> came the whispered answer from outside the darkness that surrounded me. From *inside* too, until the word filled my world and all was the word. Then, against the roaring of the word and the pain of the ice and darkness, a single voice, soft and consoling. <I'm sorry, Kite. I'm so sorry.>

Then there was nothing at all.

THREE

Cloak and Dagger

I came to, and was immediately grateful for it. Admittedly I was sprawled in the most undignified and uncomfortable position – half in and half out of bed, still wearing the clothes of the night before, my feet caught in a tangle of sheets. But I had survived, which was something I'd genuinely not expected to happen.

I sat up. My eyes were gummy, my head itched from all the dirt that had managed to slide into my hair, my clothes were crumpled and foul, but I was alive. With trepidation, because I've always been squeamish about these things, I raised my right hand and turned it over, to look at where Renna – or something pretending to be her? – had sliced open my wrist.

There wasn't even a scratch. Not a scar, not a swelling, not a bruise – nothing. In disbelief I rolled up my sleeve further, as if I'd mistaken the place where she'd cut me and in fact she'd slit a vein in my elbow without me noticing. As I did so I realised that even the old burn marks were gone from my fight in Haven with the king of nightmare. Surely they should have scarred me for the rest of my days, being caused by magic and a dying man's magic at that? But no – they too had healed.

The more I looked, the less I found any sign of what had happened in the night. I felt better, too, than I had for ages – a little tired, perhaps, but not the wreck you'd have expected.

As I moved, however, down my side there was an unpleasant tearing sensation. I froze, and looked at where dried blood clinging to my shirt had soaked through to the skin.

I don't know how long I sat there, staring at this sole proof that I hadn't imagined the whole thing. But the same words kept coming back to me.

It wasn't Renna.

I told myself this gave at least some reassurance, now that I'd never needed it so much.

I got up on automatic, pulled the shirt off and scrubbed away the blood with a determination I didn't understand but which bordered on fearfulness. It was then that the little thought wormed its way into my mind.

Why?

Why what? I demanded irritably.

Why not Renna?

Because she's gone. She isn't mortal, and would have no reason to slit my wrist.

How do you know?

Because I know her, and there an end to it!

But immediately the Silverhand side of me was protesting. Emotional involvement, it whispered.

Perhaps Renna's gone mad, perhaps she can't cope with not having a body, perhaps . . .

Perhaps it wasn't Renna at all! Perhaps it was really some mage or other dreamer. Plotting and scheming and using others like they've done before in this cursed life of mine! Face it, the possibilities are endless.

Wearily I rubbed the blood from the shirt, watching the water in the sink turn red, and in the mirror my own haggard features caught my eye. Something in that face was strange, out of place. But what? With a shudder I turned away, swearing to cast every spell I knew to try and wash off the magic of the night. Every instinct cried out to do something, to act on whatever it was that had happened.

Yet I couldn't think what to do, save carry on with life as before and hope it was a benign creature that had worn Renna's face.

If it wasn't, I'd soon find out.

It was with this sense of being utterly powerless that I departed later than planned, wearing my only other shirt and feeling pretty miserable. All the way my mind was racing with explanations. Some were absurd paranoia, some were founded at least on scraps of genuine observation. All were unlikely.

At least I had something to think about in the Void. It was one way of ignoring the silence around me.

On the second night I stopped in Towerpoint, a cold kingdom of mountains and lakes and dragons. I sat up late in my lonely bedroom, looking across a landscape where a cold wind whispered defiance to the moon, and didn't dare to sleep. Oh, I tried. I drew thick wards around my bed, slipped a sheathed dagger under my pillow and curled up beneath my sheets, hugging them to my chin and tucking my knees in as if that could shelter me from a knife in the dark or a spell from above. For hours I tossed and turned, as though afraid that if I lay on one side an attacker would stab me from the other, then rolling over to lie on my back and wishing I had more arms to wrap over my exposed chest and belly.

Eventually I did sleep, exhausted from constant ward-weaving. My racing thoughts of Haven, Renna and Sunpoint had also drained me so that, though my eyes had been half consciously wandering left and right in search of a foe, sleep still managed to slip in.

But it was a tired, tired Laenan Kite who reached Silverpoint late the next day.

A stranger who didn't know the ways of the Consortium might easily overlook Silverpoint. In the past it was just an administrative kingdom where the tax collectors had their base, and various dignitaries going to or from Haven would spend the night. As time went on the Consortium wormed its way into this small patch of reality floating in the Void, until it had become uniquely their own. On the maps it was still marked as administrative, and any strangers trying to enter the kingdom would be politely informed that they'd come to the wrong place.

It didn't look much, to tell the truth. T'omar had tarted it up a little so that the original dull wooden structures standing apart from each other, like some frontier hamlet, were now a more impressive complex of stone buildings with apartments, offices, halls and all besides, around a pleasant courtyard complete with a fountain.

'If it doesn't cost us, then why not?' he'd asked me.

'Because we're supposed to be discreet, T'omar.'

'This is bloody discreet! I'm fed up of having to do the filing in a gloomy cellar whose most interesting feature is the rat hole.'

The sun was setting by the time I entered Silverpoint. I was glum with fatigue as I gave my name at the gatehouse to the Key-bound guards on duty, summoned into being for the sole purpose of keeping people out.

'Kite!' A beaming figure was hurrying across the courtyard towards me. 'How good to see you!' He was a fellow Silverhand called Virisin, an innkeeper from Haven who'd been recruited to the Consortium long ago. Innkeepers, it has been wisely said, hear everything.

He slapped me on the back unnecessarily hard, grin widening. Once we'd both been insignificant people leading little lives. We'd sit up all night ranting about things we hated and it was a good friendship. My ascent into fame had changed that in several minor ways – for a start Virisin was eager to be seen in my company, if only to assure other Silverhands that he was more than an innkeeper who knew how to listen. I'd wanted to explain that those 'players' who spent their lives in dark alleys waiting for unlikely meetings were only there *because* they were good at listening.

'But what are *you* doing here, Kite? I thought you were taking a break?'

'I was, and wish I still were.' I shrugged, seeing the blank look on his face. 'Got recalled. T'omar says it's urgent.'

Something dawned behind his eyes, though his face remained impassive.

'Virisin? What is it?'

'Are you going to Haven?' he asked cautiously.

'I think so.'

He took a deep breath. 'Did T'omar mention Sunpoint at all?'

'No, I didn't,' said a weary voice. T'omar had come out to greet me too. He looked as tired and stressed as any leader of the Consortium might in time of crisis.

'. . . Sunpoint?' I asked as T'omar led me down a new pillared arcade towards his office.

'I'm pleased to see you too, Kite.'

'Bullshit. I want to know about Sunpoint.'

He showed me into a room that had to be his – dirty plates left from where he'd eaten at odd times without stopping work, and a seeming chaos of files strewn across the desk and other surfaces, every one in use. Clearing away some of the debris, he offered me a chair. 'You've eaten?'

'Not yet. Tell me about Sunpoint.'

He sighed. 'When did you leave there? As in, when the Void was young and you were young with it.'

'Hundreds of years ago. I was seventeen. At twenty-five I was a thief in nightmare. At twenty-eight, a shoemaker's apprentice in dreams.'

'Who ruled Sunpoint when you left?'

I cast my mind back. 'Old Giroign. Total bastard.' Even now I had a clear picture of him, one that put me in mind of a particularly stupid rhino.

'Giroign's dead.'

'Doesn't surprise me. He was getting on, even then.'

'His sons look like trouble. The older, who rules now, hardly qualifies as a mage, his magic is so weak. The younger son, Rylam . . .' He hesitated, as if uncertain how to voice his thoughts.

'Rylam,' I prompted.

'He's dirty, Kite. I can feel it. The guy turns up and he's wearing white, riding a white charger and carrying a long jewelled sword. Unclean, has to be.'

I recalled the good impression made on the two drunks in Starpoint. 'The guy turns up where?'

'Oh, in Haven. It happened almost a week ago now – thanks for hurrying, by the way. I get word from our Silverhands there that Rylam, heir to Sunpoint until his brother gets his act together and produces a son, is in Haven, as I say, and demanding an audience of the queen. He claims that in exchange for aid against his elder brother, he's prepared to swear allegiance to dreams.'

'He'd be giving us an important kingdom,' I said. 'But – what's the emergency? Why call me?'

T'omar shifted uncomfortably. 'Rylam brought a small entourage. The day after they arrive one of his two servants is found dead. At this Rylam leaps to his feet and points the finger at his brother Feilim, warning of a plot to kill the queen.

'We would have discounted it were it not that a patrolling mage found a half-finished inferno spell. Written into a room near the queen's.'

'Rylam brought a mage with him?' I asked cautiously. T'omar nodded.

'You've investigated him, I take it?'

'Hasn't been in Haven long enough to draw the spell without us noticing. Believe me, Kite, we've been watching him from the second he entered dreams.'

'Does Lisana know of this latest threat?'

'Yes, more's the pity. Locked herself away behind a wall of guards, suspects everyone, makes it impossible even for *our* men to get close.'

'Not useful . . . But what do you want me to do?'

'Find out who *did* draw the spell. See if Rylam's clean, find out if Feilim would really be so stupid as to threaten Haven itself. It's nothing you can't handle.'

'Yes, T'omar,' I said flatly.

He sighed, as if I were a child asking for one sweetie too many, and added, 'I owe you one, Kite.'

I was given a room in Silverpoint, and every Silverhand I passed stared at me openly. *That's Laenan Kite, he used to be our leader . . .*

I'd have to go to the court, of that I was certain – to speak to Lisana, to observe Rylam, to observe his mage. But there I'd be recognised as myself, and I didn't want to justify my every move to some curious courtier. I needed a pretext that got me access to the court, but left an exit route. Perhaps . . . a mages' college reunion? No, too many people would know if there was one of those. Or was I researching some complicated spell in the great library of Haven . . . again, no. It would be an easy matter for anyone to ask the librarians if they'd seen a man of my description.

But there was bound to be some way to hide in plain sight. I'd think of something.

That night, tucked up deeply beneath the sheets, I felt sleep come fast and heavy on me. To think that only two nights ago I'd been attacked by a creature who wore Renna's form, and the night after had lain shivering with fear at what might be. Even now, sleep itself seemed threatening.

Humans, those strange creatures of Earth, dream of

the Void. They can rarely remember their dream, and I am sorry to say that nightmare usually leaves a more lasting impression on their thoughts than dreams. A child dreaming of his mother will travel at the speed of thought to the woman who most resembles her in whatever kingdom of the Void where, so it's said, scarcely any human lacks a doppelganger. Somewhere, sometime, someone on Earth will always dream of somebody here, be it as their lover or their hated enemy.

For my part I dream of Earth. I've seen the Forbidden City, flown across the Pacific Ocean in an hour, watched the fashionable dog-walkers on the Parisian boulevards – and still never quite understood humans. I've used some of their scientific ideas, I admit, but apart from unreliable rifles and not very good plumbing, none of the wonders I've seen on Earth have been replicated in the Void without the use of magic.

I do have one advantage over most dreamers visiting the Void. Unlike them I remember everything I dream, and have control over where I go and what I see and hear.

Or very nearly. Only a very few times have I had the sensation, so common to humans, of being in a dream whose course is directed by another. But that someone else has to be possessed of awesome – maybe terrifying – powers, to breach the sleeping mind of Laenan Kite, or any other mage.

Not all my experiences on Earth have been good, in any case – curiosity like mine is bound to exact its price. It was as well then, that being in Silverpoint helped, by making me feel at least a little safer as I lapsed into what proved a mercifully dreamless sleep. This place was familiar ground, populated with people I knew and who

I felt, even through my walls of Silverhand mistrust, that I could depend on.

I was grateful too that when I walked out next morning for Haven it was in the company of two other Silverhands. One, Rinset, was young, energetic and ready to save the Void, whatever it took. The other, a woman everyone called Shell, must have been as old as I was, and cast disparaging looks whenever possible at Rinset. Her appearance was ordinary but not plain, average but not so dull that people would notice her for it. I soon realized that she was one of those people whose looks can make extraordinary changes in an instant.

'Shell's the best,' T'omar had said. 'She hears everything, sees everything and can bluff her way in anywhere. She knows everything there is to know about anything – just ask and she'll prove her worth.'

'What's her real name?'

'You know, I've never asked. She was born and raised in Silverpoint and if Shell is what she wants to be called, it's no problem.'

'Why haven't I seen her?'

'Nightkeep agent.'

I'd nodded, greatly impressed. The post of Nightkeep Silverhand was one of the most dangerous, and I was grateful for never having held it. If this woman had been in nightmare on those terms she'd earned nothing but respect.

On meeting her, I discovered that was indeed what she deserved.

'Feilim's not bad, as Sunpoint rulers go,' she told me as we trudged through the Void along roads growing ever heavier with traffic towards Haven. 'Certainly better than his father.' She snorted. 'Still a little pile of shit, though. Slavery, bigamy and all things besides are still legal in his kingdom. Mind you, exports are up, which keeps enough people more or less happy.'

'And Rylam?'

'Too good to be true,' she said firmly. 'He's charming, polite, a brilliant swordsman, a capable mage, wears white, probably doesn't even fart in bed. A real heart-throb. The Silverhand ladies we had watching him have got a real crush.'

'Sounds a slimy bastard.'

'It always looked that way, even in his youth. Someone must have taught him who knew the value of a well-placed smile.'

'Are you going to warn the queen?' demanded Rinset, staring hopefully at me. *If you're not dead within a month you're going to be very disappointed*, I mused.

'Warn her about what?' said Shell.

'About Rylam!'

I managed to forestall her sharp reply. 'Eager though I am to do just that,' I told him, 'we don't know that he's done anything.'

'Even though he is an odious wart,' snapped Shell.

'"Your majesty",' I continued, ignoring her, '"I mistrust this man because he's more handsome than I am, or even slightly handsome for that matter – will you have his head cut off, please?"'

'Oh.' He looked disappointed.

Things would be so much easier if the Consortium did assassination, I thought. *But that's against the charter. Assassinations make the assassin think he can just kill anyone, in a world already messy enough. Things would be easier if the Consortium had power of any kind, rather than practising a little intelligence gathering here or there! Why is life one long frustration?*

Look who got out of bed the wrong side this morning, replied the rational side of my mind. *You know the answer well enough. Sometimes change just has to be feared.*

We arrived in Haven at noon, and stepped from the Void into a glorious spring day. The City of Dreams was looking even whiter and cleaner and brighter than before. Each house was taller and more dignified, and extravagant rooftop gardens flourished everywhere. After the silence of the Void the noise hit like a hammer. A thousand – a million – voices all at once, none louder than the shouts of the traders as we wound our way down the main street that led towards the palace.

At a square where a fountain of white light rose above the roofs, showering silver sparks, we went our ways. Rinset to meet his contacts on the streets, Shell to 'labour with the other servants', which meant she was going to debrief those Silverhand informers who worked in and around the palace.

That left me to present myself at court. I resisted the temptation to send up a signal to Lisana to warn her I was coming. Just hit her with the bad news that you're staying indefinitely, I decided, and leave it at that.

I wove my way through the streets, taking in the bright faces of a population blessedly unaware of who I was or what my purpose might be in that city. Watchmen, Key-bound creatures of very little brain, stomped blindly past. Behind them trailed a few others, real watchmen this time, with their own minds and ideas, chatting together and happily leaving any hard work to their Key-bound comrades.

I reached the outer wall of the palace, where stalls pressed up against the pristine white stone and the flow was greatest of people in uniforms or fine clothes. Following the course of the wall, I found the palace gate had moved since I was last in Haven. But that was commonplace with new rulers. They wanted to arrange things in a certain way, and it was up to the rest of us to get used to it.

'Laenan Kite,' I told the gate guards. 'Warden of Stormpoint.'

Above the gate, a Key-bound hawk sat on the battlements, and on hearing my name it craned its neck to get a better look at me. Almost a second later I felt Lisana's mind brush mine as she caught onto my presence in her city.

<Kite. How *nice* of you to come so promptly.>

<For you, anything,> I sent in equally deadpan tones.

<I know why you're here.>

<Quite right too. I haven't forgotten who pays my salary.>

<Come up to my study. It won't have changed.>

So I went, not stopping to dump my bag or eat, even though by now my stomach was grumbling.

Up a flight of stairs, along a corridor, turn right, turn right again, up another, shorter flight, first door on the left, smile at the guards in what you hope is a reassuring manner, knock politely.

'Come in, Kite.' Her voice was silken as always, tempered only slightly by the iron of command. I obeyed, and found her standing behind a large desk overflowing with papers. Dressed in quite plain clothes, for her, she was every bit as regal as I remembered. It was strange that, having in effect won her the crown, I still didn't care to sit without permission, so imposing was she.

Lisana looked me up and down before speaking. 'You look like an assassin.'

I scrutinized myself and only then realised how scuffed and dirty my boots and trousers were, how loosely my jacket hung on me and how, if you looked closely at my once white shirt, you could still see a faint stain where my blood had soaked it through. For some reason even magic had failed to remove the last traces.

'I had an accident.'

'You always do.' She nodded at the chair in front of her desk, meaning that I should sit. Sitting down opposite me, she folded her arms and stared at me with barely concealed suspicion. 'The Consortium called you, then, as my illustrious Silvereye?'

'Yes.'

'I thought they might. The Consortium values its precious secrecy so much that it would only send you.'

'Does it occur to you, ma'am, that I might have come out of genuine concern?'

She laughed. 'Oh, please. Even if that were true you'd never admit it.' In an instant she was serious again. 'Tell me what the Consortium is doing. And tell me about Rylam.'

'Rylam . . .' In spite of what I'd told Rinset and Shell, I repeated what I knew. 'And a servant murdered, with an inferno spell half-complete inside a reflection shield.'

'Should I ban reflection shields in the palace?' she asked suddenly. 'Security would be easier.'

'If you did, I for one would never willingly enter these walls again.' *As you well know*.

Thwarted, she acted as if the subject had never been mentioned. 'Well, carry on, won't you?'

'I've got no evidence yet, but we can draw a few provisional conclusions.' I leaned forward, frowning. 'Firstly, the shield above the inferno spell was sustained by a complicated ward-circle. To set that up without causing an alarm would have taken time and stealth that Rylam lacked. From the second he entered Haven the Consortium has been watching him, and there's no way he could have drawn that spell in the time he's been around.'

'So he didn't do it,' stated Lisana, as if closing the subject.

'Not without being in two places at once. The second thing,' I continued, 'is also in Rylam's favour. The murdered servant was loyal enough to leave Sunpoint and go with his master into dangerous territory. Rylam would have no apparent motive to kill him.'

'But as you said, for the moment you know nothing.'

'I'm glad to see your majesty is keeping an open mind.'

She shrugged. 'I prefer not to have my life under threat. You believe Rylam – that Feilim's sending assassins?'

'I have no opinion, and will maintain that happy state until given further evidence.'

She looked me up and down for a long moment. It was the nearest she got openly to shaking off some clinging doubt. 'You will do well as a policeman,' she declared, as if contradicting something I'd just said. 'I knew you would, of course. Even though I'd only seen you as a courtier, smiling and bowing but never quite doing the right thing.'

'Hey, who crept into your room that night and found

the evidence that got you banged up under house arrest?' I asked lightly.

'One of the reasons you have this job, my dear Kite. Now, since you *are* here, what do you need?'

'An excuse.'

She raised her eyebrows. 'What kind of excuse?'

'The kind that means I can slip in and out of the palace and no one asks why.'

Her brow furrowed. 'I don't suppose you've got a dying relative?'

'Only in Sunpoint, I expect.'

'Really? Oh yes, of course . . . Well, can't you *invent* some expiring next of kin?' She considered. 'Perhaps you've got family living in the western quarter, near the barracks and traders. How thorough does this have to be?'

'Enough to convince the court and the killer not to follow me.'

'Then definitely the western quarter, if you want to shake off any self-respecting courtier.'

'I thought these days all of the City of Dreams was a testimony to wealth and luxury. Why wouldn't someone go to the western quarter?'

'It's very . . . temporary, shall we say? It's where all the traders lodge who've come halfway across the Void and, worse, where the soldiers stay. I can summon beautiful buildings and magnificent attractions, but I can't change human nature and a tired soldier or trader who's just trekked through unbroken emptiness isn't interested in keeping the noise down. Crime is just hell at night – the thieves of the town seem to know to the minute what times I wake up and go to sleep, and the second I *am* asleep and unable to watch the streets . . .' She sagged, as if saddened by the flaws of mankind. 'Sometimes I think I'm too good for this place.'

'Right. I have a dying . . . oh, make it an aunt . . . in the western quarter. She has worked all her life as . . .?'

'Do you know anything about weaving?' she asked.

'No.'

'She'd better be a baker.'

'Okay. I have a dying aunt who used to be a baker until her hands packed up. All her family have left or died and I, her favourite nephew, have come to fulfil my familial duty in their place. Now, where does she live, more exactly?'

Lisana closed her eyes, and I felt her Key stir inside her as she cast her mind around the western part of the city. 'There's an old lady who lives next to the baker's on Eagle Lane.'

'It'll do,' I said. 'Also, there may be another reason for choosing that side of town.'

'Indeed?'

'It's where the servant's body was found.' Despite myself I couldn't resist adding, 'And I thought you kept a clean city.'

Though her face showed no outward sign, her fists clenched. 'Kite, don't push your luck.'

Considering my relations with Lisana I was given quite a nice room. It was away from the hubbub of any ballrooms or sculleries and commanded a view across the richest and most handsome area of the city. Someone had even left a wrapped set of Void-proof clothes across the bed. With them was a note in Lisana's precise handwriting, which said, 'Wear it.'

Scowling, I tore open the package, expecting the worst. Mage's robes with stars, puffy pants, silly hats – everything in the court that was fashionable seemed devised to torment me.

What I pulled out was quite a pleasant surprise. The codes are fairly unambiguous concerning some of the colours traditionally worn in Haven: white for dreams, black for nightmare, and grey for someone who hasn't established any kind of loyalty. The robe in the package wasn't exactly grey, more a kind of dulled silver mixed with my favourite shade of blue, but Lisana had intended it nonetheless as a message. Get your loyalties straight, Kite, because these days I pay the wages. It also made another point – while staying here, follow palace rules. And rule no. 1 was simple. Just look grand enough to pass as one of the crowd.

The robe was still soft after being summoned directly from the Void – by quite a talented mage, judging from the quality and look of the thing. It fitted perfectly, too. But I wasn't that much of a fool – you couldn't just summon something as fine as this without someone passing several hours of sweating and struggling in the Void. Lisana had known I would come, probably before I did. *Clever queen*. My respect for her, the one positive feeling I do have, rose several notches.

Meanwhile I paid a quick visit to the scene of the inferno spell – to what would have been the exact centre of a smoking crater half a mile wide if the thing had gone off. I wasn't greatly surprised to find that it was a small bathroom next to an empty guest room. Bathrooms were common places for reflection wards to be erected, and the floors were conveniently clear for our friend to draw his symbols and do his chanting. Some over-zealous mage had scrubbed off the last traces of the spell from the walls and floor, but I could still sense the after-taste left by the magic.

Curious. I'd expected the magic to drain away faster, once the spell was dismantled. But it still clung faintly to the place as though it were one large storage space for raw power, instead of just another room in just another kingdom. *Very* curious.

Since I had to start finding answers somewhere, the next thing I did was to go in search of the city watch.

The watchmen of Haven are a mixed bunch. It's gener-ally agreed that patrolling the streets of the City of Dreams is one of the easiest jobs there are, given the nature of the place. But it's also agreed that the worst crimes are those buried deepest.

So, where in a kingdom of nightmare you'd get five minor thefts and one murder a week, in Haven you'd get one minor theft, a long period of calm and then a grisly, nasty murder to turn the stomachs of all. Just because the city itself is regarded as pleasant, it doesn't mean the people in it are all smiles and charm. The material things of this world can never entirely change people's natures.

Which makes for a very unusual watch. You realise this the second you enter the small courtyard, a place not unlike the Consortium's headquarters at Silverpoint, where the watch is based. The watchmen, those who aren't Key-bound and therefore tireless, loiter and chat, a favoured topic being the intricacies of one case or another. Let the Key-bounds bring in the criminals, they say, we'll find the evidence.

Every man is waiting for a disaster to happen, I thought, looking at the faces of men who knew too well what a bitch fate could be. *They've seen the worst that dreams has to offer, and now they're waiting for it to happen here. Well, boys, you never know . . .*

'I've come about a murder,' I said to the Key-bound watchman on a desk.

'Name?'

'Lenian Kiret.'

'I'll see if the commander's around.' The man rose, disappeared into a back room and a few minutes later re-emerged with a man with red eyes and a fatigued slouch.

'Yes?' demanded the commander. He hadn't shaved for several days, and his uniform was stained with just about every kind of sauce to be sold cheaply at the local market.

'I've come about a murder.'

'Which one?'

'This week. The servant from the Sunpoint entourage.' I gave the dead man's name. He'd been called Corbe.

'Right. We know sod all about it, so you'd better make it good.'

'Can I have a word with you in private?' I asked, glancing around us. 'I've been sent by someone from the palace.'

The commander snorted derisively at the mention of the palace, good man that he was, but led the way nevertheless into a small office that reminded me of T'omar's in almost every chaotic feature.

'The last guy,' he snapped, 'sent by the palace had orders from the chamberlain himself to keep the murder quiet. But did he give us a single connection on which to work? No! – he just said the man Corbe was of "diplomatic importance" and the situation was very delicate.' He looked at me with doubt in his tired eyes. 'You're not going to tell me to keep it quiet, are you? I've been investigating this thing "quietly" for days, and I'm getting nowhere. All we know is that he had his throat cut while in the western quarter.'

'I have a confession to make – no, not that sort,' I added hastily, seeing his face lighten. 'I was sent by the palace. But before that I came from Silverpoint.'

The light drained from his eyes. 'You're a bloody spy.'

'No, just a spy.' Briefly I explained what had brought me to see him. The murdered Corbe's identity as Rylam's servant. Rylam's petition to Lisana for aid in claiming Sunpoint. The half-drawn inferno spell near the queen's bedroom.

'The spell is disabled, Rylam arrives, Rylam's servant is found dead in a district where he shouldn't have been in the first place. Why?'

'You tell me,' he said. 'Dreams above, I *hate* politics.'

'You and me alike. And since you ask, you now know as much as I do.'

There was a long silence, in which his watchman's mind was summing me up. 'Bit blunt for a spy, aren't you?'

'When people are writing inferno spells in the queen's palace, it's easiest just to get on with things.'

'Good policy. All right, what do you want?'

'Right now, I want to know why this servant was in the western quarter.'

'You've got time on your hands?'

'Since this is probably the only lead I've got, yes. Plenty of time.'

Commander Janyvir Reshin was a man who liked his crimes solved nice and neatly, I soon discovered. For himself, he lived the life of a slob. His uniform hadn't been cleaned for years and looked as attractive as a dog after a mud bath. Debris, so it seemed, strewed his office, over desk and floor and one of the walls where he'd pinned up pictures and maps and strange spider-like diagrams that to me might as well have been in another language.

But however foul his outer garb and lifestyle, the eye soon noticed how, once you got within a few feet of him, Janyvir himself was not the mess you'd expect. He was lean from patrolling the streets for most of the day, his hands were calloused by sword practice, his eyes were alert from reading file after file and seeing things that mere mortals would never have spotted. He moved like a nervous pigeon hopeful of food – his head constantly snapping from side to side in search of danger while the rest of him almost bounced up and down with tension. Yes, there was no doubt about it – Commander Janyvir was the copper incarnate.

Which was why, when his men had found no clue to indicate the murderer, and the palace had delivered a firm 'silence' order, he'd taken over the case personally.

We started in a small, plain room where boxes were stacked floor to ceiling. He pulled a box from on top of one pile, slammed it down on an empty table and prised the lid off.

'Here's your man. One set of very unfashionable clothes cut in a foreign style.'

'Sunpoint, all right,' I said as he laid out a bundle of white garments stained with blood. Sunpoint had its own peculiar style of clothes, being about the only desert kingdom in the Void. Even when travelling the people seemed instinctively to dress if not for the desert then for high summer.

I watched him dig deeper into the box.

'One pouch, discovered empty.'

I took the small square pouch and turned it over and over. It was plain and about as useful as a winter shower.

'One bottle of green ink, only just opened.'

'Green?'

'There's more.' From the bottom of the box he extracted a money pouch, waggling it back and forth so that I could hear the jingle of coins. 'One money bag, *full*.'

I took it. 'Oh hell.'

'Exactly what I thought. What kind of murderer attacks a guy, steals whatever it was in his pouch, but doesn't take the money? What was in his pouch, for that matter, that was so much more valuable than money?' Janyvir smiled humourlessly. 'And then the palace tells me to keep quiet. So, more than an average murder. Almost an assassination, surely?'

'Committed by a very stupid assassin. The good ones *always* take the money, to make it look like a robbery.'

'Oh, the assassin is even more interesting than *that*, sir. You're not squeamish, are you?'

I gave him a long, sideways look. 'If you're proposing I stare at a body shortly before supper, forget it. Just give me the summary.'

'Have it your own way. The body was found, over in the western quarter, with the throat cut, but that wasn't all. There was no sign of a struggle, no one reported hearing a scream or cry for help, and this servant was a big man — it would have taken more than a rather shallow cut in the dark to bring him down.'

'He'd already been killed another way?'

'Yes — then had his throat cut in the most amateurish manner to make it look like a mundane attack.'

'Mundane? You mean he was killed by magic?'

'That's exactly what I mean. You know anyone magical who might want to kill him?'

'I can think of only one mage who's actually connected to him,' I said, thinking of Rylam's entourage, 'but he'd have no motive, surely. Besides, the man was being watched. You must have more idea than I what magely assassins might be in the city.'

He considered. 'A few from nightmare, perhaps. One or two mages who couldn't get a place at a college have been known to go bad.'

'I want a list of all magical residents who might have "gone bad", please.'

'That'll take some time. How many assassins do you know who'd let themselves be registered under a real name or address?'

'We've got to start somewhere, haven't we?'

The sky was turning pink and the bells in the palace were ringing for dinner, by the time I returned to my room.

Having changed, I caught sight of myself in the mirror, and nearly laughed at the stranger I saw there. Not someone plotting all kinds of base tricks for the Consortium, but a man wearing the fine robes of the palace. In all that silver and blue silk I almost looked like a proper courtier. I, who kept a dagger in my belt at all times and knew every way there was to trip an opponent into the mud. Yet here I was again, pretending to be somebody grand.

I shrugged and went in search of food.

Lisana likes dancing, and isn't bad at it. So the great hall, which I remembered mostly as a stony place with long tables staged in order of rank, was now brilliant from the light of many chandeliers, with a high musicians' gallery and a vast dance floor across which courtiers were already wheeling. There was a throne at the far end surrounded by plainer chairs which, as so often, were far more comfortable, and around the walls were tables heaped with elaborately presented food.

The place was heaving with great folk in their finest, and it was an easy matter to pick out the old and new from among the dancers. The older courtiers, those who'd been fortunate enough to survive nightmare's invasion of Haven, still shamelessly sported the extravagant garb favoured by the previous king. The young, who viewed themselves as Lisana's new generation, wore more refined clothes cut to much the same simple design as mine. But they were still a mixed bunch. Every kingdom had its own fashions, and nowhere did it show more than in this meeting place of Wardens and other official visitors.

I slipped into the hall with a crowd of others, so that the unfortunate Key-bound man announcing arrivals was unable to keep up, thus passing me by. I stuck to the edges of the room, not being the world's finest dancer, and once again the short-guy-at-the-back routine paid off. Those who noticed, simply looked me over and turned away again. I cherished invisibility while I could, and helped myself to the food. It was arty stuff – Lisana really did suffer from a surfeit of good taste – and I couldn't see how all those bite-sized pastries or delicately assembled slices of fish were going to feed the whole hall.

'Try one, sir. You'll love it, I'm sure.'

I turned, ready to refuse, and looked into the impassive face of Eisirrn. With inexplicable ease this cook-Silverhand had changed in no time, from providing huge slabs of meat for one king, to contriving jewel-like tartlets for his successor.

It was a relief to see a friendly face among the crowd, even though we had to pretend not to know each other. I took the biscuit-like thing he offered, along with a splat of reddish sauce. 'Thank you. The recipe for this must be complicated.'

'Oh, it is sir,' said Eisirrn, with every appearance of seriousness. 'And when I find out in full how it works I'll be sure to tell you.'

I suppressed my disappointment. 'You can't explain it now?'

'Sir, I am as baffled as you.'

He slipped away, at the same moment that a fanfare announced Lisana's entrance. I bowed – and stayed bowed – along with the rest of the room, watching from this greatly reduced height as she moved through the silent throng, resplendent and formal. At the end of the hall she turned gracefully, paused a for moment above the throne, and sat, gesturing as she did so for the court to rise. It was a perfectly timed display of regal authority, contrived to leave a lasting image of who was boss. The music struck up again and the roar of conversation returned.

I went on watching the queen. After all, it was my job.

A thin but constant trickle of people went up to her. Toadying youngsters tried, if nothing more, for a moment of her attention, and old councillors leaned down to exchange an occasional whisper, causing a frown or a laugh as her eyes fixed on the subject of their discourse.

People were starting to notice me, too. Several of the older lords, recognising me, were nudging their neighbours and whispering. A few of the younger and shrewder Wardens meanwhile appeared to have put two and two together, having observed how strong the magic was inside me – and also noticed, as I realised, how familiar I was with the whole court routine.

There was a movement at the end of the hall and my eyes darted again to the throne. A young man in white was kneeling before the queen. While she seemed to make level replies, he was talking urgently.

Dark hair, dark eyes, tanned skin. It had to be Rylam.

Lisana's eyes flickered towards me, and his followed. I knew then she'd mentioned that I was in Haven. From across the hall his eyes lingered on me for a long moment. Then he looked away again, as if he'd now stored the face of his enemy and would always recognise me at a glance.

After a few more words he rose, and was lost in the crowd. I helped myself to more food, and continued to watch the hall.

'My lord Kite.'

'My lord Rylam,' I replied, not bothering to turn.

I heard the faint undraping of breath and felt the barely suppressed wash of anxiety slip through his fairly standard mage's shields. Without turning I could picture several muscles tensing up in him, and felt a certain satisfaction at having caused discomfort so easily.

'The queen told me why you're here. I hope your uncle recovers soon.'

'Aunt,' I said, knowing perfectly well he'd been testing me.

There was another faint hiss of breath, as he realised how easily I'd seen through *that* most ancient of ploys.

I added, 'So do I, though it's unlikely. One can only hope she goes peacefully, now. But I'm curious – why did the queen mention me?'

'Why, as a former citizen of my kingdom.'

'My' kingdom? Your brother's, you mean. Don't get ahead of yourself, kid. And while I'm at it, Lisana only told you about my birthplace to give me a pretext for meeting you. So there.

'I fear that was a long time ago.'

'Not that long,' he said, as if you could just dismiss a few centuries here or there. 'Your family is doing well, I believe. The Kites are well respected in the rural areas.'

Just not respected for magic.

'I'm glad.'

'I hope we can meet again. I would be fascinated to hear of your exploits.'

'Exploits?' I asked, considering the word. Somehow it didn't fit my own definition of the various misadventures into which I'd been forced. But I supposed it would have to do.

Rylam left, with a tactful show of disappointment at not being able to draw out the legend. I watched him go. Shell had been right, I decided. The man was too polite, too handsome, too charming to be true. Everyone had at least one vice, and the better it was hidden, the more it was likely to be a bad one.

'They tell me you're a great mage.'

A woman, slightly taller than I was, with a tilted chin and button nose. She was staring at me as if I had committed some foul crime and she was about to pronounce sentence.

'They tell me that too, but I never believe them.'

A smile crinkled the corners of her mouth, but it was hastily suppressed.

I couldn't help staring back. What was it about her that was so different, yet utterly familiar? Something inside me was going mad. And my wrist was itching – it was getting worse every moment as I struggled to ignore it and went on scrutinizing the woman. She was young – very young – but possessed of a confidence and determination I hadn't seen in many of her age.

'Is it true you fell in love with a dreamer princess?'

'No, on at least one count.'

'Which one?'

'The princess part.'

She raised her eyebrows. 'You fell in love with a dreamer?'

'It didn't seem like love at the time.'

'Love never does,' she said. 'Only when love is gone and you're left floating adrift with no wind to fill your sails do you realise how much you came to depend on the breathing of your lover.'

I fought back a range of responses to such overwrought tosh, from sympathetic agreement to disbelief. Was language like this really her own? Managing to keep my face empty and my voice neutral, I replied, 'Sounds about right.'

I was scratching where the scar should have been, I realised, and hastily stopped. The answer to why she was familiar must be staring me straight in the face, and still I couldn't see . . .

'Miriam?'

A man, bright with magic, emerged from the crowd. I recognized him as Xavian, the mage who'd come to court from Sunpoint, with Rylam. He was a good deal older than Miriam, but not much more than me. Just for a second he froze when he saw me, before taking his charge by the arm and pulling her gently but firmly away.

'Miriam, I've been looking for you everywhere,' he chided. 'Good evening, sir. I do hope you don't mind my friend, but she's still a little unstable.'

I watched him steer her into the crowd.

Even though its unnatural itch was now fading, I turned my wrist over to see where I'd scratched. My fingers had dug so deep that they'd drawn blood, and I hadn't even noticed. Little beads of it clung to the skin, forming a straight line where Renna's knife had cut. At the sight of it, I suddenly felt the wound burn ice cold, filling my whole arm with knives. With a barely suppressed choke of pain I swept my hand over the cut, destroying in one movement the unnatural line of blood.

In the wake of my hand's passage, the scratch marks had all healed up, and there was not a trace of blood anywhere.

So. You're still after me, whoever you are.

I took a steadying breath, and looked up to make sure that no one had noticed this momentary episode.

Why did it happen now? When did it first start itching?

When Miriam came close.

But why? What is it about Miriam that triggered it?

No, wait. It itched before, when I dreamed of a place on Earth.

I looked through the crowds, searching her out again – yes, there, standing with the mage and talking earnestly to a husband and wife from a trading kingdom somewhere near the borders of nightmare. I turned my magical eyes on her, and felt it. That familiar shimmer of unreality that marked out a dreamer.

I nearly yelled with surprise, recalling my magic in a second. A dreamer! As real and stable as Renna had been – another comatose, perhaps?

But for a dreamer to become that stable she'd have to be close to something – or someone – here in the Void that corresponded to *her* dream, the object of *her* thoughts back on Earth.

It was that same proximity that gave dreamers reality, made them almost indistinguishable from us.

But if she is a comatose dreamer, does she understand what she could be? I doubted it. If Miriam had found out the potential for her own powers, she would hardly be hanging round in Haven with a mage of uncertain nature. And the way she'd questioned me . . .

'You fell in love with a dreamer?'

What did it mean? She'd heard that Laenan Kite had got involved with a dreamer, and come to me hoping for advice? The majority of dreamers were famously the most unstable creatures in the Void, not knowing where they were going or where they'd come from, forgetting almost everything and jumping from place to place at the speed of thought.

Comatose dreamers at least retained some semblance of sanity. But Renna was the first I'd ever met who'd exploited her full powers.

She's still a little unstable, the mage had said. Did that mean Miriam was seeking the full extent of what a dreamer in her state could do?

Surely no one apart from Renna and me knew what a comatose's true potential really was? Others had held her hand as she'd carried us across the Void and into the battle for Haven in the blink of an eye. But *I'd* been the one who'd nurtured her to what she was, *I'd* had the visions of a place on Earth where dreamers went who never woke up, *I'd* been the one who'd dreamt of her body's death, even as the mind lived on.

Was this mage, who looked so proprietorial towards Miriam, trying to crack the same riddle that I had?

I resolved at that moment not to let Miriam out of the sight of at least one damn good Silverhand watcher.

The evening went on.

'Oh, I *do* hope your aunt gets better soon!'

'Yes, it would be just frightful if anything bad should happen!'

'How's Stormpoint?'

'I hear the caravans are demanding more again, even though *we* won the war.'

'Sheer lunacy. The Void hasn't been safer in years!'

I hate you people. Why am I sitting with such stuck-up, self-obsessed pigs as you? Certainly not for Lisana, probably not for goodness and light, no matter how much I want to believe it, and if I am going through the torment of your company for my own sake then I think I might as well give up now.

I plastered a smile across my face and kept nodding appreciatively at all of them. The rich merchant and his pretentious wife. ('Oh, *you're* Laenan Kite! My, how full of surprises the Void is.') The old Warden laying down the law. ('Of course, it was before your time, but I remember when we showed those Swordpoint knaves who was who.') And the Warden's young heir, who knew just enough history to recall that the Swordpoint-Haven war had happened a very, very long time ago – so if his father wouldn't be dead within a week he was certainly getting frail.

I hate you all. I hate your mannerisms, your arrogance, your blind belief in your own capabilities.

'I'm going to get that shipment from Treepoint.'

'But what if the Warden won't send it?'

'He will send it.'

'But what if he doesn't?'

'He will.'

But I kept on smiling and listening, because that was my job and, ultimately, it was for the best. So I liked to believe.

But by midnight, when my head was swimming from one glass too many and I was lying on the bed with my boots only half off, I'd got no further than, *There's more to all this.*

Nothing to do with the inferno-spell threat to Lisana or with Sunpoint, I don't think. But something to do with whatever happened to me. I'd decided to treat the two as completely separate, even though I was starting to suspect some kind of connection. Silverhands don't believe in coincidence, and I was a stickler for that rule at least.

I get attacked by something wearing Renna's shape – call it 'R'. R injures me with a knife, does some kind of magic on me using my blood, I pass out in the process, thank you Laenan at least for staying awake during the useful bits.

When I come to, the injury is completely healed up without a trace, but there's blood on my clothes proving that I, or at least someone, was indeed hurt.

Still no connection to Sunpoint, save a rather unlikely conjunction of timing.

I arrive at Haven. I encounter a dreamer, and immediately have a reaction. Question – did I encounter any other dreamers along the way and have a reaction to them? I thought about this. No. So my reaction to Miriam may just be a general reaction to all dreamers brought on by whatever R did to me. Which raises the next interesting question. What did R do, why did R do it, and more to the point, is it dangerous?

If it's not dangerous, why apologise to me for doing it? Besides, what can I do about it? I can't track down something that's not there. I can't expel something from my blood with my magic – my magic is in my blood, it'd be like trying to dust a duster with the duster itself. But for all R is probably dangerous, I haven't started going mad yet, have I? And then it wore Renna's shape, talked like Renna, felt like Renna. So if it is Renna, she must have reason. Which is comforting, I guess. The problems – too much to do, not enough time or power or skill or simple basic understanding to do it!

Renna, I really, really hope it's you in there.

That night I dreamed of homesickness. Or so I thought at first.

I was surprised to wake, or as it should perhaps be put, sleep, in a forest that seemed almost magical. It was so similar to Stormpoint I nearly believed for several seconds that I'd returned home. There was the river, the sunlight catching its wavelets as they skipped over the pebbles. There were the tall trees, and the animals scampering away into the green shade of the forest.

I heard human laughter. A young woman broke from the woods nearby, giggling at a joke she'd just shared with someone unseen. Kneeling next to me by the river, she splashed water on her flushed face, oblivious of my stare. After a while though, her mirth faded, and she glanced left and right with confusion in her eyes. I wasn't surprised – humans can't generally see us, unless gifted with second-sight, but sometimes they can feel us watching. We are the freak gusts of wind, the eyes from above and the whispers in the night. She looked through me, and frowned slightly, as if chiding herself for her own childish instincts.

A man appeared from the forest, out of breath and grinning. The woman laughed to see him, rose to her feet and darted to his side, winding her fingers in his. I found myself wondering exactly *what* it was I was about to dream. There are some times, even if bodyless, when it's best not to intrude.

Then a scream shattered the peace of the wood. A second woman, wild-eyed, was running towards us. She had a look on her face that I never want to see again. At the sight of her I failed to move, indeed, so that she ran straight through me, into the arms of the other woman.

'What is it?' demanded the first woman. She was almost shouting, her features distorted by fear.

'Mary,' gasped the second.

The couple exchanged a look, as if it were some particular dread that was seeping through them and taking hold.

'Come quick,' begged the woman.

Instinctively I reached out to touch her, to offer comfort. But my hand passed through her. If anything my ghostly gesture caused her even more distress, because she suddenly gave a shudder and burst into the tears that had been welling up behind her eyes all along.

They began to run, up the slope and into the trees.

'Please God,' gasped the man, 'don't let her have done something stupid!'

I moved to follow, to where a bungalow with a wooden verandah came into view. Before I could see where they'd gone inside the building, my way was suddenly blocked, on the verandah steps. The largest, blackest cat I'd ever seen had leaped from nowhere into my path, making me jump. It stopped face on, its tail upright in greeting, and looked at me. Cats are good at seeing us disembodied intruders, just as we're good at seeing dreamers.

'Here, puss,' I murmured, even though my voice made no sound in that world. I reached out to stroke the creature, knowing my insubstantial fingers would pass through it nonetheless – and a claw shot out. It racked the air, and tore through my wrist as the empty thing it was.

Having struck out at me, the cat should have leapt away, intimidated by this intruder who passed through walls. Instead, it turned, with a look that might have passed for human, and stalked away as if with infinite purpose.

But what was my surprise?! This creature from another world had clawed through the air, its paw had passed through my arm as if it wasn't there, and yet I felt pain! Never, when dreaming of Earth, had I experienced any physical sensation. But here – here was pain!

I knew then, what the creature was. A shape-shifter, whether friend or foe. Here to tell me something that I had to know, or torment me, deceive me – what?

'What?' I shouted soundlessly. 'What is it? Who are you?'

But my surroundings were becoming shadowy, a

second world scribbled faintly across the background of this one. I recognised the signs – so great had been the humans' distress that it had started waking me. I tried to fight it, tried to stay asleep. As is the way however, the more I resisted the more conscious I became.

Earth faded entirely, and I was left lying in Haven with a head full of questions. Somewhere in the distant ocean of my raging mind, I heard the faintest trembling sound, as of a cat purring in delight.

And my white sheets were stained red with blood that poured freely from my shallowly slit wrist.

Healing magic is not my speciality, but I was quick to cast the strongest spell I had on that gash. I focused the magic with a strength that I didn't know I had. Remarkably, I felt it respond with ease. I was quite taken aback. That burst of fiery magic as it raced through my blood had felt like a healer's power ten times over. Indeed, as skin knitted back together, leaving just a long red scab to show what had happened in the night, the magic seemed to bring with it a clarity I hadn't noticed before. The world seemed somehow brighter, sounds sharper, smells . . . dreams above, I *could* smell freshly baked bread! I *could* hear the sound of my neighbour in the room next door turning over in his unbroken sleep.

It was as wonderful as it was terrifying. *I've got to get R's spells out of my system. All this is not natural.*

FOUR

A Day in Haven

I left the palace next morning wearing my plain one-of-the-crowd travelling clothes. They were almost noticeable for how unnoticeable they were, so it took a moment even for Rinset to see me among all the people and traffic. He was standing outside the palace gates, holding a basket of cheeses and running a right little business, all in the name of information. 'And you, sir?' he asked as I approached.

'How much?'

'For you, sir, I'll halve the price. Any one for two coppers.'

I handed over the coins with good grace, knowing I'd get them back, and asked, 'Any kind in particular?'

'I recommend the Waterpoint Red, sir,' he said, pointing at a neatly wrapped bundle. I took it, slipping it into my pocket and walking away with a nodded acknowledgement.

This was the easy part of the day's work. I put a good half mile between him and me before finding a pleasant little square away from the bulk of human traffic, and sat down in the shade of a fig tree. All around were tall apartments from whose windows laundry was hung out to dry. A pair of children watched me from a balcony, a dog barked somewhere, and the sound of traders trying to out-yell each other seemed a long way off.

There was something so familiar about this routine, the disguised little meetings, the searching for an obvious hiding place, which to a clever man is just so obvious that no one would ever cover it, that I found myself already slipping into the old routines I'd learnt in those first years at Silverpoint. Skirting the rooftops for watchers, check-ing the streets regularly for the same pair of boots that followed me everywhere, probing the area for anyone hiding in some nook. I was on the case again, and all the old instincts were returning with the promise of a hunt.

Unwrapping the bundle, I ate the cheese and examined without high hopes the note that had been shoved in with it. It was a watcher's report on Rylam, compiled by Shell.

Subjects are housed on the top corridor of the guest wing. Rylam shares an apartment with his servant, Corinna. The mage, Xavian, shares a room with Miriam . . .

My mind raced. Miriam was the mistress of Xavian? The mage who'd led her away from me with such furtive urgency?

Rylam requested access to the royal scribes' library, and spent most of the day there with Corinna. The librarian suggests Rylam was studying the family tree of all those who have ruled Haven, inclusive of their distant relatives. During the day Miriam and Xavian stayed under a reflection shield at all times . . .

The report bore a postscript, hastily scrawled.

Rylam went into Xavian's rooms drunk last night, and disappeared under a reflection shield. He returned half an hour later with heavy bruising and his wards in tatters. If Rylam's bad, I don't doubt that Xavian is even worse.

This morning he took his injuries to the palace healer, but tried to conceal his identity . . .

A report of mixed usefulness. Shell had done the right thing in merely reporting what had happened. But *someone* had to draw a conclusion from what she'd described. I had a disagreeable feeling it would be muggins.

I was growing very interested in Rylam, though. Why his studies in the history of Haven? And why would Xavian want to attack him? Sighing, I put the paper away and went to find Janyvir.

He met me with one of his shrewd looks – and a bad surprise to match.

'I don't suppose you lot from Silverpoint will have anything on this other dead guy?'

Against all expectations of the City of Dreams, there'd been a second murder within one week.

'He was found late last night, stabbed through the heart. The boys call him Brawn.'

'Wait, don't tell me. He's a big guy who looks like he could knock a wall down with a fist.'

Janyvir hesitated before adding, 'Only I think we should be treating both cases as one.'

'You do? Why?'

There was a thud as a box was extracted from its pile. 'Have a look at this, it may interest you.'

I fumbled through the contents. A set of plain Void-proof clothes, stained with blood. A set of knives ranging from small and refined to large meat cleavers. And a collection of leather straps that hung together without making any sense at all. 'What are these?'

'Sheaths. The corpse was found with knives hidden all over him. We also think he was a mage – some of his stuff was warded.'

'Could he be the assassin who killed Corbe?'

Janyvir paused. He wasn't going to say yes, but then, he didn't say no either. *A man so after my own heart that he was starting to drive me up the wall.*

'Not when the palace says there's diplomacy involved in Corbe's murder,' he said thoughtfully. 'This second death looks too untidy for that.'

'Do you know where Brawn was staying?'

'Nope.'

'Great.'

'Do we still have to keep it quiet?' he asked. 'No posters on the streets saying, "Have you seen this man?", no arrests?'

'Please.'

'Typical. You people who work for the palace are all the same.'

'Nonsense. I'm one of the nicer ones,' I said. 'Now, where was the body found?'

It was a little park in the western quarter, pleasant enough if it hadn't been for those details that give any neighbourhood away. The heavy iron chains on the gates of the larger houses, the way windows only started on the first floor, or the ground floor windows were all shuttered up. The griffins circling overhead at all times, searching for

anyone of a suspicious nature. The smoke rising from all
the nearby smithies. The laughter of a pair of drunken soldiers as they staggered across the park, stopping to piss on
a statue. Janyvir watched them with disgust.

'Areas around barracks are always degenerate,' he
muttered bitterly. 'Plus we've got a lot of traders from
nightmare and you know what they're like. They keep
the peace while they're here, but some of them ought to
get arrested just for what they're thinking . . .'

'The body,' I urged.

He led me to a park bench, standing in a little arbour
of trees. The wood, which was old and splintered, was
still stained from the blood. It was a safe place to commit
murder – away from all eyes but so tranquil by day that
few would think of patrolling it at night.

'What was he doing here?'

'You asking me?' demanded Janyvir as if the idea was
ludicrous.

'Make a guess.'

'What would you do here, Silverhand?'

I frowned and made no answer. Instead I started wandering around the little park, searching for the mark
which I felt in my bones had to be there.

'If you're looking for what I was, it's over there.'
Janyvir pointed at a rock garden nearby. I went and
squatted down in front of a pile of rocks between which
trailing purple and pink flowers contested for precious
space in a patch of sunlight.

Over the garden's sound of birdsong there was a
crunch of boots on gravel behind me, and Janyvir's voice
said, 'After finding that, any message from the palace
about the first murder seemed almost inevitable.'

I pushed a leaf aside and stared at the green mark. It was daubed in thick ink on one of the rocks. And below it, a small purple circle – a counter-signal if ever I saw one.

'An exchange.' I sighed. 'Things are getting more complicated, if anything.'

'What have we got then?' demanded Janyvir as we walked away from the scene of the crime, two figures bowed by heavy matters. 'Corbe comes out to the western quarter to meet someone.'

'To hand over documents?'

'Hence the empty pouch,' he agreed. 'The signal that his exchange partner is ready to meet and it's safe is a purple blot. He draws a green cross to signify that he's also safe, the two see each other's signs and the meeting goes ahead. Only it doesn't.'

'One question,' I said thoughtfully, 'is whether or not the second man got the documents before our assassin got to Corbe.'

'You care to make odds?'

I considered. 'Evens. The signalling system was clumsy – bad delivery man. But then the assassination attempt was clumsy – bad assassin. The two deserved each other.'

'All right,' he said. 'The document isn't handed over, because only one man was found murdered here, not two.'

'Dodgy reasoning – the first may have come early, been killed, the assassin flees, the second arrives, sees his partner dead . . .'

'The document isn't handed over successfully,'

repeated Janyvir firmly '– bear with me – and the assassin gets it first. The assassin – Brawn – is then murdered by . . . whom?'

'Assuming Brawn even *is* the assassin.'

We fell into a long contemplative silence, in which I realised we were also keeping pace. Somehow sharing the same thoughts had made us both slip into a copper's automatic stride, and we were even now trying to out-do each other for burdened watchman of the year.

'There is something else I can do,' I said finally.

'This Rylam bloke?'

'Exactly. I doubt if he'll tell me anything useful, though – a slippery character as ever I saw.'

'So apart from him, did anyone else know Corbe?'

I smiled despite myself – already he'd discounted Rylam as too hot to touch. Truly we were going to make a great team.

'Possibly. Over time, I'm told, fellow servants get very close to each other.'

I returned to the palace just after midday, slipping in through the tradesmens' entrance, and taking my time about it too. I'd been careful to head to the palace by a very up-and-down route and even raised a few spells of 'Who? Me?' when I reached crowded areas. I had the feeling of being followed – either that or my imagination was playing tricks. Once in the palace, I went in search of the only other person in Haven who might know anything about Corbe – Rylam's other servant, the woman named Corinna. An instinctive knowledge of how the palace was laid out – important guests at the top but a long way from the queen and, at the bottom, kitchens and other working quarters – led me without much trouble to the apartments housing the Sunpoint entourage.

Xavian's room was obvious – a thick, well-worked reflection shield surrounded it and Lisana, with her intelligent use of manners and understanding of convention, hadn't tried to break into it. I kept my own curiosity to myself, knowing how difficult it could be to get past some kinds of warding without causing a huge uproar.

Rylam's room was also shelled within a reflection shield, but of a flimsier kind. It was enough to block my probes but, as so often with these magical defences, it didn't allow for the simplest, most mundane solution to my problem. Checking that no one was coming, I knelt by the keyhole, squinted and gained a very narrow view of the room which, if I strained, I could just expand to a ten-degree width.

Somebody was standing by the far window, wearing a light shift of white. I couldn't see if anyone else was there, but there was a way to find out.

Rising, I knocked briefly on the door, then ran for the far end of the corridor. Just as I rounded the corner the door opened. I waited for a breathless second, drew a quick spell of 'Who? Me?' and rounded the corner again looking as casual as possible, eyes on the floor and hands in my pockets as though deep in thought.

A woman had stuck her head out, looking left and right with an anxious frown. The 'Who? Me?' spell usually has the effect of making people not notice you. This time I'd drawn it deliberately weak so that, though Corinna would doubt her own memory if asked to recall my features, for the moment she saw me well enough.

For a second I thought she wasn't going to fall for it.

Then a voice worn down by habitual tension asked, 'Excuse me, but did you see anyone?'

I glanced up, as if annoyed to be broken from my reverie. 'Pardon?'

She effected a bow, rising to say only that someone had knocked on the door.

'I saw the house chamberlain, if that's any help.'

'Oh. Thank you.' The door began to close.

'Corinna.'

The door stopped, then re-opened fully. She was a typical Sunpoint woman – stringy and compact, worn dark and toughened by the desert.

'You know me, sir?'

'Where's Rylam?'

She seemed to bridle at this question, probably because of something in my tone. 'In the library, sir.'

'Are you expecting him back soon?'

'My master doesn't tell me what his plans are – I simply obey.' She seemed quite proud of the fact.

'Can I come in? I was the one who knocked on your door – I wanted to catch you alone.'

I hadn't meant to say that, having planned on something far less blunt. It was probably a morning with Janyvir that did it.

'Why, sir?' she asked coldly. I'd definitely got off on the wrong foot with this woman.

'I'm from the city watch. I'm interested in the murder of a man found in the western quarter.'

A flicker of doubt crossed her face, but it was just that – a flicker. 'Why do you think I can help?'

'Because he too was a servant of your master.'

She said nothing, raising her chin proudly in the face

of my almost-accusation. I recognised the type – follow
the master until death and proud of her own pointless
silence. It's said by buffoons who don't know better that
silence is golden. The opposite is true in my business.

'Look,' I said, as reasonably as possible, 'I know how
precarious Rylam's situation is here. He's come to beg
aid for a kingdom which, in the past, has been nothing
but a thorn in Haven's side. Lisana's only considering his
request because Sunpoint's economically strong, and
positioned to hurt nightmare.

'But if she says no to your master, he'll have to throw
himself on her mercy. And I know Lisana isn't above dis-
posing of potential enemies like that. The murder of this
servant – of Corbe – and finding the inferno spell, might
just convince her Rylam's more risk than he's worth.

'Unless, that is, I can prove that the real threat comes
from Rylam's brother – that the servant, *your* fellow, was
killed by Feilim. Because,' I smiled lop-sidedly, 'let's face
it. If Feilim is just a regular guy – and *not* a tyrant threatening all of dreams – Rylam hasn't a leg to stand on.'

She didn't move for a long moment, reviewing her
choices. Eventually, though, she saw reason. 'Come in.'

The door closed behind me, and I was immediately
aware of the unsettling presence of another mage's spells.
I kept my magic down to a minimum and tried to ignore
the urge to tear apart the reflection shield from within.

'So?' she said finally.

'So?' I was pushing her to go first, though I could see
she resented it. In her position I would too.

'What do you want to know?' she asked grudgingly,
knowing that I wasn't going to budge.

'What was Corbe doing in the western quarter?'

She shook her head 'I don't know.'

'Oh come on! He must have said something!'

'I don't know! He just went!'

'With money, a pouch full of documents and a signalling system? Please, don't take me for a fool. I know about Sunpoint – servants are bonded to their masters for life, there's no choice in the matter. The servants of the Warden are either slaves or people with nowhere to go, no alternatives save those given by their masters! Rylam must have known Corbe was up to something, *you* must have known!'

'No! Perhaps Corbe thought he could make a new life in Haven,' she stammered. 'Perhaps that's why he took the money.'

'And the documents and a way of signalling to a contact?' I snapped. 'Meetings at midnight aren't exactly the best way to start a new life, are they? Unless . . . unless he was blackmailing Rylam, perhaps? What if Rylam had his own servant murdered because . . . I don't know why, perhaps he knew something that Rylam was scared of, perhaps Rylam had gone to bed with the wrong woman, arranged for the wrong person to meet with an "accident". Is that true, Corinna? Was Corbe blackmailing his own master?'

'I . . . no!'

'*Then what was he doing?*' She made no answer but stood before me shaking with a mixture of rage and frustration, while I hammered the point home. 'If Corbe wasn't blackmailing Rylam, what possible motive could he have for going into the western quarter? How can you say he wasn't blackmailing if you don't know *what* he was doing instead?! How do you know Rylam didn't have his own servant killed?'

'My master is a good man!' she burst out suddenly. 'A good, honourable man! Corbe was a good man too – he was my master's page when he was just a boy, then his squire and then his servant for a hundred years! Corbe loved Rylam, as Rylam loved Corbe!'

I relaxed slightly, releasing the breath I didn't realise I'd been holding. Corinna's outburst had the ring of truth about it – she was too upset to come up with any really convincing lies and it wasn't that unusual for servant and master to grow close over a long period of time.

'All right,' I said, softly this time. 'I believe you. Rylam didn't have Corbe killed, Corbe wasn't trying to blackmail Rylam. What then was he trying to do? He was carrying a letter pouch and money. Who were the letters for? And the money, for that matter?'

'I don't know,' she whispered, tears brimming in her eyes.

'Look, I know you must be upset about Corbe,' – *and I'm really doing a lot to help, aren't I?* – 'but if you care for your master it's important that I can prove he had nothing to do with this. If Feilim has indeed sent assassins, then to track them down I need to understand them. And to understand them, I need to know why they killed Corbe.'

'I don't know,' she repeated.

'I think you do,' I said as gently as possible. 'I think you're trying to protect someone. Corbe? Rylam? Who is it you don't want to see hurt?'

She straightened her shoulders, and I realised I'd gone just a little too soft. While she'd been angry and upset I'd been able to push her into my control – by relaxing that again I'd given her time to recover her wits.

'I have nothing more to say to you. My master didn't

kill Corbe. I don't know what Corbe was doing in the western quarter. He would *never* betray my master.'

'Telling me is the best thing,' I murmured, even though I knew my words fell on deaf ears. I'd already told her too much, trying to draw her too far, and in the process lost the advantage.

'I have nothing to say.'

'You do. You're just not saying it.'

Her face tightened, her eyes turned hard. Regretfully, I turned and left her. There would be another opportunity, though. I could wait. The longer you waited, with the enemy knowing you were there but unable to do anything about you, the stronger you became. Cruel, but true. I'd wait. For now. I was very good at waiting.

It was another dance that night. Skirting the edges of the hall I stuck to the routine of waiting for people to come to me. Watching, waiting, thinking.

I caught Lisana's eye as I passed near the throne, but if she wanted to ask me anything she didn't let it show. Besides, the illustrious queen wasn't in the habit of asking people. She expected them to do what they were told and report back without question.

'My lord Kite, might I please have a word?'

I turned, the smile already fixed on my face.

Rylam was standing behind me. 'Are you really here to see your aunt, sir?'

'Why else would I spend most of today in the western quarter?'

'It's widely known, my lord, that you have a care for the queen's safety. If there's anything you want to know to that end, feel free to ask me personally.'

'What are you implying?' I asked, as evenly as possible.

'My servant had a visitor this afternoon. A man with a face that she can't recall – even the colour of his hair is vague.'

I forced a laugh – and was disappointed at how easily it came. *Dreams above, am I really this good at lying?*

'I am here because my aunt is dying, sir. She never had children, her husband is long dead. When I first came to Haven she was the only one who showed me kindness, and I intend to repay it. My days of fighting for dreams are long over.'

'Really? And they say you're still under six hundred years old. Good for another three hundred, surely?'

'Three centuries which I intend to spend in relaxation and repose. Whoever called on your servant, I'm sure he had good cause. Your protection, for example. The queen's safety too and ultimately the well-being of dreams.'

'My protection?' he echoed. 'You mean from my brother's assassins?'

'Among others,' I murmured.

'What others, sir?'

I forced a smile and stood up straighter. He was still a good sight taller, but I wanted to give the impression of having shaken off the conversation. 'I really don't know. Sometimes we need protection from ourselves, perhaps? I hope the healer was able to help, by the way.'

He didn't even flicker. His face, like Corinna's in a similar situation, was as empty as stone. 'Good evening, sir.' He turned on his heel and disappeared into the crowd.

'Very impressive,' said Xavian, who'd been loitering nearby and pretending not to listen.

I spared him the briefest of looks, intent on spearing myself another slice of meat, before turning back to watch the dancers. All those whirling colours, those men and women completely unaware that there was a world beyond the walls of their stately manors and luxurious palaces . . .

'I don't know what I've done to earn such high praise,' I said. 'But thank you anyway.'

'I was congratulating you on how well you play the part of the harmless little man.'

'"Harmless little man"?' I echoed. I was torn between delight at hearing my acting skills so highly praised and shock at realising that yes, that was exactly the image I was trying to give.

'Oh, come now. I know what you are. A powerful, powerful mage joining games you don't really want to play. The unwilling player is always the one least blinded by the goals he's trying to achieve.'

'You think some covert agenda has been forced on me?'

'That's my impression. Otherwise, is it not strange that an expert on Sunpoint, a powerful mage, a patriot even, should arrive in Haven so soon after the queen's life is found to be under threat?'

'Almost as strange as you arriving when you did, and with such consequences.'

'Almost.'

I looked at Xavian out of the corner of my eye, and seemed to see him for the first time. He held himself as straight as a poker, and showed about as much emotion. His eyes never left the swirling hall, and he stood tall and proud as if ready to take on the world and its biased, blind opinions and, what was more, to win.

'Where do you come from?' I asked.

He glanced at me sharply, no doubt wondering where that question had sprung from. 'Sunpoint.'

'It's your place of birth?'

'Yes.'

'Your *parents'* place of birth?'

'Ah.' He smiled, and his eyes drifted back to the hall again. 'Your image as the harmless little man is shattered, I'm afraid.'

'I know about Sunpoint,' I continued, as firmly as I could. 'I know it can be pointless to generalize, but you're just . . . not from Sunpoint. You're too . . . different.'

'Too mannered? Too magely?' he suggested. Impossible to tell if he intended any irony.

'I was thinking of clever. Notwithstanding what little national pride I have as a native of Sunpoint myself.'

'I'm flattered. "Clever" and from Laenan Kite himself! I shall relish telling my grandchildren about that.'

'Where are you from?' I repeated stubbornly.

'My mother came from Sunpoint. She was just a minor mage, taught me most of what I knew. My father was from Firepoint, and he taught me everything else. I haven't seen them for a long time.'

But he'd already said enough. Firepoint was a kingdom of nightmare, famous for producing a particularly warlike breed of necromantic mages. Though I'm usually against generalization, I am prepared to say that necromancers are ninety-nine per cent stupid bastards. Here, crying out at me, was a crime just waiting to happen.

FIVE

Connections and Divides

In my dream I knew the place. A bungalow miles from everywhere, connected to the rest of its world by a dusty track. In the distance I could hear the splashing of a river and, yes, the forest came right up to a garden where a vegetable patch was being eagerly dug up by the family dog.

I'd been brought back to where I was before, but this time there was no one to be seen. Deciding it was my dream, and bugger to all manners, I drifted through the walls and into the house in search of life.

The place was in chaos.

Kitchen drawers hastily emptied and cupboards turned inside out, their contents left scattered across tables and even over the floor. A curved device that I knew worked like an electronic form of call-signature, only without the privacy or magic, hung by a long wire off a device on the wall. From it came a steady little whine, as of a trapped fairy trying to escape

I stared at a box, one of the few items which actually spoke my language. Bandages were heaped around it, along with leaflets about what to do in cases of emergency. It was what I knew from my own world as a herbalist's box, for first aid it said, and someone had been searching through it with unnatural haste. Several empty packets were strewn around it, labelled with things like 'Nurofen' and 'Anadin' and bearing stern warnings like 'do not exceed the recommended dose'.

I left the kitchen and wandered into the living room.

There was the cat again, staring at me from on top of a large padded sofa. It was watching from a distance, never blinking, only the topmost tip of its tail in motion.

And there was the pain again. This time the cat hadn't even scratched me! I stared at my wrist – three precise marks, running horizontally across the exact same place where R had cut me! And again, the pain was of ice cold fire! I tried to wipe the hurt away as I had done before, but if anything that made it worse. The cat hissed, and sprang out of the room. I raced after it, into the garden, and found myself blinking in brilliant sunlight, unable to see anything save burning whiteness . . .

It was the voice that woke me. And the shaking. And the feeling of being watched, eyes all around, eyes in every corner that were as substantial as shadow and as hard to dispel.

Although the pain would probably have woken me up just as well. The pain and the cold.

I sat bolt upright, the dagger I kept under the pillow flying into my hand and coming up to end the life of my attacker . . .

Lisana leapt back in the most undignified manner, and immediately looked embarrassed. So did I for that matter. Already I was struggling to remember what it was that had scared me so much, or what that pain was that had pursued me through the night.

'It's late,' she said. 'I was going to wait. But if you can't be bothered to wake up at the accepted time, it's your problem. I don't pay you to lie in bed.'

'You could've knocked, ma'am,' I grumbled. I was drenched with sweat, my sheets were crumpled from too much tossing and turning and the dagger was an embarrassment in my grasp.

'Do you imagine I didn't? I couldn't wait any longer for you to answer. And since this is my palace and my kingdom, I might as well come in.'

'I was having a bad dream of Earth.' I found I was still shuddering at the memory. 'I guess it carried over.'

'Earth is a strange place. What did you do to your wrist?'

I glanced down. There was a very, very thin line of blood across it. 'I didn't.'

'Then why is it cut?'

'I . . . don't know.' I brushed my hand across it, magicking the blood aside. Beneath, the skin was as whole as the day I was born. 'I did come into contact with a nasty spell,' I said cautiously.

She didn't buy it for a second. 'How nasty?'

'Pretty nasty. I took it to be something that it wasn't.'

'I thought you were the great one,' she said, her voice dripping scorn. A part of me wanted to believe that beneath Lisana's mask of aggression lurked genuine concern. If so, it was well hidden.

'I'm sure it's nothing,' I lied. 'What brings your highness into her loyal servant's bedroom at this hour?'

'Get your cloak and boots. I want to show you what the guards found this morning.'

I got up and joined Lisana outside. My pyjamas attracted a few stares, but I just glared back. There was a smell of fresh baked bread on the air, and that was odd, because the kitchens were a long way from my room. I was also colder than was normal for the average day in Haven, but I put it down to nerves. Theoretically, I knew I ought to be panicking about the events of the night, but what could I do? Surely it would only be a matter of time before the mysterious R wanted to reclaim on whatever investment it'd had in attacking me.

Then I'd be sure to wring a *real* apology.

Outside the door, two guards who'd been waiting fell into step behind us as the queen led the way down a staircase, across a courtyard, down another flight of stairs and into a large cellar.

Even before we reached the door I said, 'Someone's been killed here.'

I hadn't sensed it deliberately. But now that I extended my thoughts ahead I could feel the soldiers gathered around the body, and the emotionless Key-bound servant clearing up where some weak-hearted onlooker had lost his nerve and his breakfast.

I could also feel . . . *Rylam*?

And then the sense that this was . . . a very bad assassin? But how would a bad assassin get into the palace undiscovered?

I turned to examine the black chalk marks on the wall, in which the magic for a curse still glowed. It was a nasty curse – necromantic, complicated and requiring considerable power.

There are two kinds of spell-casting. The first, and the kind I favour, is to go directly up to your target and cast the spell then and there, not bothering with finesse and leaving such essentials as an escape route until afterwards. My thinking is that, if you do win against this target, then the escape route will invariably open up of its own accord. It's remarkable how few people are willing to fight for a dead employer.

The second kind is where symbols, incantations, chalk marks or candles are involved. Used for such things as divination, which is one of the hardest, most dangerous spells a mage can undertake, it's also employed by those assassins who want to, say, set a building on fire by magic but be well away by the time the spell starts to burn. To do this you need a large understanding of magical symbols and keys, and some kind of trigger system written into the spell itself.

But however hard I looked at the scrawls on the wall, bright with magic, I couldn't see any sign of a trigger! It was the outline of a necromantic curse all right. But nothing in it suggested the little sub-spell that might have activated the curse once the caster was away.

Either this man had a whole complicated system of magic that l have never seen before. Or he was willing to commit suicide for his cause. Or . . . the spell was never meant to be finished.

What's the point of writing a spell that can't be finished?

I gave up. There were some things on which you needed the opinion of a professional. Which was fortunate, because just as I passed through the palace gates looking for one, it came in search of me.

'Cheese, please.'

Rinset handed me a cheese from the back of his tray, took my money with a grunt of thanks and went about his work without meeting my eye. I felt the little bundle of paper folded beneath the cheese, and slipped the package into my pocket.

'I was about to come looking for you.'

I glanced up and into the face of Janyvir Reshin.

'Do I know you?' I asked, aware of the palace gates so close behind us. I'd had no time to lose any pursuers – I need at least five streets, a good crowd and a series of spells to get rid of all but the best trackers. Here, having just emerged onto the street, I was painfully conspicuous.

I'll give this to him – he did respond quickly. 'Sorry, sir. Must have mistaken you for someone else.'

<Ten minutes, Blue Moon Square? At the centre of the maze?> I sent into his mind.

'Have a good day sir,' he said, nodding slightly. 'I know how easy it is to get lost.'

'Fortunately I don't get lost,' I said smoothly.

'Neither do I.'

Good. You do know how to get through the maze.

Blue Moon Square is just a few minutes' walk from the palace. It's where jugglers, illusionists and musicians gather to entertain audiences of all ages, and at any hour of the day it's usually swollen with people. There are large and eccentric structures for clambering children to go berserk on, little groves where tired adults relax in each other's company, even a pond surrounded by weeping willows with delicate silver leaves where youngsters steal their first kiss. And in the middle of it all is an enormous maze of head-high silver bushes. For centuries the Consortium had used it as a meeting place, as much as an act of humour as for its convenience. The trick was to take the second left, then the first right over and over again, until you reached the centre. Every king or queen of Haven had kept it that way – it's my belief that they simply weren't up to designing an effective maze themselves.

So I picked my way through the narrow pathways with ease, recalling all those times down the years when I'd done exactly this. In the dead of night, perhaps, to meet some unlikely contact or plot some inspired scheme. It felt like home.

The centre of the maze was deserted, as usual. There wasn't much to recommend it anyway – a sundial, a bench and an old peach tree. The tree's fruit, just starting to splatter the ground, was edible, but I wasn't hungry.

Besides, I had cheese.

'What's that?'

'Daily report,' I replied, reading carefully and slipping it into a pocket. 'Surveillance. I see my friends are doing what I wanted.'

'I've got news for you,' said Janyvir, sitting down next to me. 'I was about to go to the mages, ask them to scry for your whereabouts. It was lucky I found you coming out of the palace.'

I didn't answer his unspoken question. *What were you doing in the palace, and leaving it as though you owned the place?*

'Very lucky,' I murmured. 'I assume you had a reason why you were looking for me?'

Indeed he did. Early that morning a distraught woman had rushed into the watch HQ, claiming that her husband had been abducted by magic.

'I wasn't going to try and interest you, until she let slip the useful information that her husband was a newly arrived citizen of Sunpoint. He'd come to the city "looking to make his fortune".'

I looked up, suddenly hopeful. 'How new?'

'Three weeks.'

'Commander Janyvir, I believe you're an unsung hero.'

'You and me both,' he said, doubt in his eyes. 'I didn't know Silverhands stayed at the palace.'

He said it casually, hoping to catch me off my guard, but I was ready for him. 'Oh, I was just collecting a few messages, nothing out of the ordinary . . . May I have a chat with the wife? It might be that her husband was connected with a body found this morning in the palace.'

Janyvir gawped at me. 'In the *palace*?!'

'I'll tell you about it. Just as soon as I've talked to this woman of yours.'

The tearful wife was sitting in Janyvir's office having her hand held by a sympathetic blue-skinned nymph who'd been summoned for the specific purpose of 'lulling'. The woman's name, which I recognized as typical of Sunpoint, was Olma Kartoui. She had to stop her tale every few minutes while she wrung her hands and tried not to weep, but somehow she forced out the facts more or less in order.

In Sunpoint, sir, her husband Borutn had been studying under a powerful mage. He'd been sent to Haven, sir, by this mage, sir, to find a series of books in the huge library at the heart of the college of mages. But the book had proven harder to find, sir, and when he did find it, the library wouldn't sell.

Borutn sent to his master, asking what he should do, and his master instructed him to start copying out the book by hand, if necessary.

'That's what we were doing here, sir. And then, last night, my husband was sitting up late, copying the book, when an actual whirlwind of magic caught him up and made him vanish, just like that. I was so frightened, sir.'

'What was the book?' asked Janyvir.

'The Carionillan.'

Janyvir glanced doubtfully at me. 'Mean anything to you?'

'Well, I am a mage,' I said as humbly as possible.

He didn't show much surprise. 'You know, you just *look* like a mage. Only without the beard and wisdom.'

I ignored him. 'The Carionillan is a book of basic technique for focusing and refining spells, nothing more. The first years of the mages' schools have to study it if they want to cast really tough, well-built spells, but it's not necessary. I don't really see what the fuss was about.'

'My husband was very loyal, sir, and his master was a good teacher. If he wanted the Carionillan copied, then my husband was going to do it. He had a good hand,' she added proudly.

'What was the name of your husband's master?' I asked.

'Xavian, sir.'

Janyvir instantly sensed me freeze. 'Mean anything?' he murmured.

I nodded without taking my eyes off the woman. 'Mistress Kertoui, I know this sounds like a strange question, but did your husband ever use purple ink?'

'Purple?' she echoed. 'No, of course not.'

'You're sure. Completely sure?'

'Yes. I'm certain.'

I took a deep breath, focusing on the image in my mind as I started moving my hands to draw the symbols for the spell I needed.

For the wife's sake I blotted out the memory of the blood and spilt guts, and tried to envisage what the dead man in the cellar would have looked like in life. The illusion started shaping itself next to me and acquired form.

I heard her gasp.

'Mistress Kertoui, is this your husband?' I asked, struggling to maintain the image.

'Yes,' she whispered.

I dissolved the image in a second. 'Thank you. That's all I wanted to know. Commander?'

'I think I'm satisfied,' he said quietly, eyes not leaving my face.

'We'll inform you as soon as we find anything,' I said politely to the woman. She recognised a request to leave, and rose to her feet.

'Private!' snapped Janyvir. The door opened and a watchman appeared. 'Take Mistress Kertoui to the kitchens. Give her a nice hot mug of something to drink and a comfortable place to sit. And close the door behind you.'

We eyed each other like stags preparing to fight, waiting until the door had shut and the sound of footsteps had faded away.

'You know, you never told me your name,' Janyvir observed finally. 'You said "Lenian Kiret" to the man on the desk, but I'll bet you'd just made that up. What's your proper name? Sometimes, surely, a Silverhand will tell you what he's really called?'

I laughed, despite the tension in the room. 'In that case, I'm Laenan Kite, mysterious master of magics, at your service.'

Once again, human perversity played itself to the full. He snorted in disbelief at the absurdity of such a notion.

'A well-sung hero, that Kite.'

'Well sung, but not well known,' I replied lightly.

'All right, *Kite*,' that heavy lilt of scepticism again, 'tell me what's going on.'

I stretched like a cat, enjoying an audience, however incredulous. 'Shall we take this in chronological order? Xavian, the loyal mage of Sunpoint, sends Kertoui to Haven to copy a book which every schoolroom already possesses. A week later, Rylam flees Sunpoint for Haven, with his mage, the mage's mistress and two servants. What happens next?'

'A few days later one of the servants – Corbe – is found dead in a part of town where he shouldn't have been. Soon after that another corpse is found – Brawn, who reeks of professional assassin. A *third* man, Kertoui, disappears late at night . . .'

'And is discovered in the palace cellars by that same Rylam, who fights and kills him.'

'Questions,' Janyvir said flatly. 'We know about the how, the where and the when. That leaves why and who.'

I jumped to my feet and began pacing. Janyvir, I

noticed, had reached for a small woollen ball which he began squeezing and tugging with nervous energy.

He saw my look. 'Hey, you pace when you're stressed, I attack bits of wool. Why not?'

I sighed. 'Questions. Why was Corbe in the western quarter?'

'To meet and conduct an exchange with . . . someone.'

'Why was Brawn found murdered?'

'Because he murdered Corbe?' He added despairingly, 'How I *hate* circumstantial evidence.'

'Why was Kertoui sent to Haven?'

'Certainly not to copy a book.'

'Yet his wife seemed genuine. Have you searched his home?'

'A couple of the boys did this morning. They found the copies, all right. Plus enough work for at least two or more weeks' writing.'

'But why would Xavian send his apprentice to Haven on such a trivial errand? And at such an unstable . . . oh my.'

We both froze, and our eyes met.

Janyvir asked softly, 'Is this Xavian a truly cunning bastard, by any chance?'

'There's no proof of what we're thinking.'

'But it is possible.' He rose to his feet, and began pacing *and* squeezing.

'What if Xavian sees that his master, Rylam, is in danger? That soon they must both flee Sunpoint? He sends his servant ahead, on a trivial errand that will keep him tied down in Haven for several weeks.

'In due course Rylam arrives at the palace in Haven. Xavian *knew* – no surprise there – that the queen would need a huge incentive before she'd commit troops to attack a potentially friendly kingdom. So Xavian arranges to get his apprentice into the palace somehow, and sends Rylam to kill him before the eyes of several witnesses.

'Bang. No more suspicion on our Rylam.'

'The curse,' I murmured. 'It didn't have a trigger mechanism, it was never meant to be cast.'

'And the man's knife – that was no assassin's weapon. Dreams above, he even had the ink stains on his hands!'

'Would Xavian really have arranged for the death of his own apprentice? Just to give Rylam a little credit around the court?'

'It seems that way.'

'But how could he have drawn the curse? He was in his rooms all night! And how could he have got Kertoui into the palace in the first place?'

'You tell me. You're the mage.'

'The only way to abduct by magic is if you can jump from place to place using . . .' My voice trailed off. I couldn't believe how furious I was at my own stupidity. 'I am a total idiot,' I murmured. 'Just because she hasn't found her powers doesn't mean he can't harness them.'

'Who? What?'

'Miriam,' I snapped, sharper than I'd meant. I was angry with myself, angry at Xavian and most of all angry that it still didn't work! 'A comatose dreamer exactly like Renna was!'

'Renna?' he echoed.

'A comatose dreamer who was pushed so far so fast that she broke the conditioning of her earthly life and became a fully fledged, bodiless dreamer who could travel at the speed of thought!'

'And this Miriam's one of them?' he stammered, out of his depth.

'No! If Miriam was like Renna she certainly wouldn't be hanging round a wart like Xavian. But he can still harness her powers.'

'He can?'

I sighed, and forced my self-reproach back under control. 'How was Haven freed from nightmare, all those years ago?'

'The forces of dreams used . . .' Janyvir's eyes widened. 'They used the teleportation powers of dreamers – yes!' His face was now one large grin. 'Xavian uses a dreamer to teleport Kertoui into the cellar, Kertoui doesn't leave because his master says it's for the best. Xavian teleports back to his rooms, sends Rylam down to the cellars to fight and kill Kertoui. And so Rylam becomes a hero and Kertoui a faceless assassin.'

'But he isn't!' I exclaimed. 'Because Xavian, for all he's a clever trickster, has made several mistakes. Kertoui is too obviously from Sunpoint, for one. The curse had no triggering mechanism, for another. It's simply *too* convenient that Rylam should be "just passing" in time to prevent Kertoui's diabolical scheme. And Kertoui brought his wife with him, who was so shocked at her husband's disappearance that she came straight to the watch, allowing us to make the connection.

'But,' I added, 'we can't confront Xavian yet.'

'What? Why not?' he demanded. 'With Mistress Kertoui's confession, and if we produce this dreamer – Miriam – we can prove what a slimeball Xavian is once and for all.'

'Yes,' I said patiently, 'I'm sure we could get him banished for trying to deceive the queen, and for deliberately endangering the life of a man. But that man was a Sunpoint citizen. *Xavian* is a Sunpoint citizen. And we still need him as a possible lead, to help us answer a host of questions. Besides . . .'

'Yes?' he demanded impatiently.

'Besides . . . I'm concerned about the dreamer, Miriam. When I first saw her I had difficulty identifying her as a dreamer, she was *that* real and *that* grounded in dreams. Renna was much the same. If we push the Xavian matter, it might also push Miriam into becoming much the same as Renna did. And if that happens . . . well, Renna acquired formidable powers, but she was a rational person, put it like that. Miriam might not respond in the same way.'

'Oh come on. We could arrange *something*.'

'Perhaps. But there's still one more problem.'

'What?'

'If Xavian has a dreamer under his control and can jump from one place to another in the blink of an eye, that makes it likely that *he* drew the inferno ward in the palace. He could have drawn the spell during the night without any absence that people would notice.'

'I can understand Xavian having Kertoui killed, to help his master look good. But why something so suspicious as drawing the inferno spell? And so soon before Rylam's arrival?'

'There it falls down.'

We both sat down together, as if it was an unspoken signal at the first sight of defeat.

'Well,' said Janyvir finally, 'we've worked out one murder – a third of the puzzle.'

'Xavian was a fool. Using Kertoui was asking for trouble as it was.'

'Not such a fool that he doesn't know there's no proof. I mean, *look* at what we've got. Hypothesis. Guesswork founded on a little magical knowledge that may not even apply.'

'There is one person who knows, though,' I murmured. 'Someone who's the key to everything.'

'Will she talk to you?'

'Dreams know,' I sighed. 'But we can try.'

SIX

Miriam

Increasingly, the thought of Renna came back to haunt me. That evening, as I watched the usual dances being spun out across the great hall to the usual tunes with the self-conscious flair of the usual lordlings, all I could think of was Renna. Clever, kind, fiery Renna who had found her destiny amid so many ever-changing dreams, and ascended to a place I couldn't reach.

The closer a dreamer gets to his or her dream, the more real the dreamer becomes, until it's almost impossible to tell that's what they really are. And there was Miriam, dancing across the hall with Xavian. Clever, cunning, evil Xavian. The evil mage who surely knew how to hold a dreamer's mind captive to his own and use it to travel at the speed of thought. Delicate Miriam, who might well gain the powers that Renna had.

Renna could summon anything at a thought, any time, wherever she was, without the least hesitation or strain. Not being bound by flesh or blood to a particular form, she could change her shape at will. She could stop the heart of men at a thought and stand unbowed against a tide of spells, never once touched or turned by their power.

Might Miriam become like that? If so, what if she stayed loyal to Xavian? Could Haven – dreams – the whole Void – afford to have her gain such terrifying power?

Oh, the problems. How to bring Xavian down but keep Miriam up? How to persuade her to tell me – and herself – the truth? How to keep her safe, from herself, from the Void?

From Xavian.

Where is Renna in all this? Hasn't she seen how closely another follows in her footsteps, and how uncertainly Miriam will cope? Thank dreams she didn't end up in nightmare, though. There I wouldn't have been able to do anything.

Again, I had the odd sensation of being watched, but I ignored it. In this place, everyone watched each other like cats.

The dance wound to an end, and I saw Miriam move away from Xavian, still with a responsive smile on her face. *That's right, little girl*, I thought darkly, *leave the nasty mage and come to me*. But instead she went to the side of the hall and helped herself to some supper. I watched her toy with some honeyed thing, spangled with tiny preserved fruits. She was eating it with a slow thoughtfulness as if all that mattered was the flavour and whether it was good or bad for her was of no concern whatever. *Of course, it isn't, is it?* At length she returned to Xavian. Damn her . . .

Shell had been right about one thing. As the evening

wore on I could see how Xavian and Rylam were keeping a steady distance, only occasionally shooting each other a look. Their shared glances were . . . cold, certainly. And once I'd noticed that, other adjectives suggested themselves, ranging from 'tense' and 'laden' all the way up to a speculative 'bitter?' and 'vengeful?'.

So intent was I on deciphering their looks that I almost missed Miriam's exit. She was headed for a back door in the hall, and the service corridor busy with servants, normal but efficient or Key-bound and magical. There were washrooms on either side of this corridor, and lounges where people could discuss their business in a quieter, more secluded environment. I waited until Miriam must have had time to go up the stairs beyond, and followed, easing my way through the crowds inconspicuously, lest Xavian or Rylam notice my passage. I saw Eisirrn playing the cook again, and nodded at him. He returned the nod, and by the time I'd left the hall he was plying Xavian with food. Xavian, I'd told Shell. He's the clever one – Rylam doesn't compete.

Confident now, I slipped out and up the stairs.

The corridor *was* long, I discovered. The stairs to the kitchen were the busiest, and a fair trickle of people passed in and out of the washrooms. Probing quickly inside various rooms peopled with old ladies powdering their faces, I couldn't sense Miriam anywhere. I hastened on, down several bustling passageways. The lounges were divided up into different environments, I soon discovered. There was a room with a tinkling pool where water nymphs sang for the amusement of those dignitaries who'd grown too weary for the dance. There was a room full of comfortable furniture where old men bemoaned their weary limbs or argued passionately about some obscure tweak of politics. There was a balcony commanding a spectacular view across the night-time city where young couples sneaked off to discover exactly how much they liked each other.

No sign of Miriam.

There was a room made of silver, copper, gold and bronze, where silver mists coiled around strange sculptures as disturbing as they were beautiful. There was a conservatory full of steam, kept at a tropical temperature by Key-bound force alone. Still no Miriam.

I reached the end of the corridor, pushed open the last door and saw her. She'd found a balcony where ivy, clematis and vines curled around fantastical ironwork, up to the roof and down again, creating a little cave of green. Miriam didn't notice me. She was leaning over the railings and looking down with an expression of such profound sorrow on her face that for a second I believed she really was going to throw herself off the edge.

'I did love her.'

She started on hearing my voice, spinning to confront this interruption in a flurry of ballgown and loose brown hair. I could see she was embarrassed to be caught alone with her own thoughts.

'I beg your pardon?' she stammered.

'The dreamer. I loved her.'

'Oh.'

Of course I felt guilty at citing my former relationship with Renna, whatever the need to keep this dreamer from the realms of horror that might lie before her. I suppressed the feeling, though, with the usual inward murmurs. The end justifies the means. It's all for the best . . .

Dreams above, but she's just a child. At least Renna knew who was who and what was what. The girl looks as if she could try to stroke a viper and think it the friendliest creature in the Void.

I leaned on the balcony beside her, trying to look like a casual passer-by. 'What are you doing here away from . . . what's his name again?'

'Xavian.'

'Xavian. You must be very close to him.'

'I am.'

'Close enough for him to make your dream come true, even?'

She hesitated, then looked away with a little laugh. 'So you've seen me for what I am. Xavian said that if anyone could, it would be you.'

'He has an unjustifiably high opinion of me . . . How long have you been comatose?'

She shrugged. 'I don't know. No time at all. Forever. At first all I remember was the Void, the feeling that I had to keep on going no matter what. Then I found him in that place with the desert, and I knew it was *right*. Even when Feilim tried to kill Rylam and we were forced to flee I stayed by him. He made me real.'

'You follow him even though people die?' I asked softly.

She tilted her chin proudly. 'He makes me whole. Every night, when I go to sleep, he'll murmur his spells over me, so that I will wake feeling better than the day before. When he touches me I can feel his power sweep through me – and it's *right*.'

I said nothing, even though her words stirred an unreasoned alarm in me. She met my eyes again, and there was the same defiance in them that I'd seen in

Corinna. *Dreams above, give me a chance with these people and their mindless loyalties!*

'He says you've come to Haven to try and get Rylam executed for a crime he didn't commit. He says you're a threat to us, because you came from Sunpoint and hate it with a passion. Rylam thinks you're harmless, just another courtier. But Xavian says you're dangerous.'

I couldn't understand why she was so confiding with me. Cautiously, I said so.

She gave me a look in which frankness jostled with mistrust. 'I want to know if you're really trying to hurt us. Sometimes I see you leaving the palace, always heading towards the western quarter – towards your aunt. Yet how convenient that your aunt should fall ill just as Corbe's body is discovered.'

'She's been ill a long time. Now she's dying,' I replied with as much emotion as I could find for someone who didn't exist. 'And no, I don't hate or want to hurt you. The evidence, what little I know of it, is still in Rylam's favour. His brother is sending assassins – maybe the man found in a cellar this morning drawing a curse was the same man who tried to cast an inferno spell. Maybe he really is a Sunpoint assassin.' I stared at her as I spoke, searching in vain for some kind of reaction.

'And you?' she repeated, stubborn girl. 'What's your interest in palace affairs, if you're only here for your aunt?'

'Who wouldn't be interested, when there's a threat to life within these very walls?' I paused, knowing I'd never find the right words for what had to be said. 'I'm also interested in you.'

She raised her eyebrows, and her voice took on an offended edge. 'Oh, are you? And why is that?'

'Because you're a dreamer who's struggling a long way out of her depth. I don't know what powers you may have found in yourself. But I do know how hard it is to break free of Earth and become real in this world – and that's something you are doing very, very well.'

'Thank you . . . I suppose.'

We leaned on the balcony together in silence. I waited breathlessly for her to speak, praying, *let her volunteer the truth. Don't force me to drag it out of her.*

Finally she asked, 'What do you mean . . . powers? I've never been able to do anything.'

My wrist was itching. I looked her up and down with open scepticism. 'Never do *anything*? You must have, even if it's something small.'

She shook her head. 'No. Nothing. Xavian say's it's because I'm still too immature. But I still wish . . .' She stopped, as if about to say something bad.

'Wish?' I prompted, as gently as possible.

'I want to go to the dream of flying. The dream of storms. I want to go skiing in Frostpoint, I want to ride on a dragon's back in Firepoint, I want to . . . But only once Rylam is restored to his own. Xavian puts duty above all things.'

Including the life of his apprentice, disembowelled in that cellar.

'Has Xavian ever tried to help you cultivate your powers?'

'The spells he says over me are to make me stronger, for when my body dies and I must lead a new life.' She turned to me with a frown of concentration. 'I'm telling you,' she said slowly, as if only just working it out, 'because you once helped a dreamer to become a goddess. She told me so herself, and I want to be like that. I want to be exactly like Renna.'

My fingers tightened around the railing. I felt my wrist being slit all over again, with a blade of ice. 'You know . . . *Renna*?'

Miriam began to back away but I caught her around the shoulders, more savagely than I'd meant. '*How* do you know Renna?'

She struggled weakly to pull free. I exclaimed, 'If you want me to help you I must know about Renna!'

'She . . . found me in the Void! Said she'd lead me to my dream, if I'd just let her. But when she saw Xavian she said that I'd taken her to a memory, not a dream, and tried to lead me away! I told her he was my heart's desire but she said I was blind!'

'And then what? *Then what*?' I snarled, shaking her like a puppet. My wrist was flaring up into raw agony. I didn't know what I was doing. All I could feel was the pain, all I could see was Renna . . .

'I . . . don't know! I tried to push Renna away, and then Xavian took my hand and together we were stronger and she disappeared and . . .' With a burst of strength Miriam wrenched free. 'Leave me alone! You're only here because you hate Sunpoint, and Xavian! You're just trying to hurt us!'

'Miriam!' I began, but she'd turned and fled. My wrist was still stinging. But the pain was far less than at that second when I'd seized and shaken her. When I'd wanted to . . . yes, hurt her. All from frustration. Because she'd seen Renna, who'd told her Xavian was bad. And still Miriam was the mage's loyal creature. *Oh dreams, what's happening to me?*

'Silver for your thoughts.'

Shell was standing in the doorway, wearing a waiting-woman's uniform and holding a tray of drinks. Wordlessly she handed one over. I drained it in a single gesture, wiped my mouth with my sleeve and passed back the glass.

'Miriam,' I said and paused, unsure which of many, many things I wanted to say '. . . is a comatose dreamer. She's unstable, uncertain about everything, fragile as a doll and . . .'

And when she joins with Xavian she's powerful enough to send Renna running for cover? Renna, who was only trying to help her?

But Miriam surely can't yet be stable or confident enough to have a dreamer's full powers. So where . . . unless Xavian somehow shaped her raw power into his own . . .

'"And"?' demanded Shell. 'There's got to be something after that "and" of yours, since you've asked me to have this woman watched at all hours.' Then something else I'd said came home to her. 'Dreams above, a *dreamer*?'

'Very close to her dream,' I agreed. 'That's why she looks so real, and it took me so long to see it.'

'But with powers like that available . . . it means Rylam could've . . .'

'Not Rylam,' I said quickly. 'Xavian. Xavian could've drawn the inferno ward, Xavian could've had Corbe murdered, Xavian could've arranged the death of an untraceable assassin from across town.

'And Xavian most definitely *did* contrive the murder of Kertoui – the man in the cellar. On the other hand, that's the only one of these "could-haves" which makes sense. Only the death of Kertoui had a motive . . .'

'Another drink?' she asked quietly.

'Thank you,' I said, and meant it. 'What are you doing dressed up as a waitress, anyway?'

She scowled. 'This is your fault, this uniform. We didn't have enough watchers to keep track of Miriam as well as Rylam, so I had to take the job. And very boring it is too. She doesn't move all day.'

I drained the drink in a gulp and returned it to the tray, feeling it doing me good as it burnt its way through my system. 'Do you know about the assassin murdered across town?' I asked finally.

'No. In fact, a lot of what you said back there made little or no sense. Don't worry, though. T'omar warned me that you had a tendency to be a secretive, mysterious git.'

'Perhaps us Silverhands ought to have a chat,' I murmured.

It was one o'clock in the morning. Eisirrn, Shell, Rinset and I had just finished an emergency conference on what we now knew, or suspected, of Rylam and his companions. The others had gone their ways: Rinset to the edge of town to try and trace Rylam's journey from Sunpoint to Haven, Shell to employ her vast knowledge in conjuring up information from whatever squalid sources she lied about using, and Eisirrn to the kitchens to prepare breakfast. I was bound for my bed, with thoughts of Renna, dreamers, murders in the night and clandestine meetings gone wrong.

I walked through darkened corridors, too tired to pay

attention to where I was or who woke at the sound of my footsteps – turned the corner of the passage off which I slept – and froze.

Xavian was sitting on the floor outside my room, a half-empty bottle in one hand. He stared at me, then gave an unwelcoming smile. 'Aunt, my bloody foot,' he muttered.

I advanced cautiously, trying not to let my sudden worry show. 'Are you all right?'

'You're one of them, aren't you? A bloody Silverhand. I'm not an idiot, I can see through the stories. What a brilliant cover, too! Laenan Kite is a legend, a great and powerful mage, he moves in the highest circles! No one would think their great mage was a glorified spy.'

'You're drunk.' I was disgusted, and surprised, too, to see such a clever, self-contained man behaving so unlike his public self.

Xavian grinned. 'I do believe I am. What else should I be, when great mages are spying on me and my master?' He sighed. 'Do you know, I admire you? I really do. You were the smart one,' he continued, staggering to his feet. 'You saw an opportunity and you took it. Became great. Everyone finds greatness somehow, for a moment, but you've managed to be great in such a casual, easy way that no one noticed it happening. Not even you.'

I edged past him towards my door, only half listening to his ramble. Just when I thought I'd made it his hand lashed out and caught my arm in a grip like steel. 'I know you're watching me, waiting for me to slip up, Silverhand. But I see things with such clarity, even if it burns my eyes. I see you watching me and I watch you in turn. Keep away from Miriam, okay? I know you know what she is, and she is *mine*. I am her only friend, her guardian. I'm going to make her the greatest woman in the Void. I *see* things. I have visions.'

'Get to bed. You'll feel better in the morning.'

He laughed, letting me go, and reeled away towards the end of the corridor. 'We're both the little men, Kite! We're the puppeteers that no one ever sees! We both know what it's like to see clearly in a universe where everyone else is blind! We both know what it's like to try and conform and still stand out in a crowd! You do nothing against me, and I'll do nothing against you, understand?'

I got inside my room as fast as I could. To my relief, he hadn't even tried breaching my wards. Somehow I managed to get my boots off, crawl into bed and curl up, hugging the sheets to my chin. It was a long time before sleep came.

SEVEN

Body and Soul

'Now, are you *sure* you want to do this?' Janyvir asked me. 'It's not a pretty business anyway, going . . . you know . . .'

'I guess it's not.'

On the dark steps to the mortuary I could feel the temperature dropping before we were within ten paces of the door. I felt the magic around it – could almost *hear* the magic, a sensation with which I wasn't entirely comfortable. Janyvir stopped outside the door, fishing in a pocket for the key.

'I hate asking my mages to do this,' he muttered. 'It stinks of necromancy.'

'No. Empathy,' I said. 'Sometimes sharing things is bound to be worse than taking them whole.'

'Still . . .' He took out key found and turned it in the lock. As the door swung open the full force of the cold met us like a glacier. Shivering already, we bundled into the mortuary and he slammed the door wide open on its hinges with a nervous distaste we both felt for our surroundings. The place, for all that everything in it was perfectly preserved, still managed to reek of death. White tiles were smudged grey in the poor light, and the windows were high and barred, like a prison to keep zombies in.

'Are you sure you want to do this?' he repeated, as we went up to the body, peaceful beneath its shroud. 'A couple of our mages tried and they hit some really tough wards.'

'They weren't Laenan Kite, were they?' I asked with a half-smile.

Instead of the derisive snort or weary sigh at hearing a 'false' name, Janyvir just seemed to tense up even more. I pulled the shroud aside, far enough to ensure that the man's limp white hand lay close to mine. The spell *did* smack of necromancy, but sometimes these things had to be done. I just wish I wasn't the one who did it.

'All right, Brawn my friend,' I murmured as confidently as I could, 'I know nothing's been done to you since you were found. So the traces of whatever you were getting up to in the night must still be around, just waiting to be discovered. *Show* me what you have.'

My hand hovered an inch above his, and I brought the spell up through my toes, into my heart and down through my outstretched fingers. It was really just a scry, but narrowed and refined to a point where it would pick up traces of utterly anything out of the ordinary, and follow them back to the point of origin.

Silver light sprang up around my fingers, danced in

the air like fire in a mist, and slithered down to touch the man's palm. Immediately I got the first sensation. Images began dancing through my mind. Hands worn rough by sand, so much sand tearing through the sky and shifting beneath your feet.

The silver magic flowed up his arm, made the sheets stir as though being tickled by a gentle draught. Traces of another's perfume, images of a darkened street near the barracks where drunken soldiers looked for a 'good' time. I forced the spell on, felt the lingering touch of spices from a market, the tang of fish from the same place, felt the spell brush the man's closed eyes, dug the magic deeper, searching out images from the past, anything that might give us a lead . . . and encountered a wall of tightly woven wards wrapped around his dead mind.

The wards that Janyvir had mentioned – blocking all but the most determined of mages from gaining access to the last thoughts and sights of a dying man, imprinted forever on the mind. Or possibly on the soul – or on a combination of both. Really powerful necromancers, so I'm told, can pick a skull out of the ground and read its history at a glance. But that would be deathly magic and I was as bad a necromancer as I was a healer.

I hammered fruitlessly at the wards, but they were locked tight by the action of the user's death, sealed forever in that searing moment of revelation when the soul parted company from the body.

Desperately I turned my attention away from the mind and started sweeping the body again, searching for a sign of something, *anything*, that might point to where he'd come from or what he was doing. The flashing smiles of the women in the western quarter, the tang of spices from the market, the clinging smell of fish, the sun setting on that last night, the final journey through the streets, the wards locked forever by the almighty hand of Death around an assassin's mind . . .

There it was. So tiny I might not have noticed it but that my endeavours were being pushed by desperation alone. So deep was I in the spell that I'd lost all sense of my own body. Whether in reality I was standing like a statue or whether I'd truly been snatched away into this world of whirling images I was in no state to say. But there it was, that tiny little anomaly that only the rushing spell and my emptied-head determination to stay in control, had indeed found.

Then, the slow turning of time as this little grain, the object of my attention, moves away from mere imagination and becomes more and more embedded in reality. The tearing free from its kingdom's soil as rough hands pull it out in huge shovel-loads. The careful touch of the potter's hands, the cries of the marketeers as they keep on selling, the shattering as the pot is raised up on high and brought crashing down towards an unseen attacker . . . *Show me the attacker!* I wailed.

The cracked remains lay spread across the floor. *Show me the floor! Show me something!* But the speck of dust from the pot, still buried under Brawn's nail, would reveal no more. And indeed what it had shown was already so much, from just a little fragment of clay, that I could feel my magic escaping in waves from me into the spell. I tried to break free, but the scry was now running away, focusing on the dirt itself that caked the man, describing the history of every grain in a searing burst of image on image.

I wrenched my hand free, breaking the tide of images in a savage jerk that made the world in front of my eyes shatter and explode. With a cry I staggered back, shielding my eyes and nearly falling. Janyvir rushed forward to help but desperately I waved him back. Then, doubling over as the full backlash hit from a spell run out of control, I bent over and emptied my stomach on the mortuary floor.

After that, I felt a lot better.

'I said it was necromancy,' said Janyvir ten minutes later, sitting back in his desk and turning a little dagger over and over in his grasp.

'Not necromancy,' I said. 'Just a spell that got a little over-powerful.'

'You seem to have a lot of those haunting you. And what have we learnt from it?' He snorted at his own question. 'That mortuaries are no places to go after breakfast, that's what.'

'We've learnt that the man had a pot. Which he tried to use to defend himself against the attacker.'

'Suggesting he picked up the first weapon which came to hand, much good it did him.'

'I almost saw the attacker's face, but not quite. My scry was following the life of a bit of clay, not of the man who owned it,' I said with wry irritation.

'A pot,' he murmured. 'Now why didn't my mages pick up on that?'

'Because they were sensible enough not to let their spell get out of control and start examining things the size of a grain of sand.'

'A pot,' he repeated. 'Suggesting . . . quite pleasant living quarters?'

'There was also a trace of fish. And spices.'

'A market. Lots of markets sell those two things.'

'And he was definitely in the western quarter,' I finished.

We fell into silence, the kind where two minds work towards the same conclusion in different ways but at the same speed. We were alike enough for me to feel that if I hadn't ended up a mage, I'd probably have found myself in Janyvir's place. We both did other people's dirty work.

'What bothers me most,' said Janyvir finally, 'is that this guy's been dead for a week. We know assassins like to move around. But if he was attacked at his home then surely someone, by now, would have noticed that he'd disappeared off the face of the Void. *And* that there was a broken pot all across the floor.'

'And reported it to you.'

'Unless they were too afraid to report it.' Our eyes met. 'Or,' murmured Janyvir, 'too illegal. Dreams above, I hate people who don't report things. Means I have to waste good ideas just *finding* the crimes, and that's not my job. You know what I want?'

'What?'

'The bloody Key. The queen is all very well, but she's tied down with running dreams. I want the Key of Haven so that the watch can see the streets night and day. I'm fed up with crime starting the second Lisana goes to sleep and finishing just as she wakes. It makes my patrolling schedule a mere perversity. Lisana can't watch the streets when asleep, that's the problem.'

I didn't meet his eyes. 'You know, there is a way we *could* borrow the Key for a while.'

He looked me up and down. 'What? Going to scry are we, pretend you're using the Key?'

'No. I was thinking of a more obvious solution. Though it's understandable that it's evaded you.' I couldn't help sounding just a bit haughty. 'Tell me, have you ever met the queen?'

His eyes widened. 'You know, I *thought* there was something strange about you. A Silverhand mage powerful enough to scry things that the combined efforts of the fools in my department couldn't even suggest after a whole hour's work. No. The Silverhand Consortium is made up of crooks and beggars, not mages who could have been *court* mages. I'm thinking *court mages*, here, people who *come out of the palace*.'

'Worse than that,' I said modestly 'It's about the name, I'm afraid. Lenian Kiret or Laenan Kite, it's still so obvious that no man would believe it. That's one of the wonders of being a Silverhand and a legend. People are so suspicious the second you tell them, they'll disbelieve everything you say as a matter of principle. The best place to hide something is usually in plain view.'

He'd found his ball of wool and was tugging at it anxiously. 'I refuse to believe that any legend could look quite as messy and harmless as you,' he insisted.

'Oh dear. And I thought watchmen kept open minds.'

I didn't kneel, so neither did Janyvir. We just told Lisana everything we knew straight out, and waited for her to take it all in.

It took a lot of taking, however much she pretended otherwise.

'So . . . you still don't know if Rylam's the principal

villain,' she concluded, having taken in our flood of information.

'No.'

'And we can't arrest Xavian because Miriam will become even more unstable.'

'Yes.'

'And besides, there's still no motive for Xavian to have drawn the inferno spell.'

'No.'

'So? I assume you do have a reason for coming to me?'

'Yes, ma'am. We need your help.'

She raised her eyebrows, a short laugh of disbelief escaping her. '*You*, Kite, need *my* help?'

'Ma'am.'

Her eyes flickered to Janyvir, standing by my side with his head respectfully bowed. 'Commander,' she said, radiating imperial wisdom. 'I have never to this day met you, I believe. Yet you do what I should do, ensure that the streets are safe and that bad men are brought to justice. For this I thank you.'

He bowed his head deeper, but said nothing. She indicated me and demanded, 'What do you think of my Silvereye, Commander?'

'Very . . . unlikely, ma'am.'

'Unlikely?' she repeated, enjoying my mutinous silence. 'How so?'

'He . . . is such a prominent figure that no one realises how little is known about him, ma'am. So prominent in fact, that he can use his own name and everyone will believe it to be false.'

'True. You know I had Kite arrested for treason once?'

His eyes darted surreptitiously to me. 'No, ma'am, I did not.'

'Really? A pity. I tried to make the news as public as possible. But you were leader of the Consortium at the time, I believe, Kite? I don't doubt you managed to cover it up well.'

'Not so well that you didn't lose me my job, friends and position,' I murmured sourly.

She had the grace to look a little taken aback. 'Well, that's behind us now.'

Behind you, maybe.

'Ask what you want,' she said, radiating magnanimity. 'I will provide it.'

'The murdered man known as Brawn,' Janyvir said simply. 'We want to find the place where he lived. And then . . .' He shrugged helplessly. 'Well, after that it depends on what we find.'

Rinset was outside the room as Lisana, Janyvir and I were leaving in the direction of what Lisana termed 'somewhere more private'. This was another thing I remembered from my long association with the queen – for one reason or another she liked doing her spells away from the eyes of men. Over the years it had become a habit.

Rinset was doing his best to blend in with the background of the corridor – he was wearing a servant's livery and watering a large pot containing bright blue flowers. *Poor fool.* I didn't have the heart to tell him that all flowers in the palace were part of Lisana's imagination and renewed from second to second by the power of the Key.

Lisana glanced at him and passed on, deciding that he was no threat and it was his problem if he wanted to waste time on a fool's errand. I waved Janyvir onwards, and slipped up to Rinset's side. The commander gave me a questioning look, his eyes flickering to Rinset, and I could see him struggling to remember the boy's features for another time. I glared at him in warning, and he looked away.

'Quickly,' I hissed to Rinset as the commander hastened round the corner after Lisana.

'I've got something,' he replied, trying to keep his voice down against his own excitement.

'Something in particular, or just a general piece of information?' I asked sourly. I was more annoyed by his enthusiasm itself than by his unprofessionalism at showing it.

'Xavian, Rylam and Miriam were robbed on the road. A precise job, too. A gang of ten or so, at least five mages. Slipped into their room at an inn in Crystalpoint.'

'Professional robbers?'

'As professional as they get.'

'How did you find out?'

'The innkeeper's daughter is one of our intermediaries. She received a general description of the three for forwarding to our Sunpoint sources, and recognised them instantly. Ten armed thieves in black isn't the kind of thing you forget.'

I nearly laughed out loud with delight. 'Rinset, whatever nasty things I've said in the past, I retract them all. Now, what did they steal?'

His blush of joy at being praised faded almost at once. 'I don't know,' he confessed. 'Something small – that's all

I could find out. Documents, maybe? It was a precise job. Apparently Xavian was furious.'

'Documents? Is that *it*?'

'There's more!' he said hastily. 'Ten men were sighted by one of the elementals on the road towards Sunpoint.'

'Sunpoint? Do you think Feilim sent them?'

'Possibly.'

I sighed. 'You've done well. But keep trying for more on these men. I want everything that might be of any use whatsoever!'

'I'll try.' And he scurried off.

I hurried after Janyvir and the queen, who was unlocking a large door. Lisana didn't even glance up. 'Anything useful from your pet spies, Kite?'

'Could be. I don't suppose Rylam mentioned a robbery on the road?'

'No.'

That was it. Just a flat 'no', as if she was disappointed that I could ask such a trivial question.

'Has he mentioned any documents?'

She considered for a second or so, pushing open the door as she did so and stepping into the small room. 'He requested access to the scribes' library to search out several documents of "historical interest". But he didn't specify what. He gave the impression that he wanted to broaden his knowledge of Haven.'

'He's good at giving impressions,' I murmured.

The room into which Lisana led us was small, round and windowless. The only source of light came from a large ball of fire, tinged purple, hanging in the domed space of the roof. Around the length of the curved walls, on deep shelves breaking only at the door, were the instruments of any good mage. Magic mirrors, bottled spells, candles, bits of chalk, scrying crystals, and little boxes labelled with the names of people on whom she might one day want to cast a spell. In each box no doubt was a piece of hair or skin or some small possession personal to the subject. I noticed the names of several Wardens and minor courtiers, plus a few particularly annoying merchants – and, to my dismay, a box with my name. I snatched it off the shelf, opened it and stared in astonishment at a little silver half-moon that I'd been awarded on graduation from the college of mages.

'I thought I'd lost this centuries ago!'

Lisana shrugged. 'I tried casting a spell over it once, but your shielding was too tight and all my spells were deflected.'

'You could look bashful, your majesty!'

She stared at me. 'Why should I? Having at least some kind of hold is a necessary part of rule. One must always be prepared to cope with rebellion.'

I glowered back at her for a long moment. Janyvir shifted from foot to nervous foot, aware of the tension.

'You know I don't like you, your majesty,' I finally announced.

'The feeling is mutual. If there were anyone as good as you, with so many unusual connections . . . be assured he'd have your job while I packed you off to the furthest corner of dreams. I owe you, Kite, that's all.'

'I don't owe you, though.'

'No,' she said with a wry little smile. 'You don't, do you?'

For a second I considered storming from the room and

leaving her to her own wretched problems. My tenuous restraint, in any case as fragile as a child's too-tight grip on wet soap, was about to go, and Lisana's seemed close to following. Janyvir looked out of his depth, suddenly finding himself caught by a centuries-old vendetta between the queen and the man who had almost been king, once upon a time.

I could have taken the crown, I reflected bitterly, knowing that even without my thoughts being projected she could hear them as though they were her own. *Even if I hadn't been offered it by a dying king, I could have turned around at any moment, mustered up my allies and bathed my enemies in fire. I could have been a conqueror, and no one would have been able to stop me.*

But instead I backed down because I was too cowardly to take the responsibility of ruling, and you got the job instead. What should I blame now for this situation? My own cowardice, or your ambition? Or both?

Then the even stranger thought came home. *Dreams above. You need me, don't you? And I, in my own peculiar way, need you. Everyone needs someone else, as much to hate as to love.*

'Let's get on with this,' I muttered finally. There was a general sigh, almost inaudible, as though by speaking I had expelled the atmosphere of ill-will and it was surging from the room in a rush.

Lisana said nothing, but with a show of zombie-like dispassion she raised her dainty hands before her, as though expecting us to kneel and kiss them. I reached out and took her left hand, then turned to Janyvir. 'Never held the hand of a queen before?' I asked.

'Never,' he replied, reaching out nervously to take Lisana's right hand, as though it might shatter at his rough touch. I joined my left hand with his right, to connect us in a circle. Almost immediately I could feel the warmth of her magic as she opened contact with the Key. I opened my magic too, easing it through the link of hand to hand into Janyvir so that he could share the spell.

And suddenly I had forgotten what it was to have a body. There was no warmth, no cold, no ache in my wrist, no buzz in my weary head. I was one with Lisana and Janyvir, and we were flying across the city of Haven in a blur of magic towards the western quarter, seen only as a passing shadow by the mages, and not perceived at all by anyone else.

Lisana focused on the markets first, and as if the Key could read her intents, we found ourselves hanging above a market where a good selection of the stalls were selling fish and spices. Janyvir, unaccustomed to magic, tried to frame a question using his tongue, but we sensed his question even before he realised what he was trying to do, and Lisana soared in closer. Yes. A market selling spices, fishes and, on a stall a few yards away, pots.

Find a place where a man would hide. Find a criminal.

Here Janyvir took over, guiding Lisana with his masterly understanding of the darker, less frequented streets of the city. Images flashed across my eyes from his mind. Faces, houses, shops –the fronts of some criminal businesses. Lisana received the information gratefully, pleased to be learning about her city from an expert. I thought that she might have resented the watchman's greater knowledge, but even in the link we were now sharing I felt nothing but a truly regal appreciation for him.

Already, it seemed, we'd danced through three whole streets of houses, taking in room after room in a blur, discarding each one in a rush. I tried to keep track of them, but my reaction was sluggish – Lisana was the bearer of the Key, Lisana could carry us through these things so much faster.

Sensing my struggle to keep up, she slowed our pace and the images steadied to a rate I could deal with – until abruptly we slammed up against a reflection shield. It was in a house on Centon Passage. A house bearing a plaque declaring: Isla Barrant's Fine Lodging for Travellers, and set in a dark street not wide enough to let two carts pass each other. Lisana swooped below the room which magic had shut away from her and took in the unprotected floor below.

It was a seedy place. Any paintwork was peeling, and feeble wards had been inscribed here and there to ward off the overly curious. I felt Janyvir's mind again, as he recognised the passage. The thieves who lived here were sensible enough to conduct their activities at a distance. People never went missing here, and no kind of crime was reported within half a mile. But Janyvir had known nonetheless that this was a bad place.

Break it down, I thought with sudden intensity. The shield holding us back had suddenly transformed itself into a thing of urgency, and I was desperate to get rid of it. *Tear it down right now!*

We charged at it, Lisana narrowing her Key-bound senses to a sharp and deadly point of thought as I refined my magic to tear a passage through the shield. We struck, and I felt it buckle, magic flaring up in distress at our attack. Then Janyvir was behind me, lending his force of purpose to bolster my own magical strength. I seized his help gratefully, even knowing that he would feel like hell when I was done, and charged again. My magic struck the shield, tore a gash down one side. Lisana soared through it in an instant, dragging us along with her, and we were inside the room.

It was the place. I knew it in an instant, every instinct and the remainder of my scrying spell yelling out triumphantly that here was where Brawn and his pot had ended their respective lives. And once we looked closer, it became obvious. There was a stain on the floor where someone had tried to clean up the blood, there was a fireplace containing the ashes from some burnt paper. There were shelves devoid of all dust – swept bare by someone trying to cover up for a murder. There was even, shoved inside a drawer that we could see through as though it weren't there, a documents pouch, and a little bottle of purple ink.

Alarm. Burning alarm as Janyvir's mind and my own connected. A bottle of purple ink, ink used in meeting Corbe. Brawn was Corbe's connection, not his murderer. We hadn't known what connection he was before, but now the bottle of ink was a sure sign . . .

Don't get carried away. It might have been a trick.

But such a knowing trick!

Reality changed as Lisana felt our desires and summoned a group of four elven guards in the top room to stand watch over the place, and another ten guards downstairs to pick up the people who'd housed Brawn and not reported his disappearance. The yells as guards appeared out of nowhere was matched by the still-ringing alarm and distress coming from the commander.

If Brawn had been Corbe's contact, not his murderer, our theory was wrong and the true killer was still on the loose. *Not our entire theory. We thought the two were connected, we just didn't know how.*

We withdrew. The link strained and broke, and with horrible speed I had arms and legs again and was staggering slightly with the shock of returning to my body. Janyvir was extremely pale, but otherwise showed no ill effects.

Lisana was standing with neatly folded hands, not even slightly drained by the effect of using her Key. 'Is there anything more you require, gentlemen?'

I was incredibly tired. The day had been packed full of events and now all I wanted was sleep.

Janyvir and I must have made a strange pair, sitting in the interrogation room. We were staring at the woman in that reproachful 'this is going to hurt me more than it hurts you' way which only seasoned questioners can manage. I wasn't an outstanding interrogator, but I could sense a lie with startling clarity. Indeed, when we'd sat down and asked 'what is your name', I'd felt her answer was a lie even before it had been given. It was nothing magical, just . . . undeniable knowledge.

Isla Barrent, for such proved to be her name, was the podgy woman, wearing too much make-up, who'd so considerately allowed Brawn to lodge in her rooms. Her sons, Janyvir had explained in my ear, had frequently been in trouble with the law, and her husband had run off to nightmare. Life had been too hard for him without the luxury of slaves, or the law of survival of the fittest with its peculiar appeal to the criminal mind.

'Why didn't you report his death to the watchmen?'

'I didn't know he was dead. He just disappeared, that's all.'

Janyvir contrived the most sincerely regretful look I've seen on any man's face. At the sight of it I felt my stomach turn. *I wouldn't like to have you as an enemy interrogating me, that's for sure.*

'Now, Mistress Barrent, we know he was murdered in your rooms. We're not accusing you or your sons, there's no question of that. We just want to know what you did when you found the body?'

At first she evaded. But Janyvir was a paragon of gentle firmness, offering a series of hypotheses to speed her confession like, 'perhaps you were afraid? Perhaps your lodger had been going out for a long time at night? Perhaps you'd seen the knives he carried? Perhaps you were scared that he was part of something bigger than you could handle?'

He was getting through to her – that much was soon evident. She was more tense with every second, the blood draining from her face, her answers becoming faster and less convincing until finally she blurted the truth. She had come up one morning to find her lodger with a cut throat, his room all smashed up and searched from top to toe and a pile of papers burning in the fireplace. And oh, most curious of facts, he had arrived on the same day as Rylam and in the evening would often indulge in long strolls. No, he hadn't had any visitors. Yes, she'd been afraid. He never spoke to anyone about anything and paid in large collections of metal coins of a kind she had never seen before.

'Can I look at these coins?' I asked quickly.

She showed me one, and I recognised it instantly. Small,

a dull silver, made from the highly valued correnite that only a select coven of highly defensive mages knew how to summon from the Void. It was not found naturally in any kingdom, and those Wardens who'd tried to summon it had always failed. A substantial payment indeed.

Janyvir urged her on – though, truth to tell, the floodgates to the truth had now been opened anyway, and she couldn't help but spurt it all out. The man had just appeared one night and told her he wanted to hire rooms. No one was to know he was there, and she was to speak to no one about a lodger of any kind. Every morning she would bring him breakfast and he would always be crouched over a small collection of crystals, using magic. She spoke the word 'magic' as if it was a dirty thing and he a necromancer summoning the dead.

At the mention of crystals I glanced curiously at Janyvir, but he shook his head. 'We didn't find anything.'

To Isla Barrent he said, 'Tell me about the last night he was there.'

She licked her dry lips. 'He went out at eight. Came back just after midnight. He looked scared and upset, so I thought that something really bad had happened. He was carrying a collection of letters and looked as if he'd just run a mile. He went up to his room, locked the door and sat up all night writing spells around his room.'

A reaction to the failed meeting with Corbe. He made the connection, picked up those letters Corbe was supposed to deliver. Then Corbe got himself killed and Brawn took to his heels. We can tell Brawn knew who the killer was, because Brawn was scared of the killer and it's rare to find assassins who are really, really scared of other assassins. Especially anyone as inexpert –

seemingly – as the fellow who killed Corbe and left all that money to damn himself.

He must also have known that the killer was a mage, if he came back and wrote all those spells.

'What name did the man give?' asked Janyvir.

'Lesourn.'

'Did you see the murderer?'

'No. No one came in or out of *my* door, I'm sure.'

'The window was locked,' murmured the commander to me. 'Our invisible, traceless killer strikes again.'

'What do you think?'

I shrugged, leaning over the balcony. 'I like this tower, I must admit.'

'It's useful. We've got a host of phoenixes and the like for aerial patrols,' said Janyvir, leaning on the railing next to me. 'And it gives us a good view.' Indeed it did – from here Haven at night was splendid.

I'd gone straight up to the tower on leaving the interrogation rooms, feeling the need for fresh air. Something in me was feeling bitter and old, and it wasn't just my recent close association with death.

'It's all changed now. Whatever else we now know, the case of Corbe and Brawn – sorry, Lesourn – is now changed.'

'You take Corbe, I'll do Brawn/Lesourn,' said Janyvir flatly.

I leaned back against the railing, trying to think like Corbe. 'It's evening. I'm nervous – I've had to slip out of the palace under all kinds of noses, I'm carrying hot letters that require a signal system. I am out of my depth, and scared.'

'It's evening,' Janyvir said, contriving his way into the character of Brawn/Lesourn. 'I'm calm, I'm as cold as a cat. A magely assassin, trained in the arts of survival. I'm to meet a servant using a signal system that I understand perfectly to pick up extremely important documents. I'm paying my way using small amounts of extremely valuable currency. Your turn,' he nodded at me.

'I'm in the western quarter. I leave my signal and go away again until the arranged time of meeting.'

'I see your signal, mark mine.'

'I come back, see your signal, continue to the meeting point.'

'We meet. Handover is successful – after all, there were no documents on Corbe, not that it matters. The assassin got them both so probably has the papers anyway – but wait! At the moment of handover, someone is coming through the darkness.'

'I don't run. Either I'm not given time or I recognise who's coming.'

'Or both,' added Janyvir.

'Neither you nor I move a muscle as the killer comes close.'

'Then I, mage that I am,' said Janyvir still in Brawn/Lesourn's role, 'recognise the touch of killing magic, feel it closing around Corbe's heart. I see its strength, its power and skill, and suddenly realise how much in danger I am. I'm an assassin, true, but against that kind of magic I'm completely lost.

'I turn and run,' he continued, 'using every assassin's trick I have to evade this follower. Yet the things I've just seen in the night make me so scared that I'm shaken and frightened. I draw spells around my room, then sit down, feeling slightly happier at being able to read my newly acquired documents.

'Then I sense something behind me. Being on edge I reach out for the nearest weapon to hand, but it's too late. Though I struggle, the magic is too strong for me, and I'm another body in the mortuary.'

'Who sent you?' I asked Janyvir as though he were indeed Brawn/Lesourn risen from the dead.

'A wealthy employer. Certainly I'm not acting alone, and it's unlikely that I even know my contact, or understand what kind of an enemy I'm up against.'

'Are you connected with the attack on the road which resulted in the loss of documents from Rylam?'

'No, because ten men carried out the attack and ten men returned towards Sunpoint.'

'But in both cases the target has been documents. Is it possible the same person paid you who sent the ten men?'

'It's possible. He'd need considerable resources and would have to know about Rylam and his plans for Sunpoint. He'd also need a method of contact other than letters or codes.'

Our eyes met. 'Did Feilim send you to purchase, steal or exchange documents with Corbe?' I asked softly. *Did Feilim send Brawn to get those damned papers?*

'It is possible. In which case Feilim is now as much a murder suspect as his brother.'

I changed tack. 'Are you connected with the inferno spell found drawn in the palace?'

'No, because I arrived after it.'

'How were you murdered, if the windows were locked, doors barred and spells erected?'

'The same way the inferno spell was drawn, I guess. An enemy who can sneak through the Void in the blink of an eye. Someone who has the power to scare a well-trained assassin. Someone with the motive to kill a possible servant of Feilim.'

I said nothing, but the words unspoken were ringing in my ears. Brawn was Feilim's servant, sent to meet Corbe and, on the way, met by death.

Janyvir tensed up. He said, 'Let me ask you a few questions now. You're Xavian.'

'Go ahead,' I replied, imagining the shrewd face of the mage and wondering what thoughts went on behind those intelligent eyes.

'A pair of dreamers, Renna and Miriam, appear out of nowhere. Renna announces that she is Miriam's guardian, looks Xavian up and down and tells Miriam that Xavian won't do. What do you do, as Xavian?'

'Piss my pants and run away screaming.'

'Kite,' he said reproachfully. 'You're an ambitious mage on the make.'

I sighed. 'I am surprised and delighted to encounter a magical phenomenon I've never before seen. I have heard the stories of the power of dreamers but never before encountered it. I mistrust Renna, as she seems more in control than Miriam, but I long to study how dreamers work, maybe even use some of their power myself.

'Miriam cleaves to me, and I encourage her to stay. Renna tries to pull her away, but Miriam keeps on coming to me. I'm fearful of Renna, try to play polite to her, try to convince her to leave Miriam with me. Renna will have none of it. Words fly as I try to talk them out of leaving, Miriam grabs hold of my hand and suddenly I am so full of power I feel as if I am about to burst. I shove Renna back and, to my surprise, she departs. She is scared, almost as scared as I am, for I have never felt such power as that which I briefly held when Miriam opened to me.'

'What happened next?' Janyvir asked. 'Remember, as Xavian you're an ambitious mage, high on a new victory. I'm asking you, Kite, because you understand better than anyone the workings of a dreamer. You understand what binds a dreamer to a real man. What does Xavian the triumphant do next?'

'I . . . I try to get that power again, filling Miriam's ears with honeyed words, trying to draw close to her even as I try to find that core of power that so briefly she showed to me. It is easy to make her do what I want. She's so fragile and dependent that I can tell her anything and she'll believe me.

'Yet, though I share her worries, hopes and bed, I cannot get the power out of her again, and she will do none of the things that dreamers are supposed to do.'

'How do you know she can't?'

Is it true you fell in love with a dreamer princess?

No, on at least one count.

Which one?

The princess part.

You fell in love with a dreamer?

'I know,' I murmured, remembering. 'It's not that she doesn't want to, she's incapable of it. Until . . . until . . .'

Every night, when I go to sleep he'll murmur his spells over me so that I will wake feeling better than the day before. When he touches me I can feel his power, sweeping through me – and it's right.

'I discover,' I murmured, 'a way of tapping her powers using spells. Don't ask me how, but I do it. When she's asleep at night I cast my spells over her, draining her power into me so that for a brief period I can jump from place to place as though I were a dreamer and her power is mine.

'That's how I get Kertoui into the cellar. That's how I can draw an inferno spell and a reflection shield at the same time, leave no trace of my passage. That's how I can so easily murder Corbe and scare the assassin Brawn/Lesourn so greatly before murdering him. I drain Miriam bit by bit, and she doesn't notice. I was the one who interrupted contact, I killed them both because I don't want Rylam contacting his brother.

'Oh, dreams above. Xavian's a semi-dreamer, he's found a way to make her powers his. A mage with a comatose's powers behind him is . . . well-nigh unstoppable.'

'But you don't use them,' Janyvir said softly, pressing the point home. 'Something holds you back from taking whatever it is you've always wanted. You could draw an inferno spell, but there's no reason to, and you leave it uncompleted, vulnerable to discovery even though you could have finished it and killed the queen, the Wardens and all. Why do you leave it unfinished?'

'Because . . . because even if I killed the queen I would gain nothing by it. I am too shrewd a man to hold a grudge and not want something out of it. I leave it unfinished because circumstances are not ripe.'

'Why aren't they ripe?'

I said nothing.

'Why aren't they ripe, Xavian? Think!'

I closed my eyes, thinking feverishly. I was so tired, it

was hard to think like Xavian. 'I started the inferno spell. I am a clever man, I would never leave something unfinished unless I had a very good reason. Something must have changed to force me to leave the spell undone. Something drastic . . .'

My eyes flew open. 'We were robbed at Crystalpoint.'

'All of three days' journey from Haven.'

'I arrived in Haven three days after the spell was discovered! In Crystalpoint I abandoned my spell because something precious was stolen from me!'

'Excellent!' His eyes were alive, he looked like a hound who has smelt the scent. 'Documents have been stolen from you. They were vital to your plan. What do these documents say?'

'I . . . don't know. How to cast the spell that allows me to steal Miriam's powers, some form of blackmail, some means of bribery – how should I know?'

'All right,' he sighed, recognising that I too couldn't guess the answer. 'Documents are stolen. They are vital to you for whatever reason. You are forced to abandon your spell and continue on to Haven. Why?'

'No choice? Feilim is still sending assassins, Haven is the better place to be?'

'You send Rylam to the royal scribes' library to find documents.'

'Possibly the same documents that I lost on the road!' I agreed triumphantly. 'And now Rylam begins to play a more important role. In Haven he repeatedly petitions Lisana for retribution against Feilim and spends all his free time looking for these documents.'

'Corbe makes his night-time run into the western quarter.'

'I – Xavian – discover his absence. Suspecting the worst I muster Miriam's powers to follow him. I see Corbe hand over letters of some kind to Brawn/Lesourn. For their pains I kill them both and burn these same letters, because I want Rylam firmly under my boot.'

'Shortly after, our Silverhand agent, patrolling the corridors of the palace, spots Rylam leaving the healer with his shields and pride in tatters.'

'Rylam has argued with me, Rylam suspects that I killed his servant Corbe. I use Miriam's powers and Rylam can argue no more. However the death of Corbe has caused even more suspicion to land on my head, so I play the last trick I had in store – Kertoui. It was an act of desperation and flawed from the start.'

'Why are you so desperate?'

I shrugged. 'Rylam – for whatever reason – is turning against me. Laenan Kite is in the palace and snooping around – Kite knows about dreamers and may zoom in on Miriam unless I'm careful. Lisana is hedging the issue, I know it is only a matter of time before she turns round to Rylam and says, "you're lying, tell me the truth". I need a further mystery to delay that event until such time as I can find these oh-so-important documents. Kertoui was my first mistake.'

'In the meantime you continue to drain Miriam's power and search for these missing documents. You know that whoever sent the thieves is aware of your game, you know that Kite is paying undue attention both to Miriam, Rylam and the western quarter.' Janyvir thought long and hard, considering his next question. 'What are you doing about Renna?'

I jumped in surprise. 'I really don't know. I've scared

her off, of that I'm sure. I keep on taking Miriam's power, I guess, just in case she comes back. I'm not sure what Renna is going to do next. I'm even uncertain whether she's genuinely connected to Kite, or whether that's just another myth that's sprung up around the man.'

'All right, a question for Renna. Don't look like that – you're the best man to ask in the whole Void.'

'Go ahead.'

'You've been beaten back by a combination of mage and dreamer. You care for the dreamer and don't want to see her hurt. You couldn't give a stuff for the mage, but can't get to the dreamer without going through him first. What do you do?'

'I . . . I try to talk Miriam round. But I can't get to her, so I guess I don't.'

'You try to talk Miriam round,' he repeated flatly. 'But you can't get to her, so you send someone else. Someone who you know to be reliable, powerful, intelligent and curious about everything and anything.'

'Janyvir, if you think . . .'

He reached forwards suddenly, grabbed my wrist and yanked the sleeve up. His eyes were burning, his face intense.

'A spell got out of control with you, Kite. You vomited, but that was all. You're a legend – the greatest mage ever to throw fire. A mere spell wouldn't have caused you to slit a wrist. And if you were suicidal, which I don't think you are, you'd have slit more than one wrist. Tell me what happened to you!'

I didn't make a move. His fingers tightened over my wrist until they hurt. 'Tell me!'

'She came to me. On the road.' I wrenched myself free
of him and backed away, violently rubbing my wrist.
'She was scared, told me I mustn't hurt someone, cut my
wrist with a blade of ice, and suddenly it was very
cold . . .'

I told him everything about the encounter at
Starpoint, right up to waking next day to find no sign
that Renna had ever been there. When I was done, he
was staring at me with a look I found hard to meet.

'She's inside you, Kite, isn't she? You're sensing things
like a dreamer, feeling things that you'd never have felt
before. Renna is inside your blood because it was the
only place she knew to hide. Dreamers can only become
free of Earth when they genuinely find *their* dream, their
unique paradise. She went to you, because it was in you
that she found that place. She went to you, because you
can stop Xavian in whatever mad game he's playing and,
dreamer or no, you're still the most powerful man in the
Void.'

I nearly laughed out loud at that, but didn't. A curious
calm had descended over me. My wrist was itching, but
not nearly as much as it had. I could hear the bark of a
dog several crowded streets away and, if I strained, the
padding of a cat's feet on a nearby roof and the rush of its
breath. I could smell, more sharply than I once could, the
foul soup served in the watch canteen. Even though it
was night, I could see every quartering on the coat of
arms adorning a merchant's dignified mansion across the
street.

'Powerful?' I echoed softly. 'Do you even know what
power is? Power is the ability to command, to sway
men's hearts to do your will and do it completely.

Power is the thing that makes sane men mad and makes a musician swell with pride as his audience weeps for the hero of a sad song. I have none of that. I have the power to end a life, maybe, but that is more . . . control than power. Limited control of the things around me.

'But there are things within me that I cannot control. And they cry no at the idea of power, so I have none. Power is the most addictive wine and the sweetest poison. It is served in a silver chalice that never dries up. But the chalice only stays full because those who drink too deep soon give it back all their power. Maybe because they're dead. Or mad. Or torn apart by betrayal. Or shattered by the memory of what was once theirs, and never can be again. Or brought to despair by what they want to be, but never can. Don't talk to me of power, Commander Janyvir, for the only power I have is my own, and the less for that.'

'No,' he said quietly. 'You have power. Enough to see what it is that binds Miriam to Xavian, and to break that bond once and for all. You have the power to make her free.'

For a long while we stared as if about to challenge each other. Then Janyvir shook himself out of his thoughts, stood up straighter and snapped in a military voice, 'Question for Xavian. When you've found these documents, what will you do?'

I had no answer. What was there to say that he didn't already know?

And walking through the streets with Janyvir to the palace, at a pace that increased at every street corner until we were almost running, fearful of 'if's and 'maybe's' and circumstances just too neat to be true, I had the sense of being watched.

Was it Xavian? Did he know? Had I started seeing dangers where there weren't any? So many questions, and not time enough or certainty to answer any of them.

I am being watched. I feel you watching me.

And though I tried every trick I knew to lose the invisible eyes in the sky, still the feeling wouldn't go away.

EIGHT

Renna

'I can have him arrested.'

'You could try,' I muttered. 'Good luck to you, though.'

Lisana glared. 'Well, what do you want me to do?'

'Separate them out. All of them. Stop Rylam from going to the library, woo him away from Xavian with whatever device you see fit. Keep them busy while I try and get to Miriam. But whatever you do, don't let them near any kind of document.'

'I don't suppose, *you* know what these documents might be, ma'am?' asked Janyvir quietly.

'No,' she replied, stiffly as usual when she had to admit ignorance. She turned to me. 'What will you do?'

'Miriam,' I repeated. 'I've got to get Miriam away from Xavian without pushing her too far. If she was strong enough to repel Renna then she'll almost certainly be strong enough to repel me.'

'Almost,' murmured Janyvir, for my ears only.

'What will happen if Xavian finds these "documents" you keep referring to?'

'Most probably he'll try to kill you,' said Janyvir. I noted his quiet amusement at being able to say so.

'Why can't we just arrest him now?'

'We can soon,' I insisted. 'But first we need to know what these important documents are, who was clever enough to steal them, and how we can prevent Miriam from turning into – who knows what force? – under the pressure of events. Do anything to keep them busy. There's just one, maybe two more people I want to speak to, but Xavian and Rylam need to be out of the way first.'

'By lunch tomorrow,' she promised, 'I'll have them running around so fast they can't tell which way's north and which way's south.'

This time, I'll have you.

The thoughts going through my mind were not pleasant as I stomped through the corridors of the palace. They tended worryingly towards shaking certain people, hitting others and possibly dispensing with both of the above and going straight to spells designed to tear minds apart.

This time, I know what's going on, I thought angrily. *Corinna. You've got to help me now, woman.*

I'd asked Lisana – is Rylam asleep now? To my surprise, she'd said no. 'He's in the library. It's as though he's afraid to leave it.'

'And his servant Corinna? Where is she?'

Lisana had closed her eyes, listened to the Key inside her and replied, 'Awake. She's in the fountain cloister, in a state of some distraction.'

'Some distraction', in Lisana's book, could mean anything from being irritated by a fly to assaulted by a bear.

And there Corinna was, pacing up and down alone. A basket of dirty clothes had been dumped on the flagstones as though she'd reached the courtyard and lost the will to go on. I watched her a long while from the shadows, trying to read her every move. At one point she stopped and snatched up the basket again, as though she would move, before having second thoughts and dropping it again.

'Your chores are getting too much?' I asked from where I'd been observing her.

She jumped at my voice, and for a second there was a look of real terror on her face.

You thought I was someone else, didn't you? I realized with a strange sense of triumph. *I know you know something, Corinna.*

'I've been thinking,' I said, coming out into the open. She stared at me, and I could see her tensing up, ready for battle. I ignored her response, and began wandering round the darkened cloister as though I wasn't aware she existed.

Her eyes followed my every step. *I wonder if she'll make a dash for it.*

It was the old routine, the one I'd practised a thousand times. On Dislas and his kind, on all those faceless assassins and thugs and murderers I'd sought out in my youth, traipsing the length of the Void. I'd even had it practised on me a few times. That kind voice, the pretence at foolishness, the pressure rising steadily until the kindness is cruel, the fool is harsh and the full force of my questioner's knowledge falls on hapless Corinna, forcing from her the tiny gem that is the truth.

'I've been thinking,' I repeated, firmer now, commanding her attention. 'And I have reached the conclusion that maybe I was wrong.'

Her head snapped up like a snake's, but still she said nothing.

'You see, I might actually be willing to say that I was wrong, and Rylam was right, and maybe he's not a villain but simply a little . . . misguided.'

Silence.

'I might be willing to let him off, in fact. If someone made it worth my while.'

'How . . . worth your while?' she asked, not meeting my eyes.

'I'd need a good reason why he's an innocent party. I would also need an alternative bad guy.'

'I don't know why you've come to me. I'm a servant.'

'But you are in the unusual position of holding the key to your master's continued existence,' I urged.

Now she did meet my eyes, and I was startled to see how like Rylam's they were. They had that same anger, just below the surface, but hers was stronger. Much stronger.

'You total bastard,' she said quietly. 'You twist and you turn, you manipulate this way, that way, up and down. You pretend, even to yourself, to be nice. But when it suits you, you hide in the shadows and leap out ready to stab – to turn the blade in the wound. You think you can make me talk? I *love* Rylam! I love him more than you can ever understand, in ways you will never experience! You can't even begin to imagine what passes between us!'

'The imagination reels,' I murmured.

She grabbed the basket and made to move, but I was faster. I caught her wrist and twisted her round hard, so that she was forced to face me.

'Don't you run,' I warned. 'I know things. I've worked it out. All I need is a proof, just a little more information. I need to know what those documents were. Tell me that, and there's a good chance I can save Rylam's life.'

She yanked, but I held on, ignoring her grimace of pain as my fingers tightened. 'Don't you dare run!' I snapped. 'If you really love Rylam you'll bloody well help him now and tell me! It hangs together so well, but the thread that's holding it is pure conjecture. I need you to make it certain! Tell me!'

She hit me. It wasn't her action that surprised me, but the strength behind it. Though it was a slap, nothing more, it was still enough to bring water to my eyes.

There was a long silence, during which Corinna was trembling with rage. Was it just imagination, or did she almost *look* like her master in the darkness? Had she spent so much time with him that even his features were written onto her hard, defiant face?

I let her go. There didn't seem much point in holding her there. She grabbed the basket and began to back away, staring at me, feeling her way out of the garden.

'I can help him,' I said quietly as she retreated. 'You know I can.'

'I'll think about it,' she replied.

'It's all I can ask.'

She ran.

Which left just one more person to be questioned. And that one was inside me.

I am doing this for you, I thought reluctantly as I lay

down to sleep that night. *For you, Renna, because you are inside me, and because you wish it.*

Show me what it is you have been trying to show all along. I am prepared to listen, no matter what forces try to hinder you.

Sleep came all too fast – another sign that Renna was in me? And with sleep, dreams.

I was in a large hospital ward, in darkness broken only by the night nurse's light in her small office at the end of the room. In the distance I could hear the roar of heavy traffic. This was where the humans sent their coma patients to die. I'd dreamed before of such a place, when Renna's mortal body had been dying a slow, painless death. But now, there was that cat. It purred ahead of me, its bright green eyes glowing from a source that dimly shone from everywhere and nowhere. I followed it without complaint down the ward, to a bed. The cat purred again, springing up onto the bed and sliding up to the head of a figure, almost entirely covered by a sheet. I followed it, feeling my non-existent knees knock and non-existent sweat trickle down my non-existent back. *This is a dream, it's not real. Get a grip, for goodness' sake!*

I looked at the name-tag on the wrist of the patient. Mary Sutherfield. Overdose. Even dreaming, I was alert enough to make the connection. Mary. The packets of chemicals lying on the floor of the empty house near the river. I leaned over the bed to stare into the woman's face. And fell back with a cry that made the cat rise up in distress.

The empty face of Corbe was staring at me from those sheets, pale and lifeless. And . . . now that I looked closer, it *wasn't* Corbe, but Kertoui . . . but not Kertoui but the stocky features of Brawn as I'd always imagined he'd look.

I staggered back, squeezing my eyes shut. But if anything the darkness was worse, full of all those swimming faces that I might be shown, that *might* come back to haunt me. I opened my eyes, beheld T'omar's empty face, gave a cry of dismay. *He's not dead!* Then Lisana's face, the beauty all gone as though some thief had stolen it and wrapped it up to sell. Then Saenia – I turned my back, but every single person in the ward had rolled over to stare at me, and they all wore Saenia's face.

The cat mewed, whether in recognition or warning, the figures sat up and changed again, accusing in the darkness. The cat sprung away from them and sat at their side, twitching its tail nervously. I took a deep breath and faced the first figure.

'You failed me, Kite.'

'No sir,' I told the ghost of Talsin, long-dead king of Haven. 'The only person I failed was myself.'

'You let me die.'

'That's irrational, and you know it.'

Confident now. Somewhere at the end of this dark tunnel of ghosts and accusations, I knew I'd find an answer. It was simply a question of hanging on that far.

Next, the grinning features of Serein, the king of nightmare who had come so close to killing me. 'So, you survived?'

'And you didn't,' I replied levelly, adding, as much to assure myself as anything, 'ghost.'

'You fear me still.'

'No. I never feared you, Serein. Even when I thought

I was going to die, it was never *you* who made me shake.
You were a mad idiot.'

'You're going to die, Kite. You and all of yours.'

If I was startled to hear a twisted version of my own
words from another battle, another time, I didn't show it.
Whatever defences Miriam herself, or maybe Xavian,
had erected to keep me away from Miriam, I knew them
now for what they were. Hereafter it was a simple
matter to overcome each ploy. I just had to stand through
them, close my eyes and ears and it would all be
resolved. This was Xavian's work, these figures. But
Xavian was not as strong as he thought he was, though
he might pretend the world itself was struggling to keep
me away, trying to make me close my eyes against whatever it was that lay between these illusions.

The faces changed again, and abruptly my own features stared sombrely back at me.

If anything this made me calmer. 'You've misjudged
that one!' I yelled at my unseen tormentor. 'I've seen this
vision a thousand times over and it's lost its edge!' I had
the feeling that if I could just keep my eyes open and live
the faces out, then I could see whatever I was meant not
to see.

I looked down at the patient again. This time she bore
the sleeping, empty face of Miriam, and I breathed a sigh
of relief. I had known all along. 'What now?' I murmured to the cat. 'I am ready to know all of it, however
unwillingly.' I couldn't help smiling. 'You could just
have asked, you know. I would have stayed for you,
Renna.' It was a guess, but a good one. And even if I was
wrong, the cat was a good enough creature to address to
make my suspicions known.

Soon enough, on her feet a few yards off, there too was Miriam, and I knew as certainly as only a mage can, that she was the last ghost before freedom. She stood before me, wrapped in a hospital blanket as though it were a shroud, and stared at me with the same uncertain appraisal she'd shown in Haven.

'Do you ever give in?'

'I never get much choice.'

'You're an illusion, Kite.'

'No, you're the illusion – a trick of either the real Miriam, or Xavian, to keep me away. But I know what you are, Miriam, and that kind of knowledge is a deadly weapon.'

She snorted. 'I live a real life. I know who my friends are, I sleep a black, refreshing sleep of nothingness, I have no blood on my hands.'

'Indirectly you have shed blood, if through no fault of yours,' I replied. 'And what blood stains *my* hands was shed by other men for other causes. I have never struck out against another in anything but self-defence.'

'Then why did you strike at Serein?'

'Because he was going to undo my world, *had* undone my world. I had to restore sanity.'

'"I had". "To have to" is a verb used only by the weak-willed.'

'To describe people as "weak-willed" is merely to see in their souls the fear that resides in every man.'

'In you?'

'In me more than most,' I admitted. 'Everyone's afraid of something. The longer you live, the more enemies you have, the more that fear can grow. Not every life is tempered by a good padding of contentment.'

'And you – you have none of that padding,' she said, quick to bear down on my words and twist them to her own devices. 'Lisana manipulated the prince who you thought was your friend. He had you locked away and beaten, breaking every bond of companionship. You were reconciled only when he died, and by then it was too late. You've spent your life being attacked, wading through a river of blood that grows all the deeper the closer you try to get ashore. Poor Laenan Kite. A good man gone bad, who remembers what he once was.'

'I haven't gone bad, not entirely.'

'Everyone goes bad, with power.'

'I don't have power.'

'Don't give me the speech you gave Janyvir. You have power. You're just too much of a coward to use it.'

'Don't push me, Miriam, else you'll find out just how cowardly I am.'

She laughed. 'Oh dear. That's another bad habit, isn't it? Only when you are drained to the point of collapsing, only when you've been betrayed, slandered, abused and broken does your power *ever* show through. You've locked it away behind walls of iron, and it takes considerable heat to make those walls melt away.'

I was trembling with a whole tumult of emotions, but I didn't move a muscle. She advanced. 'Aren't you going to shake me, yell, curse or cry?'

'What use would that be, illusion? If by standing here against all your deadly barbs I can break the bond between a good dreamer and a bad mage, then stand I will. There. Is *that* power enough for you – the power to chose my own path, this once?'

And strangely, she smiled. It was a smile of contentment I had never seen before.

'Yes. It is enough.'

Abruptly, even she was gone.

I was standing alone in a darkened room, and indeed
I wasn't sure if I was standing, falling or floating,
because I felt nothing below my feet nor did I have any
sense of movement. My phantoms were all gone.

And now it was the turn of Miriam's own ghosts. As
they came to the fore, the whole world seemed to
dissolve.

A rushing river. Faces – some I recognised. The
woman, in a flowery dress, laying out a picnic with her
man. The second woman, as serene as her companions.
Miriam, smiling too, while they all turned to greet a man
whose voice we could hear, approaching on the path
from the house.

Show me.

How had Mary, as they called her here, descended
from this happy, happy state into the comatose, fragile
Miriam I knew?

Show me.

It was dark. The house was silent, four coats were
hanging up – the happy party of five must have lost a
member for the night. From the kitchen I could heard
murmuring

The black cat brushed against my legs. I started, and
looked down, but I shouldn't really have been surprised
that the creature could make a physical impression on
me. It bounded up the stairs in easy leaps and I followed,
drifting through the floor in a breeze of non-existence.

There she was. Miriam. Mary. Whatever it was I was

supposed to call her. She was sitting on the bed in her lonely room. The place was disordered – clothes strewed the floor, the windows were flung open and a cold wind plucked at the curtains.

Miriam herself was perched on the end of her double bed, face strewn with tears.

Double bed? Are you married, my little Miriam?

In one sweat-soaked hand she held a framed picture, shaking it up and down as her grip tightened, and went on tightening, until I was afraid for her. I wanted to move to her side and comfort her, but what good would that be? This was a dream and, what was more, a dream of the past. Nonetheless on impulse I sat down next to her, reached out and tried to brush away the tears that stained her flushed face, bloated with grief.

At my touch, half sensed, she leaped up. With a shriek of anger, frustration and a host of other unreadable emotions, she drew back her hand and threw the picture hard at the wall. I ducked instinctively, even though I didn't need to, as it sailed over my head and smashed. Glass went everywhere.

So far from calming Miriam, the violence seemed to drive her mad. She flung herself round the room in a blaze of anger, tearing books from their shelf and ripping out pages, kicking over the wastepaper basket, hurling pillows at walls and knocking over the bedside lamp, which crashed onto the floor, sending the room into darkness.

In the gloom I still saw clearly, something else I attributed to Renna. As Miriam threw herself on the bed and sobbed her heart out, the door opened, and the woman who was later to run wild-eyed to the river was framed in it. Wordlessly she flew to Miriam's side, folded her in her arms and just held her as Miriam cried and cried. I moved away, knowing I could do nothing. My glance fell on the picture in its bed of shattered glass.

Curious, I knelt down and tried to pick up the photo. My hand passed straight through it, of course. Bending over until my nose was just a few inches from the floor, I peered closer.

Miriam, wearing a bride's white dress and grinning like an idiot, was hanging on the arm of an almost militarily upright older man who could only be the double of Xavian.

There was no cry of eureka, no blaze of sudden understanding, no smug smile or snide thought announcing, 'I told you so'. Just an empty regret and the realisation that even when I first met Miriam, I'd known. She had dreamed of a memory, but in the Void her mind, twisted by grief or drugs or both, had found a corrupted version of that memory.

Renna, back in Sunpoint, had recognised that Xavian was not what he seemed, and had tried to take Miriam away from him. Why?

Bloody hell! Miriam's going to die in the most corrupt, twisted nightmare her own mind can devise. You can only become free of Earth if you find your perfect dream. What if she's found her perfect nightmare? What happens then?

Renna, why don't you talk to me? Why don't you help me?!

But even in asking the silent question, I knew the answer. A combination of mage and dreamer had beaten her back. To repel it, she had made me her partner in war. And since we were one, physically, mentally, spiritually – however it was two beings *could* be ultimately joined, surely we surpassed Xavian and Miriam, who were bound only by the flimsy rules of magic.

Promise me though, that you won't hurt the child.

Isn't that what she'd said before so rudely slitting my wrist? And there was something else. *I need your mortality, Kite. I need to equal them.*

'Bloody nice way of showing it,' I murmured, but even when I tried to I couldn't stay angry with her. Ultimately, what she – or was it 'we' now? – whatever the word was to describe this unlikely Kite-Renna union, we were fighting for the better cause. To get Miriam to her dream, before her body died and her mind was wrenched into whatever world it was that those dreamers who died in nightmare went into. Ultimately, all the intrigue, all those murders, all those long hours spent mulling over assassins, documents and princes was nothing compared to the simple fact that if Xavian could get his way with Miriam, no one would be left in one piece.

But if Renna was in me to give me enough power to equal Xavian . . . surely that meant I could do some of the things Xavian could? More even, since we were one?

A long time ago I had told a comatose, scared Renna to forget all about Earth. The rules of Earth don't apply here, and if you want to travel at the speed of thought then you can. I'd thought she was being foolish, living by her own rules. Now I began to understand how hard it was.

I want to wake up, I thought fervently, trying to will it on. *By my magic, by Renna's power, by everything that is good in this hell-cursed madhouse, I want to wake up.*

Was that a tremor of something? The vaguest tingle in my fingers, the fleeting awareness of my body in the distance? I'd never before been able to will my own waking, but surely if I could see in the night, hear the breathing of a distant cat, smell freshly baked bread from half a mile off – surely I could wake myself? Using Renna's powers, if not my own.

I want to wake up. More, I believe that I am capable of waking up. I believe it. I really, really believe it.

Who am I kidding? Just repeating something over and over doesn't make it true.

All right. I don't believe it. But Renna believes it, and she's somewhere inside me. If I can't get out of this by my own means I'm sure as hell prepared to use someone else's.

I want to wake up.

A tingle in my fingers. The faintest touch of warmth, the gentlest tickle across my palms and up my arms. An aching in my wrist. An itching in hair that hadn't been washed for far too long and was usually neglected anyway. A heaviness in my eyes that were still reluctant to open. The certain knowledge that somewhere, somehow, I was being watched.

I lay utterly still, feeling life return to me along with the real world, kept my breathing level and tried to identify the source of this disturbance to my magical senses. Someone was sitting in the dark, in the chair next to my bed, watching me. Fast breathing, shallow. I drew my magic round me like a cloak and gently probed.

Corinna. Wrapped tightly in a blanket, her face swollen as if by much recent weeping. Taken by surprise, I rolled over, and stared at her through the darkness. I could see her in perfect detail, maybe even better than if it had been by day. She stared back at me, blinking regularly in the gloom as if that could help her penetrate it.

'Hi,' I murmured finally.

'Hello.' Conversation lulled.

'How?'

'Your wards keep out those with hostile intent,' she murmured. 'So I got in.'

'Why?'

'I know who killed Corbe.'

I sat up. 'So do I. It'd have been nice if you helped me before, but we got there anyway.'

'I also know who the man was that Rylam killed.'

'So do I.'

She seemed taken aback at all this. 'I also know what it was that Feilim had stolen from us.'

'Ah. Now I am interested. Why have you decided to come to me?'

'Because Corbe is dead, Rylam in danger, Miriam dying, and I think I'm going to be next. Followed promptly of course by you and the queen.'

'Xavian's still experimenting with his powers,' said Corinna flatly. Sitting in front of me in my room, her face illuminated by the glow of hanging magelight, she'd somehow turned off, as people do when reporting unwelcome news. 'I don't know what he can do, but Rylam says it's nothing compared to what he *could* do. He could make a whole kingdom of his own, if he wanted to, Rylam says. But he doesn't want to.'

'What does he want?' I asked softly.

'Revenge.'

'For what? On what?'

'For everything. For his life as half a necromancer, half a mage. For a world that didn't want him. For a world where he was a nothing and a nobody. He wants to wear the crown of Nightkeep and of Haven, even though he has only one head and it's big enough as it is.'

'How does he want to rule Haven? Without bloody war, that is?'

She smiled, a narrow, knowing smile possessing as much humour as a snake. 'Through Rylam. Xavian's no fool. He knows that if he tries to seize Haven by force, you'll do to him as you did to the former king of nightmare – to Serein. But to take it legally, without bloodshed – that's his ideal. With Miriam's powers not only can he make the queen die, but he can twist her mind first so that she declares Rylam her heir.'

'She'd never do that. Even with a twisted head.' I spoke with certainty, for Lisana had children of her own and stoutly believed that she stemmed from the purest line of kings there was.

'She would if Xavian could produce proof that Rylam was in fact an heir of King Talsin. Her claim to the crown is strong, but shadowed by a long history where her line was regarded as little more than the Wardens of Waterpoint.'

I raised my hand. 'This is probably irrelevant, but *is* Rylam the heir of Talsin?'

'An heir. There are more running around than you'd think.'

'How do you know?'

She smiled again, a gentle creasing around the corners of a mouth that again smacked of no humour. 'He's my brother.'

Corinna's story started a long, long way in the past, at a

time when I was still a junior mage on my way to meet destiny, and Talsin was a young man learning exactly what it meant to be prince. A diplomatic visit from Sunpoint to Haven. A young and beautiful wife of old Giroign. A meeting in the dark, words exchanged, hearts emptied. I could see it all – the young prince looking for someone to talk to who didn't regard him as an idol or unfinished statue to be carved in his father's shape. The young princess unhappy with her husband, as anyone would be with any sense, reluctant to return to Sunpoint, desperate for a little company. One thing leading to another.

Then would come the complicated part. Convincing Giroign that the pregnancy was his own doing, not even sure yourself if it was. Talking to mages in the dark, convincing them to cast spells to delay the birth long enough for the old Warden to be taken in. Dangerous spells, to try and suppress a dangerous secret.

Then twins are born. Fortunately Rylam takes after the mother, not the father. The boy is fostered as Giroign's own, and though the Warden suspects, he never takes action because Rylam is everything he wants in a son. He's strong, powerful, confident – qualities Giroign believes are all his own rather than stemming from a different father.

But the girl who's born that night possesses Talsin's features and as she grows older the likeness will only become more pronounced. So the mother hides her, pretends she is just a servant girl.

'She couldn't look after me forever, though. And she was scared of being betrayed if she tried to give me to someone else,' said Corinna softly. 'So she wrote to

Talsin, telling him everything. But he sent her letters back and said he could do nothing. He was already in the thrall of Lisana.'

And on her deathbed, Corinna's mother confessed. Not everything, admittedly. Even at the last she kept the secret of Corinna's birth hidden from public knowledge. But Giroign learnt that Rylam, his favourite son, was a bastard. So did Feilim. So did Xavian.

'Giroign was a short-sighted fool. He didn't seem to realise the potential Rylam gave him, nor could he find it in his heart to throw Rylam out utterly. But Xavian – Xavian began scheming then and there.'

'When did this happen?' I asked.

'Seven years ago. It took the arrival of Miriam for Xavian to hatch his scheme properly. That, and the death of Giroign. Xavian needs Rylam to make his claim to the throne of Haven complete. Once Lisana is gone, Rylam takes her place. And when Rylam mysteriously dies of a "perfectly natural" illness, the whole Void will be shocked to find that he leaves the Key to Xavian. But no one will argue with a king's wish.'

'What went wrong?'

'Feilim wasn't stupid. When Rylam left with Xavian to try and claim his own, Feilim stole the letters from my mother to Talsin, making his claim void. Doubtless he's burnt them, by now. I'm betting that sent Xavian into a furious rage, which is why he had Rylam trawling the libraries in search of some proof, however fragile, for the connection between Talsin and Rylam.

'Rylam wouldn't have liked being ordered around, but by now he's scared of Xavian – he's realized what the mage is after. So he sends Corbe to meet up with one of

Feilim's spies. Xavian kills Corbe, beats Rylam almost to death, and sends his puppet king back into the libraries.' She spoke with savage bitterness.

'Will Rylam find anything? Proof of what he is, I mean.'

'I don't know.'

I sat there for a long while, my face as empty as hers. When I think, the rest of the world becomes as nothing to me. Right now I was thinking very hard. With Corinna's confession, we had enough.

We've got to arrest Xavian now. He must know that I know. With Miriam . . . well, I'll just have to make that up as I go along, as all these things are made up.

I rose to my feet, strode to the bedroom door, took my jacket off its peg and pulled it on. Corinna's eyes hadn't left me all the way, and suddenly I had the sense of being the great mage after all. Was that fear in her eyes, masked only by a thin layer of awe at seeing a legend starting to work?

'What are you going to do?'

'Wake up Lisana,' I replied.

'What will she do?'

'I have no idea, but we can't allow Xavian to run around loose for the rest . . .' My voice trailed off. 'Did you hear that?'

'Hear what?' she asked in a hushed, wrought voice.

I frowned, and heard it again. The little hum of distant magic being worked, just on the edge of my mage's ears. And a brush against the wards of my room, so gentle it might have been imagination.

But my imagination was not in the habit of playing tricks of this sort . . .

Instinct, or possibly Renna inside me, took over. I was at my bedside in three good strides, had drawn a dagger and was already removing it from its sheath, discarding the slim leather package that kept the blade safe and throwing it to the floor. I went to a desk and produced another dagger, larger and heavier, which I only ever used in emergencies, and handed it to Corinna. I suddenly felt very, very exposed.

<Lisana?> I sent in a hushed burst of thought. <Your majesty!> Louder, calling out this time, sending my thoughts in desperation through the palace. <Lisana! Wake up! Say something!>

No reply. I turned to Corinna, mouth opening to deliver a warning, to ask her if she knew what was going on. But she was smiling a strange little smile which quite upset all the words I'd had in store. The dagger fell from her fingers, and she yawned and began to stagger in a zigzag towards the bed.

Now I was sure of it, the definite press and pull of magic, spreading through the palace in a tide of more-than spells. There was a dreamer's power behind it too, twisting reality itself to bring sleep. I caught Corinna as she fell by the bed and tried shaking her.

'Corinna! Corinna, you've done really well, don't spoil it now by getting caught out by a little sleep spell!'

Or even a huge, unnatural, impossible spell, for that matter.

'Corinna!' I tried to cover her in my own powers, somehow shield her from the effects of the spell. The wards around the room were warping, but not breaking or sounding any alarms. My wrist hurt like hell – another sign that a dreamer was at work? That it was a dreamer's power at work I was sure, for it felt not like magic but something else being refined *by* spells – in this case to produce a deadly efficient slumber. Corinna's eyes drifted shut and though I shook her and called her name, she wouldn't stir.

Seeing how futile my effort was, I let her slip onto the bed, gathered up my dagger and on a second thought strode to a large wardrobe and flung it open. In it I found a set of slightly battered clothes, a trunk full of the usual debris you get in spare bedrooms, and, shoved at the back and swathed in rough, oily leather, a large staff.

The dreamer in me had shut out the effect of Xavian's spell, and already the mage was trying to find a way to break it. I began to wonder at the extent of the spell as I hefted the staff and felt the magic warm my hands through the old wood. Usually I don't carry a staff, but this was the same lump of wood that I had carried with me into Haven when nightmare ruled, and I had grown attached to it for more than practical reasons.

Out of curiosity I tried summoning T'omar. The answer was sluggish, but it came.

<Dreams above, Kite, what time do you call this?>

<We're under attack, T'omar. The whole palace is under bloody Xavian's spell.>

He became fully aware. <Explain.> Not a wild cry of disbelief, nor exclamations or protestations of doom and despair – that wasn't T'omar's style. There's a disaster on your hands, why then! Let's talk calmly about it, and go out and kill the baddies in a cool, logical manner, preferably without raising too great a cleaning bill in the process. I strode towards the door, automatically twirling the staff in case any demons leapt out of the shadows. I was alone in an empty palace with one mad mage, a sleeping queen, an abused dreamer and a whole host of courtiers – of relative innocents – besides.

I was breathing faster now as adrenaline made my heart race. Xavian might appear behind me at any moment, might leap out of the darkness, might shimmer out of the invisible cover of his magic to strike me dead . . . *No! You start thinking like that and you freeze up with fear. Kite, please, please don't freeze up with fear* . . .

It was hard to hold onto my staff with the sweat pouring off my palms. My breathing seemed the loudest thing in the world, my knees were shaking with each step, I was feeling hot and clammy . . .

<Kite! Answer me!> T'omar's voice, a reassurance out of nowhere that I wasn't alone, that not everyone in the Void was asleep.

<I'm . . . just trying to remember who I am,> I replied as confidently as possible. *Yes, that's right. Remember – you are the great mage. You're still alive, you're still what you are and that is a certainty to give strength.* <Xavian's bad, T'omar. He's been draining Miriam's powers and now he's using them to try and take revenge on an unloving world. The whole palace is asleep, except me.>

<Asleep? Has he enough power to cast a spell of that size alone . . .>

<That and more!> I snapped, angry all of a sudden. Or was it fear, making me angry through some twist of the mind?

<All right.> He spoke levelly, but I could hear the shortening of each syllable, the prolonging of each space that suggested a man growing frantic and trying to suppress it. <So Xavian's the bad guy. He's cast a sleep spell. What's his target? What's he trying to achieve?>

<I . . . I don't know. Either the queen or . . . or me.>
Laenan Kite, the expert on dreamers, the one man who might possibly stand a chance against the mad, mad mage.

I reached the door, kicked it open. My heart missed a beat, my blood ran to ice and I'm pretty sure that I nearly dropped my staff. Xavian raised his head, smiled a toothy little smile and drew his long, jet-black staff across his body in an attack position.

'You would be the one who stayed awake all night,' he murmured.

<Kite! Kite! What's going on?> demanded T'omar, sensing through our link the fear that had suddenly seized me.

<I'll call back,> I sent, breaking the link before he could protest. Slowly, dagger clutched in my left hand, staff in my right, I began to back away. Xavian followed, entering the room slowly as he methodically and easily tore apart the wards around my room.

'How are you resisting the spell, Laenan Kite?' he asked softly.

'That's Warden Kite to you!' I snapped, more defiantly than I felt. 'Perhaps I'm simply so much more powerful than you are, *little* mage.'

He raised his eyebrows, feigning aloofness. But his muscles had bunched at the 'little' and his eyes flashed anger. 'I am so much more than you think, Kite.'

'So am I. And my power comes from a legitimate bargain, rather than your night-time spell-casting over a sleeping girl.'

Something about me made him frown with concern. 'You're bluffing,' he declared finally. '. . . But you're not. There *is* something protecting you.' He looked me up and down as though I might be wearing some explanation on a placard round my neck. 'What is it?'

'Charm and charisma?'

'If you just tell me it'll make this process a lot easier,' he said evenly. He really did believe that with this grand offer, he was doing me a favour.

'This process?' I repeated, testing my personal shielding to ensure its strength. 'You mean the one by which you kill the queen, put a puppet king on the throne and take your revenge on "an unloving Void"? I have got that right, haven't I?'

'I'll be doing the Void a favour, Kite. Tell me, how are you at Earth history?' He began to advance on me, and I gave ground steadily. We began to circle, each grasping his staff, ready to repel any attack.

'I've dreamed a few things here or there.'

'The kingdom called Germany,' he said, in the level manner of a teacher addressing an un-cooperative student. 'It used to be scattered, divided, a thing of petty feuds and wars. Then one day, a man of steel, cunning, unappreciated, the last individual the world would have thought of as a conqueror, came onto the scene. Through guile and intrigue he united his nation into a great power.' He added, as if it were a triviality, 'Of course there had to be sacrifices, but it was all for the better.'

If anything his arrogance made me more confident. At least, if I beat the hell out of this man I wouldn't feel a thing about it.

'Germany?' I repeated. 'Unified in bloodshed, yes. But peaceable ever after? We are talking of the same place?'

'All my life,' he hissed, 'I've lived with the common people . . .'

'If you had you wouldn't use the word "common".'

He ignored me, eyes glowing at some inner vision. 'When I have dreams and nightmare united as one, think how much happier they'll be. When I have every kingdom under *my* rule there will be no more war, no more feuding or hatred!'

'Think *diversity*, my dear Xavian. Every kingdom in the Void living by your set of rules, following everything you say, be it the bravest idea or the most irrational bias – no. Half of man is the individual, the other is cooperation. Your scheme involves neither. You take all without asking, and give nothing in return.'

'Maybe not *now*,' he insisted, 'but think later! When I am king I'll be the greatest monarch of a united Void ever! I'll bring back the old laws and make sure that everyone lives happily . . .'

'"Make sure"?! What do you know about "make sure"?' I snapped, my anger overpowering my fear. 'Your schemes are all screwed, Xavian! Look at the fiasco with Kertoui! Look how easy it was to work out the truth about Corbe and Lesourn! Look how Feilim made an idiot of you, just by stealing a few papers!'

He scowled. 'Feilim will die by my hand, Kite, have no fear of that! He will die, just as you will, who could have been my closest ally!'

'I've heard all this before, Xavian. Your power is really Miriam's power, and for all you pretend to the contrary it's you who depend on *her*! Do you really think a minor mage from Sunpoint with a grudge can just walk into Haven and expect to take the crown?'

'Isn't that what you did?' he yelled. 'A little mage from Sunpoint, a nothing, arrives in Haven! Four hundred years later and a dying king turns to this common-born larva and murmurs that if anyone should take the crown, it should be him!'

'Those who want to rule shouldn't be allowed to,' I growled. 'And you, Xavian, are the incarnation of why.'

It came, as I had known it would. The little tensing, the silent roar, the spring. The flash of the staff slicing through the air, the jolt as I brought my own weapon up in one out-flung hand to deflect the blow, bringing my dagger under and down to try and disembowel the bastard in that split second of chaos. Our staffs met with the force of two giants, and I felt something akin to an electric shock, a static current passing up my arm and filling my whole body. I was aware of a wetness around my wrist as, beneath the bandage, the healed wound began to bleed again.

I had blocked a two-handed attack with only one hand, and expected to pay for it. But Xavian had released his staff with one hand just before connection, and caught hold of my wrist only inches from me puncturing his gut with the dagger.

At the touch of skin on skin, images passed between the dreamers in us, using our bodies as conduits for the exchange.

A rushing river, laughter. Picnics beneath the hot sun, a perfect life in a perfect, unspoiled world . . .

I broke free, spinning away with unexpected agility. I've never been one for hand-to-hand fighting, preferring the good old policy of standing well back and throwing fire. But now that my skills were put to the test, I found I could keep up. Again, I suspected Renna of being part of that.

It was the fastest, sharpest, most noiseless battle ever fought between two men, of that I am certain. There was no yelling, no roaring, no dramatic gasping for breath nor yelps of pain when a thrust got through Just silent, determined combat in a sleeping palace. Even the thump of staff on staff seemed quiet – the somnolent silence seemed to smother it all.

The dreamers' powers in us had speeded up our reflexes tenfold, I quickly noticed. While I retained possession of my dagger, Xavian had also drawn a slim little weapon and went into the attack using this and his staff with horrible efficiency. A cut towards my feet, from which I scrambled back, a counter-thrust towards my shoulder which I blocked with my staff, followed by a wild thrust towards my belly with the dagger. I caught the blade on my own weapon and tried to twist it down, but he was physically much stronger and twisted the other way, so that I could feel bone grating against bone and saw my skin go white as blood was forced away. My dagger fell – yet somehow I had managed to bat away Xavian's blade with my staff, bend, retrieve the dagger and spring back into guard position, all before my weapon hit the floor.

We broke away, panting for breath, our shocked minds just beginning to register the extreme workout inflicted on our bodies.

'How do you move like a dreamer?' he hissed. 'What is it protecting you?!'

'Wit and sophistication, isn't it obvious?' I exclaimed between great gasps of breath.

He gave another snarl and came in at the attack again. I resigned myself to grim defence: parry, twist, parry, thrust, recoil, parry, step, twist, parry, turn – an endless succession of automatic moves that I had never been taught, in a never-ending attempt to thwart my own extinction. Parry, twist, parry . . .

My wrist was burning, the blood now seeping through the bandage. Something was happening inside my body, a thing quite apart from the heat and sweat of the fight. Magic was raging through my veins, as it always did when I fought. But behind it swept another power, dry and ancient and about as sympathetic to my plight as a hammer is to the anvil. Through it I was aware that Xavian's blade and mine were locked hilt-to-hilt, so I gave a great heave that left my whole arm aching dully, and heard a dull clatter an eternity later as the daggers fell away. Xavian retreated, bent low over his staff like an animal taking human shape. A gasping, panting, furious animal, eyeing up its prey.

'Call it quits?' I asked with an un-felt grin.

He brushed the sweat out of his eyes with his left hand, and I saw the little line of blood. I was sure I hadn't cut him, but it wasn't necessary that I had. Wasn't my own wrist bleeding for no reason?

'You can't kill me,' he hissed. 'We're too evenly matched, you and I.'

'I can't kill you yet, but I will kill you.'

'So then you'll kill Miriam. For she is in me, and unless I release her she'll die as I do.'

'Then I suppose I'll have to satisfy myself with beating you into unconsciousness,' I retorted. 'I can't hope you've like inhibitions about killing me. No doubt your own life is too unfair to allow you that kind of balance.'

'We both know, you and I, about life's shortcomings.'

'Of course. That's why you seem to go through it in a trail of death.'

'For the greater good!' he spat with conviction. This time he didn't spring forwards, but brought his free hand up, glowing with fire. Necromantic fire.

So, you bastard, you did study the black arts too.

I raised my shields, bracing myself for the shock of impact and at the same time directed a series of probes in the direction of his wards. They were rock-hard.

So what if I am widely accepted as a powerful mage? If people discovered how much of that so-called 'power' rested merely on a different tack in combat, I'd lose my reputation overnight. Magic and science cannot mix, they say. Magic is illogical. So what, I say? That doesn't mean the person who deploys it can't use reason.

So I tried to think, as logically as possible, how to dismantle the wards in front of me. Could I simply stand still and let Xavian wear himself out, with trying all night to break down my spells? No – not with Miriam's power in him. I wasn't sure of my defences anyway – I was improvising as I went along, whereas Xavian had had more practice with his dreamer's powers. Should I spend all my magic on one life-or-death gamble? Or go for the simplistic you-hit, I-hit, you-hit, time-honoured method of duelling mages?

Or should I try to wake up the palace while he's distracted with getting through my shields? I wonder . . .

Then there wasn't time to wonder any more, because a ball of black fire, something that seemed to be made of flame and spider's web and sticky crude oil all in one ugly sphere, impacted across my shields. I shuddered as the spell crawled across my wards, trying to find a way in, but stood fast.

Xavian frowned. Under normal circumstances, that spell would most likely have torn my shields apart. I took a firmer grip on my staff, tucking my head into my chest and locking my elbows into place to provide some support should I stagger. Another spell hit, followed by a hiss of frustration from Xavian as it had no effect.

I extended my mind outwards, to wrap him in a cloud of foggy thought that crawled across his shields and made all his senses blind. He responded with a gust of wind that tore the shutters off their hinges, and picked up books and papers and threw them around the room. I smiled despite myself as my hair was plucked upwards and my clothes flapped wildly in the semi-magical wind. Xavian was the kind of fighter who liked to waste big magic on big, impressive spells. If he'd been thinking, he could just have burnt away my spell in localized patches – but, no, drunk on power, he'd gone for the whole hog.

I stood fast as the wind roared in anger and hatred, and struck back through it, using it to my advantage, playing my lesson of logic against his mage's old lessons of chaos and hammering power. I made the wind cold, feeding off a spell he'd created to expend minimum power, and filled it full of ice which shattered off his shields in a thousand deadly shards. For myself, I didn't try to deflect the ice face-on, but instructed the wind to flow round in a different way. It took less work.

Xavian was not only drunk on power, I realised, but he was one of those weak mages who was used to winning a contest by *looking* good. Which meant that whenever he cast a spell there was usually a bit of chanting and gesturing. Ritual gestures are all very well for opening up pathways. But in a fight, when dealing with forces of the size we each deployed, it was better just to stand as still as a statue and focus on employing your mind, not your hands. I felt like chiding him for his lack of technique.

The last ice splinters flew off into the walls and embedded themselves. The wind died down. There followed a cracking, crunching sound as the ice seemed to take root, and began to expand across the walls, over the ceiling, along the floor. Where it crawled up to the ceiling it began to form deadly icicles, stabbing down towards my head. Where it raced across the floor in a silver-blue tide of sparkling frost, it acquired a life of its own and tried to wrap itself round my feet and crawl up my body. I summoned fire, a thin but substantial outer-shield to dome me. As a result, the stabbing icicles above me turned to water, with an effect like standing in a sudden and very localised rainstorm. Uncomfortably hot water began to swirl around my ankles, melted by the fire.

Xavian readied his next spell. To distract him I raised my staff and brought it crashing down with a thud. In its vibration the icicles across the ceiling cracked as one and fell, all angling roughly in his direction. He saw the coming threat and dived for cover, frantically raising a spell.

I used that second of distraction for all I was worth, and launched an attack on his shields, running my senses over them and dragging behind me a trail of tearing, jagged force to scratch and pull my way through to his exposed soul. What I sought was a certain spell of his, just cast and still running, so that I could snap the tender thread between him and it, and wake the palace.

But Xavian perceived it as a general attack on his defences, and tried to throw off my attack by shoving lines of power in my way. I stayed stubbornly attached to his shields, digging my way slowly deeper. My head began to ring and my hands trembled from the shock of his counter-attacks, which grew more chaotic and savage the further I went. Unconsciously I began to draw on my staff's limited magical energy to bolster my own, and for a brief moment I was accelerating through his shields.

Then my questing magic came up hard against a wall of force. I felt as if a thousand daggers were pricking my flesh and a pile of bricks was balanced on my head. But through the pain, from two magics inter-locked so tightly it was almost impossible to distinguish one from the other, I saw it. The little, almost forgotten thread of magic that sustained the sleeping spell covering the whole palace. I reached out a mental hand and snapped it, almost at the exact second that a wall of Xavian's magic bore down and expelled me from my quest.

I was vaguely aware that I'd slumped to my knees, and that warm water was sloshing around me. The staff, lifeless, all its magic drained, lay a few feet to one side. Xavian was in a corner retching from the force of my attack, but I didn't feel much better. Lined up side-to-side, we would have left any onlooker hard pressed to say which one looked worse off. The magical blaze of light and colour illuminating the room during our contest had died, and his shield and mine were each a faint glow, perceptible only out of the corner of the eye. Shockingly cold water ran down the back of my neck – the ice around the room was melting fast, no longer sustained by magic.

Xavian finished retching and was somehow pulling himself upright. I groped feebly until my fingers closed over the staff, but it was now a dead weight in my hands or, at best, a purely physical weapon.

<Lisana,> I sent feebly, leaning all my weight on the staff in an effort to pull myself upright. <Lisana, wake up!>

Xavian was staggering towards me, his eyes slightly out of focus. Somehow I made it to my feet, relying on the staff for support and wanting to do exactly as he'd done and empty my guts across the soaked and scorched floor. He came within a few feet of me, hesitated, and knocked my staff from my hands with a savage wrench. I staggered, but remarkably didn't fall. His hands closed round mine, and there was the sense of electricity again. He twisted my right wrist over and I saw that there was blood freely flowing down my arm.

The same was happening with his hand. Our eyes met. <Lisana. Wake up.>

'I am not sure who is weaker,' he confessed. 'You or I.'

'Let's not find out,' I said feebly. 'I'm sure you've learnt your lesson.' <Lisana!>

His eyes flickered in sudden doubt, and his grip tightened around my wrist, extracting from me a small gasp of pain. 'What have you done?' he hissed.

And I felt it. The twisting of reality around us, the faint pressure of something being changed. Lisana's reassuring presence somewhere overhead, the feeling of the Key, oh yes! The feeling of the Key bringing guards into existence to bear down on us with purpose in their eyes, the warping of the room as windows and doors disappeared to create an effective prison, the wrenching of the floor as a gash opened up between Xavian and me. I yanked hard and his grip, made slippery by blood – whether his or mine I couldn't tell – no longer held. Falling backwards, I sprawled across the floor as the reality around us went on changing.

And I felt something else too. Something besides the Key, something stemming out from Xavian. I tried to suppress it, extending my magic with what little strength I had remaining, but it was no good. Wrapping his dreamer's powers – *Miriam's* dreamer's powers – around him like a cloak, Xavian raised his head, focused . . . focused . . . and was gone. He had travelled at the speed of thought to a place that I could not divine.

I raised my trembling arm and stared at the blood. I rolled sluggishly onto my hands and knees. I wondered if I really was going to be sick. I shivered at the ice-cold water pouring off the ceiling and washing around my hands. I looked into Corinna's terrified face as she woke from the Xavian-imposed sleep.

I smiled a strange little smile, and, tucking my bleeding wrist under my arm and exerting as much pressure as I dared, I went in search of a way out.

NINE

The Uncomfortable Truth

<Kite! Kite, tell me what's happening?!>
<It's all right, T'omar. Everything's over.>

Commander Janyvir had been summoned to the palace to make the arrest personally. I *don't want word of this to get out any further than it must*, Lisana had specified. If my magic-shocked mind, after a duel with a necromantic mage, was still thinking straight at three o'clock in the morning, that meant that the circle of knowledge about what had transpired was now sitting in its entirety in the queen's study. Or at least was represented in full: Lisana, Janyvir, Shell and I, with a pair of empty-eyed Key-bound elves guarding the door. Shell had refused to allow any other Silverhand to come, and even so sat in the corner behind a distorting illusion.

My wrist had been re-bandaged, and had again begun to heal with unnatural speed. The bleeding had stopped almost as soon as Xavian had vanished. I was now sitting in the queen's most comfortable chair, wearing a large blanket and waiting for people to volunteer their love and support.

Lisana, as always, put other things first. 'Where is Xavian now?' she demanded.

A series of doubtful looks was passed round the assembly. 'No idea,' said Shell.

'That's not helpful.'

'I apologize, your majesty, for not being able to trace a mage of unprecedented power through the Void on one hour's notice,' she replied smoothly. 'It's the warts who call themselves scryers, you see.'

Janyvir gave me a shocked look at Shell's blunt words, and I hid a smile. Lisana tried not to appear rattled, then smiled faintly herself. She could see that she and Shell had the same black disposition. 'What about Miriam?' she asked.

'Asleep, and under constant guard,' said Janyvir. 'In case Xavian tries to come back, your majesty.'

'Asleep? Why hasn't anyone woken her?'

'Because we can't,' I said wearily. 'Xavian has wrapped her so tightly in spells that even beginning to tamper with them would cause incalculable damage.'

She sighed, and delivered the painful speech I feared was coming. 'You say Xavian is feeding off her, using her to make him strong. Kite, you especially must know how dangerous he is, and I feel that if we can't break the link any other way . . .'

'If you kill Miriam, your majesty, chances are you'll hurt me,' I said. 'Renna is inside me. She entered my blood so that I could help her defeat Xavian, but save Miriam. If Miriam dies, I'll know I've failed both of them. *Renna* will know I've failed. And she just might be annoyed.'

Lisana's eyes widened at the things I wasn't saying. *She slit my wrist to get in, why not slit it to get out?* 'Come on, Kite. Renna and you were close – she would never deal with you in anger.'

'Who can tell?' *Who knows anything any more?* 'I'll do what she wants anyway.'

'Why?'

I smiled and said nothing. *Leave it to their imagination,* I reasoned. *Those who think they know me will say it's fear. Those with more imagination might call it love. Since I don't know what makes me wish Renna my own, I will not speak on this. But whatever it is, my favoured explanation would be love.*

There was a long silence, in which there was nothing but the buzz of four minds thinking the same thoughts. 'Kite,' said Lisana finally. 'I know you and I don't always agree. But hasn't Renna already pushed you past the boundaries of reason?'

Facing calamity, as we are, I thought, *perhaps that's what it takes.*

Sleep. It came all too easily now, and I knew too well what was going to happen, who I was going to see, where and why.

The river bounced over the little pebbles, crystal-clear meltwater from the mountains above. The trees waved in a gentle breeze and the landscape seemed, in a flight of fancy from my too-burdened mind, almost illusionary, it was so untouched by evil or corruption. *This is the canvas on which mankind paints, and what do they make with their indelicate brush? Forests carved down, animals driven away, skies darkened with pollution.*

Hell, I'm growing old.

'You did well. You always do.'

'Hello, Serein.'

The ex-king of nightmare sat down by my side, picked up a pebble that had strayed up the bank and threw it back into the river with a plop. 'You've got a peculiar brand of fighting, you know that?'

'Yes. It's called winning. What are you doing in my dream, ghost?'

'Answering your summons, since you ask. The laws are different for dreamers – they affect the physical, remember, we affect the mental. I am here because you're creating a physical illusion of me on Earth, because you're summoning me into being.'

'No. I'm not. Renna is.'

He smiled faintly. 'Ah yes. Renna is the catalyst for all this.'

'Catalyst? Hell, Renna started it all! Renna is the reason I'm here, Renna is the reason my wrist is one large scar, Renna is the reason I've just fought for life or death or both, whatever the outcome was meant to be that never came!' I raised my voice defiantly. 'Why don't you come to me directly, Renna? Powerful, clever Renna, why don't you come and show yourself?'

'She won't,' said Serein calmly. 'She's scared you won't like what you see.'

I met his eyes, startled. Licking dry lips, I asked in as rational and reasonable voice as I could, 'You mean, compared to the king of nightmare who damn near killed me all those years ago?'

'She's not what you remember, Kite.'

'Like I give a toss. She found her dream. In *me*. Does she really believe that her, *her* dream can change so much? For I am hers, just as she is mine and we are one.'

'And you forgive her?' asked Serein. 'For doing what she's done?'

I laughed. 'I can't believe this. I am having a sincere little *chat* with my long-dead enemy in a dream.'

'Can you forgive her?' he repeated.

'Of course. I have some idea of the fate of dreamers whose bodies die whilst their minds are still in nightmare. Miriam is so fragile – trying to save her from that fate is a noble cause.'

'Renna has been helping comatose dreamers for many years now, and not just in this dimension. There are a million, billion universes out there, Kite. But I think she'll always be slightly biased in favour of this one. Where her dream lies.'

'Serein . . . *Renna*, since that's who you are, however indirectly, I know this is gonna sound a little out of place, considering the circumstances, but have you ever considered making a dream come true?'

Renna was sitting by the banks of the river, exactly in the manner and place of Serein, but somehow it looked as though she had always been there. I hadn't even noticed the change take place between the two. She was hugging her knees to her chest, looking at me sideways with her toes pointing towards the river. 'It was necessary to use you,' she said finally. 'For Miriam's sake.'

'I understand that. I suppose the . . .' I drew a sharp line across my wrist, 'was an essential part of making us one so that together we could overcome Xavian?'

'I'm afraid so. I needed a large amount of your blood to make contact, so that I could mingle.'

'It's isn't permanent, I hope?'

'No. You and I are closely joined, and I expect that when I leave you, some of what I am will rub off, but I can leave whenever I want. You'll recognise the signs when it happens.'

'Thanks.' I stretched. 'What do you want me to do now?'

She eased her way closer and buried her head against my shoulder. 'Nothing. This is your dream.' Her eyes sparkled with mischief. 'I'm just a piece of scenery.'

Silence. Then, 'Renna?'

'Yes?'

'Why are you doing this?'

She took a long time to answer. 'I . . . think it's partly because I do want to help the girl. I like to believe that, anyway. It makes me feel more . . . more human. Her plight calls to me, that kind of thing. I've almost been in her situation. Trapped between life and death, confused, afraid.'

'But?'

She smiled. 'There are a lot of worlds out there. A shadow separates the Void from Earth, but there are so *many* shadows to cross. And many dreamers like me. Miriam . . . disrupts things. She is so close to becoming one of us, but in a way that's twisted. Can you imagine the power of a God in Miriam – what it would do?'

'You're afraid of her,' I said accusingly.

'Yes. I'm afraid she'll hurt more than just herself. I'm afraid she's going to hurt my dream.' She smiled, not meeting my eyes. 'I'm afraid she's going to hurt you.'

'Is this why you're doing all this? Fighting Xavian, through me?'

'Yes.'

'And that's why you needed me? Because Xavian and Miriam combined are too strong for you, you needed my magic? You needed a mortal to fight a mortal, while you engage Miriam, the immortal?'

'Yes. Kite?'

'Mm?'

'Why are *you* doing this?'

I took a long time to answer. 'Like you, I'd prefer to think it's because I've no choice. Lisana would have dragged me in anyway, T'omar would have screamed until I got involved, and you'd have slit my wrist and I'd still have been unable to stop you. But . . . there is, as always, more.'

'Tell me. I'm your dream, you're mine. And for the moment we are together.'

'I'm doing it . . . because I miss you.'

'That statement requires elaboration, Kite, and you know it.'

'Shut up and let me sentimentalize,' I said. 'You think this is easy? When I first saw Miriam, I recognized her as a dreamer where before only Xavian had. I thought I could do for her what I did for you. I thought that by helping her it would bring you closer to me – don't ask me why. I guess, in a sense, I was trying to substitute Miriam for you. The same fragile dreamer, caught between worlds. The same confusion. The same growing into something more. When I first saw Miriam and real-ized that she was a dreamer, I thought for a second that she was you. But then it was someone else And now it's too late for me to stop and take account of that. I'm too involved.'

She stared at me, then smiled faintly. 'Kite?'

'Yes?'

'For what it's worth, I missed you too.'

I sighed. 'Thanks a bundle, Renna.'

'Kite?'

'Yes?'

'I'm sorry. I'm sorry for everything. But every good dream must come to an end.'

I shook my head. 'Of all people, Renna, you should know better than that.'

We sat, dreaming of dreams.

'Are you sure you're up to this?' asked Janyvir as we strode through the palace. I gave him a reproving look, and pointedly rubbed my wrist. The bandage was clean, and we both knew that overnight the gash had healed itself.

'I mean, how do you know it'll work?' he demanded.

'It'll work because Xavian has only taken a bit of Miriam, and there's still something left to talk to. It'll work because I'm going to make it work. How's our Rylam this morning?'

'You are infuriating!'

'Just expressing an interest, my dear commander.'

'He's fine. So's Corinna. They're under house arrest together and getting on fine. It's fine,' he snapped.

It was just past midday, and the whole palace was buzzing with tension. Lisana now went everywhere with at least four guards, and a message had been dispatched to every dignitary in the land to follow suit. Because of renegade mage activity, the note had said. And I had slept the deepest, most peaceful sleep of my life, and woken with not a mark to show for the night, save a slight scar on my ego and a reluctance to touch my over-taxed magic. And the worry at the knowledge that somehow, I'd have to put Renna's instructions into action without flaw or fault.

Xavian has taken a lot of her, but there's still enough of Miriam left to talk to. You'll just need the guts to listen.

Which was why, after a hearty lunch and a splash in the face of cold water, I was marching down the corridor with four guards, Commander Janyvir Reshin and the key to the room where Miriam was kept under close watch. I looked a bit pasty, sure, and I felt like . . . well, a mage who'd had a good chunk of his magic torn from him in a mighty duel . . . but I was *alive*. And more than that, I had an enemy to direct all my hatred at, and a plan. The combination of these two made me feel more alive than if I never even had my shields torn apart by Xavian.

'You've let her off, then?'

'What?' I asked, startled by Janyvir's words.

'Renna. You're not annoyed about the inconvenience of having your wrist slashed. '

I shrugged. 'People often say the end justifies the means. In this case, I'm afraid I agree.'

'Even though you might die.'

I smiled despite myself. 'I would have come to Haven with or without Renna urging me along. What would I have done differently, once we'd worked out the truth and Xavian came after me? Without Renna's powers I would have been just another commiseration.'

We reached Miriam's room. I knocked twice, then

unlocked the door. Five Key-bound guards stared at me, registered who I was and let me pass. Janyvir started again to try and dissuade me from what I planned. Even though I was grateful that he cared, he was tempting me to lose patience.

'*Yes!*' I exclaimed at him. 'Yes, I'm tired. Yes, Xavian is out there, as you put it. Yes, I'm not totally sure what I'm doing. But Renna says it'll work. And I believe her – I think.'

Miriam was lying on a bed, her eyes shut and her breathing regular. Even without looking I could sense the tangle of spells woven tightly around her, and my anger at Xavian grew. *He's even tied in death-spells, just in case she tries to break free. Bastard.*

I went and sat down by her side. As most sleeping people do, she looked remarkably peaceful. It was hard to believe that a large part of her essence was now trapped inside Xavian, either to be released when he willed, or destroyed with him.

Keeping his distance, Janyvir muttered, 'Shall I call in the healers now, or wait until you're vomiting across the floor?'

'My dear commander, this is a very small spell,' I said, trying to indulge my not-quite-blossoming ego by putting him in his place. 'It's not really a spell at all, merely a . . . communion.'

Seeing him wear the unhappy look of the semi-ignorant, I was moved to say consolingly, 'Look, if I start screaming and shaking, feel free to hit me round the head with whatever comes to hand.'

'You're not going to, are you?'

'I can't think of any reason *why*.'

He let out a sigh of relief.

'But then magic is so unpredictable.'

The sigh was drawn back in again.

'Joking, joking . . .'

Carefully, I reached out and took Miriam's unresisting, cold hand in my own. There rushed in the memory of Renna doing almost exactly the same to me, palm to palm, and on an impulse I turned back to Janyvir.

'Have you ever dreamed of someone called Shakespeare?' I asked him.

'Who?'

'Earth.'

'Oh. No, I don't dream that much.'

'Really?'

'"Really"? What the hell is "really" supposed to mean?'

'Commander Janyvir, you are too much on edge.'

'It's called common sense. This is a fruitless exercise, and you should be . . . relaxing.'

'Look,' I said, 'if I'm feeling well only twelve hours after having my magic bashed to bits, then Xavian is feeling well, if not better. And if Xavian is feeling well, it's because he's tapping Miriam's regenerative powers. And if he's tapping Miriam, then the only way to weaken him is to try and get Miriam to stop him.'

'So you're going to reach like *that* through a blanket of magic, into a sleeping mind and . . . invite her to chat about it, perhaps? As if over a three-course meal?'

'Your sense of humour is out of place, Commander. Now shut up and watch a *real* mage at work.'

He muttered something, but I didn't hear what and wasn't inclined to ask. I closed my eyes, ignored my itching wrist . . . *give it a rest, will you?* . . . and closed my fingers around Miriam's own. I wasn't sure what was I was doing, and didn't dare use magic, in case I activated the web of power that surrounded the sleeping girl. But I knew that somehow, if I tried, if I believed . . .

<Miriam? I know you're not all in Xavian. I know you can hear me. Please. We have to talk.>

No answer.

<I know about your husband. I know about the overdose. I know about Renna. I can help.>

Can I? If that wasn't a blatant lie, what was it? Let it be at least an un-blatant lie.

<Hell, maybe I can't help, but unless you listen, a lot of innocent people might get hurt.> Possibly some guilty ones too, I thought sourly, remembering how high up the strike list Lisana was.

<Miriam, I know you can hear me. Now, I may not know much about Earth, but I can guess how the human mind works. You take an overdose, try to commit suicide. Brave, if a little selfish. It doesn't work – you end up in hospital, in a coma. Your life is overshadowed by grief, you start to dream. The dream is twisted, Miriam. It's cruel, as cruel as the chemicals that you used to try and end it all. Now either you're going to die in this twisted dream, or you're going to listen to me and let us find you a *real* dream. Miriam, answer me. I know there's something of you left in there that hasn't been taken by Xavian. You must have realized he was draining you, you must have felt it. Why didn't you try to stop him?>

No answer.

<Fine. I'm just going to sit here, keeping this connection open until you get bored of hiding and answer me. I

don't care if Xavian appears right now and kills the queen, then dances round naked waving her head in the air and singing *Old Man River* in a soprano voice, I'll just hang around here, waiting. You know I mean it.>

There it was. The change. I was ready for it, and let it carry me. It was as though I'd dropped off and was now inside a dream. But though I felt detached and insubstantial, as always when dreaming, I was aware enough to recognise it for what it was. There was the same clarity that I had experienced when talking to Renna – this was no dream, but a dreamer's vision.

A church. I knew enough about Earth to recognise that. Someone, wearing black, was praying before the altar. Sunlight smote through the stained-glass windows and patterned the floor with brilliance as Christ looked mournfully down on his one worshipper. The cross, stark symbol of a bloody past, hung above Miriam's head. I walked down the aisle and dropped as quietly as possible to my knees beside her.

'Thank you,' I murmured.

'For what?'

'Listening.'

She gave a strange uncheerful smile. 'The church is empty. I remember when it used to be so full, not so long ago. But Xavian has taken all the people. I don't want to be alone.'

No one ever does. 'I'm here.'

'You're trying to destroy my dream.'

'Not your dream. Your nightmare, or something near. An evil man who steals what's left of a fragile girl's heart. Who uses the best of a good woman to his own ends.'

'I could crush you now,' she whispered. 'Even though

that . . . other woman . . . is inside you, you are inside me. You're vulnerable. Exposed. Unwilling to strike back. I could smother you so fast you wouldn't know what had happened.'

I tilted my chin and tried to hold myself taller. 'Do it, then. I came here – *Renna* came here – to help you. Kill me, let Xavian take what little power you still possess, and die in nightmare. If you really love him so much, if you were really so *blind* as to think he cared an inch for you save as a resource to be drained, you wouldn't have consented to listen.'

'I've listened. Now I just want to be left alone!'

'So you can destroy yourself completely? In the selfish manner of an immature girl?'

She drew up straighter, eyes flashing with anger. Instinct warned that I was pushing too hard, but I knew that if I stopped I'd lose her. So much of Miriam was now in Xavian, it was all I could do to keep my tenuous hold.

'Wake up, Miriam! Only you can't, can you? Because on Earth the man you loved is gone and your body will never recover from the mischief you did it in your blind rage. And here the illusion you thought you loved has wrapped you in malicious spells that I won't dare to break!'

'You pretend so well!' she snarled. 'You think you can trick me with your words, but you can't! You're trying to kill Xavian!'

'Yes! Yes I am! Because he's trying to kill me, the queen, Feilim, Rylam, and eventually you. He's a vampire, Miriam, sucking your blood, your life, and you are so *stupid* you refuse to see it!'

'How?' she retorted. 'I am here! I am still Miriam, I am still talking!'

I sat back, trying to relax, only half aware of the tingle in my palm from where my hand in the real world still held hers. 'But you could be so much more.'

Her eyes narrowed, and when she spoke it was with the still calm of hatred. Irrational hatred, sure, but so deep it corrupted the bones themselves. 'You're a cruel man, Laenan Kite. You offer so much, but none of it is real.'

'Is that what he told you?'

She declined to answer.

'You're dying, Miriam. Do you know that?' I asked as gently as possible. Death is one of those things it's hard to tune down. 'On Earth your body is slowly slipping away – you took too many chemicals, the damage is too deep to be reversed and it's only a matter of time before your organs all pack up. No medical procedure can sustain you there.'

I was trying to be conciliatory now, like an impartial doctor spelling out possibilities to a patient in the manner of, 'well, this is a choice, but alternatively' or 'you could if you really, really wanted'. 'And here, Xavian is draining your life bit by bit. Sure, we're going to keep you under tight guard so that he can't come back. But by the looks of things he'll go on using you up anyway, wherever he is.'

Sometimes I hated myself. But the truth, harsh and unrelenting, had sneaked onto my tongue and was ready, if need be, to fill the air with fire. I paused, then said, quiet and deliberate, 'I need your help.'

A brief flicker of surprise, but at what I couldn't tell. I hoped it was because I'd said 'need'.

'I still don't understand dreamers. But I know this is all in your mind, and for a brief period so am I. And part of you is in Xavian.'

Arguing with an irrational person is the hardest thing in the world. For anything but this, I wouldn't think of it. Now I found myself wishing I was more persuasive, like T'omar or Lisana. They could have my position, power and magic at a moment's notice, and I'd be happy.

'All I want you to do is help me find him. That's it.'

'No.'

Great. Thank you most mightily.

'Miriam, you're a stupid girl wrapped up in some very thick spells ... Please. I know you can still feel him. Please.'

Her eyes locked onto mine. I found it impossible to look away.

She said, 'You're like an actor. People can't tell if they're talking to the real person behind all those disguises, or a character assumed for the occasion. But I know. I *know*, Kite.'

I stood up, wanting to hit her. She rose with me, defiant to the last.

'Is that it?' I demanded. 'You're just going to let us all die because you're too cowardly to stop believing and start seeing for yourself?'

'Get out of my head, Kite!'

I raised my hands. 'Look! I'm defenceless – a mortal, still dependent on my body, here only by the grace of someone else's powers, by the grace of Renna who risked her life for *you*, ungrateful child that you are!' I advanced on her, forgetting all tact, forgetting every small flattery I'd had ready.

'So expel me, Miriam. Break the link. Go on believing in your stupid little fantasy, because I am done! I will find Xavian in another way and I will kill him with no regard for the part of you that dies when he does!'

She was shaking with anger, or possibly grief. It was impossible to tell. As I came within a foot of her she raised her hands in defence. I lashed out and caught them, crushing her fingers in mine. 'Why don't you ever *listen*?' I hissed.

Her fingers twitched in mine. I suddenly felt very chilled. The pools of sunlight were dimming, disappearing. The whole church was turning cold and filling with shadows that strained against the corners of darkness binding them, reaching out at us with clawed insubstantiality. I staggered as my veins ran with ice-cold fire, felt it touch my heart, turn my lips blue and fill my skull with angry bees.

Miriam's eyes were wide. She staggered back from me, hands slipping from my grasp. *She doesn't know what she's done. Shit, she doesn't know . . .*

The only warmth came from my wrist, which was reassurance of a kind. The marble of the aisle was icy as Laenan Kite crumpled like a paper man, the buzz in my head escalating to a roar.

And soon, oh blessedly soon, it was peace again, as if the ice hadn't been. Now, when I looked, if I dared, there were *things* in my mind that hadn't been there before. Miriam was crouching by my side, her face a study in fear. Gently she prodded me, then recoiled as though I were about to bite her. I was reminded of a fearful child prodding the dead insect with a stick to see if it moved, and rolled onto my back as much to reassure her that I

was alive as to test the hypothesis myself. There were . . .
images.

Xavian's face dominated most of them and, if I
focused, memories that weren't mine came flooding to
the fore of my mind. They were hard to keep still, as
though they were a living thing that didn't want to be fin-
gered by mere thought, but I held onto them tightly and
let Miriam's memories play out through my mind in a
rush.

They ran from that first moment, when she'd seen him
and run towards her fate, to that last night when he'd
pulled on his boots, murmured soothing spells over her
and slipped silently through the door in a palace buzzing
with magic to put an end to his enemies once and for all.
All those images and more besides, feelings, snatches of
thoughts, half-heard sounds and quickly suppressed suspicions, of me, of Xavian – they ran smoothly past my
eyes and ears as though a skilled mage had created some
illusion and I was merely the admiring onlooker.

When they were done, I became aware of something
else. A feeling of violation almost, of having had something scrutinized that no one else had even glimpsed.
Once I was aware of this, the memories came fast again.
My memories this time, of Renna. As I had broken into
her memories of Xavian, so Miriam had taken a piece of
my past.

For a long time we just sat there, or in my case lay,
inwardly inspecting what had just passed between us.
The floor was almost comfortable once you got used to it.
Finally I decided I had to speak. Miriam wore a dumb-
founded look that was far from healthy.

'Let's . . . not do that again, shall we?' I asked.

'I didn't do it.'

'Bloody hell, could have fooled me.'

'Renna did it. She's about as uncompromising as you are. Must be why you two got on so well. Your wrist is bleeding,' she added after another tortured pause. I suspected that she too had been going over those shared memories, wondering if they showed her up in a good light. It's a strange thing that, even when our enemies learn something of us, we want to impress.

I didn't even bother to look. 'It'll heal. It always does.'

She ran her hands across her eyes, and for the first time I saw how tired she looked. 'Xavian . . .' Her voice trailed off.

'I won't ask,' I said as kindly as possible. 'I won't trouble you again until this is over.'

'No.' She looked up sharply. 'No. I love him, but what he's about to do . . .'

I was suddenly very nervous. 'Do?'

'Sunpoint. He's in Sunpoint.'

I was on my feet already, reaching through Renna's powers for my body, feeling the world whirl and dissolve. 'Who's his target? Feilim?'

'And others. You know who else.'

I didn't even say goodbye.

The connection snapped with violence. I was on my feet and racing for the door before Janyvir had even taken in my return to normal consciousness.

'Kite!' He started from his chair, where he'd been languishing like an old man. 'Hey, wait for me!' he yelled as I barrelled from the room.

Sunpoint. Feilim. And others, oh , dreams why didn't I think of that before? It would be exactly the kind of thing he'd do. We warned all people of importance, T'omar, Saenia, everyone, not to go around without a guard, but they're not important, are they? Dreams above . . .

Janyvir caught up with me, confused as ever. 'Where are you going? What did Miriam say? Was there a Miriam to say anything?'

'Sunpoint!'

Running to keep up, he had just enough breath to demand, 'How?'

'Same way Xavian got there.'

I stopped dead. I hadn't realized until that moment that I was going to do exactly that.

Same . . . way.

Janyvir was saying something. 'What?' I asked.

'I said that if it's a war party you need, I'm coming.'

'A war party?' *Hell, yes, that is what I need.*

'You did give me permission to hit you over the head if you started screaming and shaking. I'd say that if you try charging off by yourself that also qualifies.' He tried to be conciliatory. 'Look, I'm way out of my depth here. I don't understand what you great mages are playing at. I hardly understand the criminal side of things, and I'm a watchman! But I can use a sword, and when it comes to working out who stole something from someone else there's not a man better.'

'And if he's going, so are we.'

It was Shell and Rinset, one in servant's livery, the other wearing his scruffy cheese-seller garb.

Shell shrugged apologetically. 'T'omar said one thing you did a lot was go around independently.'

My eyes narrowed. 'You've had a trail on me, haven't you? I've felt someone watching . . .'

'T'omar's orders. You get into trouble too easily.'

'And you complained of being over-worked,' I muttered, uncertain whether to be grateful or infuriated. *I am perfectly capable of looking after myself!*

A dry little voice inside me stirred in response. *Haha. Give us another.*

'How are we getting to Sunpoint?' demanded Janyvir.

'*We're* going by magic,' snapped Shell, surveying him like an avenging queen of darkness. 'You can walk if you feel so inclined. We're going because Renna is inside Kite and she can travel at the speed of thought. And if Kite is too foolish to notice the bloody obvious, we're going with him anyway to show him *he* can!'

'That's nice and simple,' I murmured.

She scowled and grabbed my hand without a word. Yanking at Rinset's hand, she nodded curtly at Janyvir. 'Well, come on if you're coming!'

Rinset was grinning like an idiot – he seemed to be having the time of his life. *You'll learn.*

Shrugging, Janyvir put his hand on my shoulder in good old watchman style, as if making an arrest of a delinquent mage. All three turned to look at me.

'What happens now?' asked Janyvir. *A rational man completely out of his element*, I thought with sympathy. *Poor guy.*

I opened my mouth to argue, but Shell gave me a warning look and I realized how fruitless it would be to resist her. Hadn't T'omar said she was one of the best? 'I warn you, I've never done this before.'

'You haven't. Renna has,' said someone, probably Janyvir. Already I could feel ice-cold power stirring inside me, warming to a comfortable body temperature then moving beyond, spreading out to encompass the kingdom, the Void itself, the whole universe in a single blanket of power. We weren't moving, I realized with a start. The whole universe was in motion and we were simply taking advantage of that movement to stand still, and wait for a different place, a different land, to come to us.

'This is all going to end in tears,' I murmured, but my words were muffled by a great, suffocating blanket that pressed down on us from all sides. It was hard to breathe, though at the same time air didn't really seem necessary.

The floor moves like a living thing, snakes into the distance, writhes and shimmers in a silent dance. The walls bend outwards and stretch into infinity, a million colours playing across their endless surfaces. The buzz of the city, half-heard, never perceived, is gone, to be replaced by roaring, deafening silence which manages to make louder the noise which had come before.

A patch of red bends up before us, lightens into yellow, acquires a dull smear of brown. A streak of purple above us curls over into a dark sky. A curve of green becomes firm, hard, takes on edges and corners and shape. A distant sound, like the hum of a far-off spell being cast. The return of warmth, sudden, hard, baking warmth that knocks all moisture from the body so that you can't even sweat. The feeling of sand biting the air. The feeling of home, long forgotten. The fading of the Void. The arrival of Sunpoint.

Memories returned in a rush, along with the shocking truth. The corner of this street, where the tanner and the baker rivalled each other for space in the mud-brick world of cramped Sunpoint, hadn't changed in all those years. How neglectful were the Wardens, not to have cast their mind over this place, to remedy even slightly the piles of rubbish that spewed from dark alleys into the streets. The buzz of flies, the mewing of a distressed cat – even the bark of an ancient dog, the great, great, great grandsire of which had often scared away the young Kite – none of it had changed.

I knew where we were. I had never seen the inside of the palace, so I hadn't known how or where to focus. But I had known this place, just a few blocks from the palace wall. I'd outrun a thousand childhood torments in this street.

'Bloody hell,' someone breathed, breaking the embrace of a past, not all smiles, that had wrapped around me. It was Rinset, looking round with astonishment at what had just come to pass. 'How . . . what . . .?'

'Ignorant boy,' muttered Shell. To me she said, 'Couldn't have brought us down nearer Feilim, could you?'

I glared back. 'You're lucky we're here at all.'

Janyvir was also looking shocked. 'I don't understand anything,' he announced. 'When this is over I shall demand an explanation.'

Looking around, uneasily for her, Shell said, 'Let's find Feilim.'

The first thing that struck me were the streets. Bare. None of the normal traders, none of the mounted knights on their way to yet another war, none of the playing children. Even the rats (another pest the illustrious Wardens had failed to remove) had run for cover. Sand trickled like water around the buildings and lay several inches deep across the pavement. Had there been a sandstorm? And why would Feilim summon a sandstorm, unless there was something he wanted to harm?

We reached the palace, and there wasn't a guard on the heavy wooden gates. I suddenly felt extremely exposed. Rinset raised his hand to knock, but Shell batted it down. Her eyes were fixed on me and there was fear there. 'Is it always like this?' she asked softly.

I shook my head, raising a hand to my lips for silence. Carefully I placed my hands on the gate, feeling through the ancient wood for signs of life, listening to the slow, lumbering bricks and planks of the palace just in case something stirred inside there. Not a soul.

There was a gentle thump. Something rolled from the edge of the battlements, fell spinning to the ground and lay in the sand a few metres off. By the time we'd reached it, the blood was already pooling.

Someone was being sick. It was Rinset. Even Shell looked away.

Janyvir, with a much more pragmatic view to death, knelt by Feilim's side and gently closed his eyes.

'The kingdom hasn't fallen apart, with its Warden's death,' he murmured, looking up from his place. 'So who has the Key?'

Our eyes met. In a second I'd caught his hand and grabbed Shell by the shoulder, summoning all of Renna's powers to speed us away. There was a roar as the ground came alive. Too late I saw the yellow warriors of the desert rise up from the streets with blades of sand. Too late I yelled Rinset's name. Too late he turned.

And now I was aware of the people. A dozen pairs of eyes peered or squinted through every barred shutter. A thousand minds whispered their fear, a thousand hearts thudded in terror of the Warden who'd come out of nowhere and was as substantial as air.

As Rinset's body fell, I had Renna's powers ready. A sword arced through the air on a line straight to my throat, but I was faster. I didn't try to shield, I didn't try to repel. I just focused on not being.

It came easier this time. *Warriors shimmer into shapeless forms, dance around each other in a whirlpool of light. A tingle as a blade no thicker than a shadow passes through my throat, but I am already gone.*

You've won this battle, Xavian, but now I know where you are. I will find you no matter what. I am stronger than you think, for your trap has failed. I am the greater mage, coupled with the stronger dreamer. You cannot hide forever.

Roads fade and just as soon re-appear. Buildings dance into different shapes, different colours. Browns become vibrant blues and green, swirl and twist and weave. Blues and greens darken and dull, crawl and worm their way into new buildings in a new form.

Shell wept, as Silverpoint rose around us. Immediately a dozen crossbows were levelled at our faces, a dozen Key-bound guards were ready to shoot, alerted by the queen's warning against teleporters.

I raised my weary hands. 'We're here,' I murmured.

It's strange how the toughest people in this life have the softest hearts. Shell had worn an illusion of strength, but clearly in all the time she'd spent with Rinset something had wormed through it, since she cared enough to cry.

Janyvir was wearing an empty, weary look. He'd seen murders, but never one that hit home so hard. We'd tried to bring the attack to the enemy, and it had failed.

'Kite!'

T'omar, rushing down the corridor, seeing the shock

on our faces and the blood on Janyvir's hands from where he'd closed Feilim's eyes.

'I can't stay,' I said softly. 'If he's got Sunpoint he's got other things.'

T'omar tried to grab me but I was backing away fast, raising magic around me. Revenge was in my heart now, revenge for Feilim, Corbe, Brawn – people I hadn't even met save in their afterlife. Revenge for Rinset.

Revenge for the family I had long ago forsaken and who were now trapped at the mercy of Xavian.

T'omar knew. As head of the Consortium, he had his sources and knew where I'd come from. I had left my family in Sunpoint all those years ago, trekked off to danger and occasionally received its rewards. Now the danger had come home, and a good deal of it was due to me.

'Kite, wait!'

I didn't.

TEN

Past, Present and Future Tenses

This time I knew what to expect. I had the scry-block raised the second that Sunpoint came into existence, and I was confident. This was *my* kingdom, albeit not in the literal sense. I knew the ground, and if Xavian fancied he'd scared me off, he had another thought coming.

And hadn't Miriam said he had only just taken control? He couldn't have found my family yet. They didn't look like me, and I doubted he'd had time to interview his newfound subjects. Not so soon after he'd just murdered their liege lord.

Scry-blocks are one of the only ways to deceive a Warden with a Key. It shows him what he expects to see, and twists his mind in a small but subtle way, sending out little subversive tendrils of magic through the fabric of the kingdom itself. As such, it's remarkably effective.

It was almost easy to forget that Rinset had just been

murdered, when I appeared in the desert. The shuttered and silent city lay a few miles off, clearly visible from the shadow of the sand-coloured rocks where I'd arrived. When I was a child I had pretended these rocks were alive. Why else would they seek to hide themselves so well in the sand? As all my Silverhand experience had swiftly come back in Haven, so the rules of the desert returned in a rush. Emergency or no, I knew that staying out in the open without protection was a fool's policy. I also knew that, scry-block or no, if Xavian bothered to look with his real eyes he'd see the trail I left behind me. And I'd have exposed not only myself, but my family.

'*My*' *family*, I thought without any emotion. The oddness of the expression struck a chord somewhere inside, but there were too many obstacles for me to make anything of it. '*My*' *family*.

I slipped and scrambled through the sand, careful to stay in the shade of the rocks as much as possible while I set out in the opposite direction to the city. Farming an ordinary crop in this barren land was hopeless, I knew that. But Sunpoint had never been a place for the ordinary. As I rounded the base of the rocks I saw the little farming town where, dreams help me, I had grown up.

Here too nothing had changed. The same sand-coloured, sun-blasted vines crawled up their long poles, looking about as nourishing as a lump of stone, but bursting with the sweetest juice once split open. These plants needed water but once a month, and a minimum at that. What genius had set their evolution in process I do not know, but their production had kept my family in business for centuries.

Beyond the huge fields that were one with the desert,

there stood large mud houses. They'd been improved since I last saw them, expanded to include a stable and courtyard with that most luxurious of objects, a well. The Kite family had become quite the thing, in the time I was gone.

And even here, the doors were shut and no children played in the streets.

Keeping my scry-block raised and checking that not a slip nor a bump existed in its smooth shelter of magic, I slipped into the street. I ran, past one locked house after another, until I reached the courtyard that housed my own large family. The gates were locked here too, but this was a problem easily overcome. I didn't even bother with fancy magic, but simply glared at the lock and willed it open with all the faith and certainty I had to bear.

Renna is a dreamer. Dreamers affect the physical, we affect the mental. That is why they make machines and we make magic.

The lock clicked, and indeed contrived to look as if it always had been open. I pushed the gate back – someone had oiled it, which seemed to ruin the effect. I would have felt comforted by the rusty old whine I remembered from my youth.

The courtyard was empty. Shutters were across every window, every door was locked. I stood in the centre of the courtyard for a long while, thinking *someone must have seen me. Why don't they answer?* My imagination began to throw up the worst possibilities. Xavian had found my family, had killed them all. This was just another trap. My family had run away, this trip was in vain. My family had long ago left Sunpoint and I was none the wiser. What if, what if, what if?!

There was the faintest click. I wouldn't have heard it

under normal circumstances. But the silence, and Renna's presence in me, made it sound to my ears like a gunshot. It was the subtle little sound of someone clicking the safety catch off a rifle. Within a second my eyes had pinpointed the source of it. A rifle end was sticking out from under a shutter, a pair of suspicious eyes were lost in the darkness behind. I stared at my invisible watcher, and my invisible watcher stared back.

Extending the scry-block carefully, to cover the whole house, I raised my voice.

'I'm here to help.' The sound echoed back at me, as if reminding me over and over that this was the first time I'd made such an offer to this particular family. A hundred times before, I'd helped strangers, but never my own. I hadn't been back for so long. I'd scryed and listened to the rumours. But to return and find so little changed . . .

'I can get you out of here. Please.' *Odd, how you have to beg to your family as you begged to Miriam.*

There was the sense of movement behind walls. *Do I tell them I'm Laenan? Will they shoot if I don't? Will they shoot if I do?* I tried to remember the names of all my many, many sisters and brothers, long ago shoved to the back of my mind in a file classified as 'do not wish to remember' along with all those monsters and deaths and dramas that had dogged me through my meagre little existence.

I tried to remember which ones might be more sympathetic towards me. 'Elsa! Iorion! Queria! I can get you out, to safety!'

A door opened a crack. I could feel a dozen searching gazes on me. Then the door opened a little further, invitingly so. Trying to radiate confidence, and ignoring my natural doubt at going into a dark, enclosed space with unseen people, I marched towards it and into the half-lit relative gloom of the Kite family 'mansion', as we'd loved to call it. We are the grand family Kite, we'd used to say. We are the best farmers in Sunpoint! No, in the Void itself!

The door clicked shut behind me. In the bright light that crept through the shutters I saw the whole family assembled. Old grannies, babies, women, children, young men, old men – the lot.

Whoever had been watching me in the courtyard still wasn't satisfied. I could feel the rifle brushing the back of my neck. Despite everything that had happened, my stomach rolled over at the idea.

'Who are you?' demanded a young lady with the typical dark skin and dark eyes of the Kites. I didn't recognise her.

'Laenan.'

There was a general murmur of disbelief at this. The over-eager boy with the rifle started searching ruthlessly for weapons which I did not have. The best he could come up with was my dagger, which in any case I had made no attempt to hide. The thought hadn't even crossed my mind.

'The mage?' whispered someone.

'Laenan,' agreed someone else. A walking wall of muscle pushed his way to the front of the throng. Brernt, eldest and most favoured of my father's many sons, one of the many torments of my youth. The boy who'd beaten the living daylights out of me until the day when I turned round with magic in my hands and nearly broke his neck with a gesture.

'The bastard son who ran away,' he hissed. To Brernt, all children were bastards who'd been fathered out of any of my father's nine other wives. It seemed he'd proven his point too, and was now wearing the mantle of father figure himself.

'And lookee now,' I said conversationally. 'At risk of my own life I've run back. How nice. When did Feilim die?'

'He's definitely dead?' demanded someone.

I rolled my eyes. 'Why are you indoors, then?'

'Warriors of sand came marching through the streets. They told us that if we left our houses, we would die,' said someone else. My eyes picked the face of Queria out of the gloom. She was carrying a baby, and a throng of kids crowded round her feet. Someone had certainly been busy. I remembered her as a scruffy teenager with spots, not this motherly figure.

'What are you doing here, Laenan?' she asked. 'You left us long ago.'

'Just trying to save you from a madman. Er . . . is the rifle really necessary?'

'Put it down, Tierne.'

I glanced over my shoulder at the young man who'd been so eager with his precious gun, and looked into a pair of bright blue eyes. Only Saenia and I have eyes like those. Only Saenia and I are mages. And yes, there was the glow, the faint shimmer of power visible only to my eyes. Still small, but with the potential to grow. Given time, given training. Did he know? I couldn't tell.

I talked fast, fearful of losing my audience. Even the babies had been silenced. 'Feilim's been killed all right.' With no time to spare for anything, nonetheless I spared them nothing of who or what Xavian was, how he'd decided it was his duty to kill just about everyone who moved.

'This includes me. If I'm not top of his list right now, I'm close. By association, you might be in danger. Certainly you're in danger by the sheer misfortune of living here. By everything that can drive a man mad and make him hungry for power, whether over higher forces, himself or other people's lives, you are all in danger.'

'Then by coming here you bring that danger on us!' yelled someone from the back.

'He doesn't know I'm here. But he'll be looking to find out about my family. Even now I don't doubt he's tearing through every record of this kingdom, scrying every house, searching every room for a clue as to where the Kite family is based. And when he finds you he'll kill you, have no doubt of that. I have got here first, I am going to get you out.'

Rinset died for you. Feilim, Kertoui, Corbe, Brawn — they all died in a way, for you. I may die for you, although I'm still debating that one. Do not pass up this opportunity, because by all that dreams, you're unlikely to get a better one.

'How will you do that?' Brernt said.

Ever the pragmatist. 'I have a way. It's safe, it'll work.'

'How?' he demanded again. 'What makes you think we believe you anyway?'

I met his eyes squarely. It was a shocking experience, something I'd never done before.

'Because the streets are full of warriors of sand who've promised to kill those who do not stay indoors. Because the whole kingdom is silent. Because the two sons of Giroign are either dead or have fled. Because I have never lied to my own family and I don't intend to start now. Because if you're wrong I won't have the satisfaction of saying "I told you so". I'll be the most silent of workers – the grave-digger.'

The family itself didn't have any part in the decision-making. It had always been the way. I had to address the leader of the family and no one else, and Brernt was the leader.

I knew then, as I had known from the moment when Rinset died and Xavian revealed his power, that he wouldn't agree. If someone else had appeared out of nowhere and suggested that they depart, he would have said yes. But not me. Not the kid who ran away.

'You're not wanted here.'

'You're a fool, Brernt. Stuck in your own little world where you can't say anything for fear it isn't macho enough. Having to be the tough lad every hour dreams send. I'm offering you a way out. I'm offering you a longer life, dreams know why.'

'Get out,' he hissed.

'And then what? I'll go and fight this mad mage for you, and the kingdom will turn to fire and when you die in the flames you won't think of the children you've condemned to death! But you will remember that this disaster happened under *your* leadership. Your "guidance" as I suppose you call it.'

I advanced on him. 'I'm not the little boy you used to boss around, Brernt. I've killed kings, and I'm perfectly prepared to knock you unconscious for the sake of doing just this once what I want. Don't think I'm beholden to you or to anyone else. I am here because there's been enough bloodshed, and I have no desire to see it go on spreading, like a disease.'

He was backing away. From me! The sheer exhilaration

of it was almost more than I could take. Brernt was scared of *me*!

'You're lying.'

'Others have said that,' I replied, striving not to let anger darken my voice. I was thinking mostly of Miriam. 'But they've come round to my way of seeing things. Maybe we simply swapped thoughts. But in your case it'll have to be magic time.'

He backed away further and came up against a wall of relatives. The contact seemed to make him recall himself, and he stood defiant again.

'If you care for us so deeply, *brother*, you'll leave now!'

'To what purpose? I've already risked my neck for you – don't think I'll let it be in vain.'

His hand flew to a knife; I was there faster. I gripped with all of Renna's strength and his fingers turned white. The blade fell from his grasp, but I caught it before it hit the floor and held it against his throat. Dreams, but my blood was hot, and made hotter still by the memories of all those long years when I'd longed to do exactly this.

'Will you let this whole family die because you're too stupid to see your own failures, huh?' My voice was light, and made lighter by the boiling fury beneath whose mastery demanded every fragment of my self-control. 'Will you really, really refuse to do anything because the little boy from your past, the one you made do all your errands because he was weak and cowardly and couldn't fight back – will you really lose all this because he's the one who brings you salvation?'

There was the click of the rifle again. I felt it brushing the back of my neck. 'Family don't hurt family,' said Tierne softly.

I backed away slowly, keeping my hands raised. With or without Renna, I doubted if I could get out faster than a bullet could travel an inch. Besides, I didn't want to.

Brernt, shaking with humiliation, snatched the knife from my hand and spun me round. I was shoved to a tabletop and confronted with his furious face and, worse, his alcohol-soaked breath. *So. The son goes as the father does*. The knife tickled my throat, became a painful itch.

'Get out of my house, Laenan,' he hissed. 'Get out and never come back. We don't want your help, we don't need it.'

Then his eyes widened.

'Family don't hurt family,' repeated Tierne. His hand was shaking, but he held the rifle more or less steadily at his father's head.

Dreams above. What has this kid been through?

'I'm with Laenan,' said someone suddenly. It was Queria. Sensible, rational Queria, who in her teenage years had been a horror to outrank them all. Motherhood had done her good. 'Sunpoint isn't safe.'

Brernt had another argument, though. *Not so much an argument*, I thought with loathing of my own kin. *Just a complaint. Just another bit of macho, stupid defiance.*

'How did you get here so fast, little brother?' he demanded. 'How did you come so quickly unless you knew this would happen?'

'You never understood magic,' I spat in return. 'You never understood the nature of dreaming!'

'If you knew, you could have warned us!'

'Know? Know how to predict the future? I can travel far, *brother*,' I threw the word at him, burdening it with the hatred and rivalry of the past, 'but I cannot travel in directions that are not yet charted.'

'How did you get here so soon unless you knew?' he repeated, seeing his one lifeline to respect and grasping it.

'The same way I'll get you out.'

There was no time to give a more explicit answer. There would be chaos if I demonstrated Renna's powers, and I was pretty sure that once I had initiated the tele-port, however small, my scry-block would fail. Would Xavian notice the flicker as I disappeared and re-appeared in the blink of an eye? Would he sense the flash of Renna's powers, which I had already been using with abandon?

Queria had pushed to the front of the rabble. 'If we go, we all go. Including Father.'

I must confess, I came this close to blurting out, 'He's still alive?!' The idea that he might have died had never occurred to me in the hard, rush-of-blood-to-the-head sense. At the same time, I'd always known the Father wouldn't live forever. I guess that somewhere on my travels, I'd come to believe it and accept it without ever noticing what I did.

'Where is he?'

'Upstairs.'

'Are the rest of you all here?'

There was a general look-around, followed by a murmur of agreement. I raised my hands, taking Queria's in my own. I had never before tried transport-ing so many people, but, as far as I reasoned, it was just the same as transporting one. All I had to do was believe in Renna and she, through me, would make it happen.

It was the ultimate religion, and disturbing at the same time. No priest ever likes to know the truth, the real truth, not just some make-believe, about their God. *When this is all over, Renna, much as I love you, out. Can you hear me in there? No more holiday for you, my dear. From now on, do your own dirty work.*

Queria, in moving forward, had emboldened the others, and now they came in a tide, clinging onto each other like spiders attaching claws to their prey. Some of their grips were borne of the desperation that says they'll never let go. Only Brernt remained behind, and with him lurked Tierne and a collection of watery-eyed women, far too young for Brernt, whom I took to be his wives.

'If we go,' repeated Queria, a note of pleading in her voice, 'we all go.'

'Then no one leave,' said Brernt.

I bit my lip in a frenzy of suppressed annoyance. 'Don't be a bloody idiot,' I hissed. It wasn't the best thing I could have said, but it was all that came to mind. *I could force him. I could throw magic around until he . . . no.*

My eyes wandered to Tierne. *Does he know? Dare I harm family, to save family?* 'I'll be back,' I warned him, and before Queria or anyone else could protest, I had raised Renna's power, checked my scry-block, cast my mind out far to be sure that Xavian's attention was elsewhere, and begun to teleport.

There was a feeling of weight this time, which I took to be all the other people clinging onto each other, man, woman, child. But apart from that, the teleport was no different from any other. The rush of the Void. The still-ness of not-being. The loss of all thought, of all physical sensation for a few seconds that stretch to years and contract again within the blink of an eye. The swirl of colours, perceived by eyes that are not there. The melting and re-assembling of reality. The look of astonishment on Saenia's face and the crack as she instinctively raises her shields. The yowl of terrified children, the buzz of frightened adults. The slow shift from surprise to astonishment as, bit by bit, Saenia recognises faces from her past.

The silence between us as brother and sister share their thoughts in a single burst of magic. The slow dawning of a smile on Saenia's face.

'Well,' she said finally. 'Thank you for the warning.'

Saenia hadn't done anything to change Stormpoint – not as far as I could tell. But I wasn't there long enough to look hard.

I transmitted all I knew in a single burst of thought, watched her digest it. Finally she nodded. 'Then go back to Sunpoint. I'll look after the ones here.' Saenia would cope, as she always did, usually a good deal better than I could.

So alone I returned to Sunpoint, and arrived in a room now a lot emptier. I hadn't realized until that second just how big my family had become. Seeing the room without its press of bodies, I realized how many people must have filled it.

Brernt exploded at me as I reappeared. 'What have you done?' he yelled, leaping forward as though he might attack.

I sprang backwards defensively, raising my hands to shield myself. Fire played around my fingers, and for a second I caught a look of such wonder and longing on young Tierne's face that I almost lost concentration.

'They're safe! For dream's sake, why can't you trust me just once in your life?'

'Where are they?' he roared like a lion deprived of its cubs.

'In my kingdom!'

He fell suddenly silent. Though his breathing stayed fast, his face red and fists clenched, his eyes showed the blow I'd unwittingly dealt.

'You have a kingdom?'

'A small kingdom, a few miles of land,' I said. 'It's safe there, brother. It rains often there, too. The grass is green and, as far as the eye can see, there isn't a grain of sand.'

When he finally spoke, it was with barely masked resignation. 'I don't trust you, Laenan.'

I ignored him. 'Wait here while I go and get the Father. If he refuses to come, I swear I'll just have to carry him.'

'Tierne, go with him,' snapped Brernt.

'What the hell do you think I'll do?' I asked, only a little surprised at his distrust. 'Kill my own father?' *Well? Do you?*

He said nothing, which spoke louder than if he'd made an hour-long speech. Shrugging inwardly, the usual resort of a man trying to prove his mettle where there is none, I climbed the stairs, my silent nephew in tow. Tierne pointed to the appropriate bedroom, but I paused before the door. *Do you really want to do this?*

Do you have any choice?

I pushed it open and crossed the threshold with the speed of a man who knew that, once you slow down, once you lose momentum, you're doomed. You'll never make it.

The room was gloomy, the shutters closed. A single

bed rested in the centre of the floor, in it a man with his back turned to me.

The Father. Formerly a titan of a man, possessing at one point twelve wives, at least seven of whom he'd won by his charms as well as purchased. Now his white, thinning hair crawled across the pillows, his breathing was shallow and only my memories had supplied the rest. An old drunk, who hadn't known the names of half his children. Once, he'd vaguely recognised Saenia, and she'd been so scared she hid in the desert until she nearly died.

He'd learnt my name the day I nearly broke Brernt's neck. He'd cursed me from the rooftops the day I'd left, and I doubt not that he'd cursed me since.

I prayed that he was asleep but no, as the floor squeaked under me, he turned. A pair of eyes still sane, speaking of a working mind trapped in a dying body. They peered at me, and widened. He recognised me still.

I looked round the room for a stick or something like for him to lean on, and saw a staff in the corner. Even now, my father doubtless liked to show his strength.

He wore a night robe but no shoes, so I nodded at Tierne. 'Help him up.' Tierne didn't move a muscle.

Understanding dawned. The boy was a mage, having more than a few characteristics in common with the other two young mages who, all those years ago, had fled. What had he experienced at the hands of the Father, as recompense for a sin he hadn't committed?

'Get his boots and stick,' I said as kindly as possible. 'I'll help.'

I advanced to the bed – and the Father seemed to shy away from my touch. He was scared of me.

Clearly some of the stories had filtered through to

even his ancient ears. 'It's all right,' I said, hating the reassurance even as I gave it. 'We're getting you to safety.'

He was an incredible weight for such a frail old man. I struggled and sweated until he was sitting upright, and helped him lean on his staff. He didn't say a word. But those sane, those horribly sane, knowing eyes never once faltered from scrutiny of my face.

As we helped him limp downstairs, each one holding an arm, I felt it. So did Tierne. We froze just a few steps above Brernt, and our eyes met. Reality was changing, warped by the Key.

In a frantic rush I checked my scry-block. Yes, it was still there and I was certain Xavian hadn't sensed anything amiss with it. Nor had he perceived my previous teleport out – for surely he would have done something about it. We staggered the last few steps and practically threw the Father into Brernt's arms. Brernt looked shocked at the violation, that *he*, who was head of the family in the aged Father's place, should have to mother his own parent!

I was at a shutter, Tierne also, kneeling down to peer through the cracks. The sand was moving, blurring and rising. But instead of the army of sand-soldiers who had slain Rinset, a single figure appeared. A herald. All over the kingdom, outside every door and in every street, a like figure was rising out of the sand, and when they spoke the kingdom shook with the force of so many speaking, over such a sweep of land, the same words at the same time.

'People of Sunpoint!' they roared. I covered my ears in pain. The vibrations coursed up through my feet. 'Your new Warden greets you!'

I moved back from the window, catching Tierne by the shoulder and pulling the fascinated boy into the centre of the room. 'We don't have time for this!'

'This is the start,' continued the voice outside, 'of a revolution against sin that shall cleanse the Void!'

He's utterly, utterly mad, I thought. *Totally round the twist, a nutter if ever I saw one. Oh, dreams, what am I going to do?*

A hand, strong as steel, gripped mine. Brernt's now scared eyes met my own and he nodded frantically. *Still the leader giving permission to his troops.*

I looked round the room one last time, and felt no sorrow at leaving it.

Sound fades, dwindles, is gone. The memory fades too, and there are no ears for it to ring in, no feet to feel the vibrations. Sunpoint melts, dissolves, blends to a point, winks out. There is only swirling colour and light. Nothing else matters. Nothing else remains.

Reassemble the light. Vortexes of colour twist around each other, trying to pull their neighbour into a new shape. There's a whole universe out there, but now is not the time to explore it. Stormpoint. The storm, the lightning, the thunder. The memory of home, of safety. The memory of a time before all this began, when the world was a happier place. The memory assembles itself, builds itself up piece by piece into . . .

A tower. No, a room in the tower itself. Round and light, with windows open to let in the last rays of setting sunlight. You have been to Haven to Sunpoint to Silverpoint to Sunpoint to Stormpoint to Sunpoint and now, finally, are home.

As Stormpoint built itself out of impossibility, there was a gasp from Tierne, and the Father slid unconscious into his arms.

ELEVEN

Priorities

Saenia has always been a better healer than I. Me, I've been the fighter. So when she emerged from the top bedroom of the tower, I could see in her eyes that the news was bad. 'He's suffering from age, for which there's no cure.'

The rest of the Kite family had been housed in a tower only just summoned. Around it circled griffins and even a small dragon. Inside, the passages were full of wary spirits, watchful sprites and a host of spells besides. We were taking no chances.

'Will he die?' I asked as she descended the stairs to the kitchen, and a hastily prepared meal.

'Everyone dies, sooner or later. There's nothing I can do.'

In the kitchen, which was illuminated by magelight alone, she sat down heavily at the table. Outside, the stars of Stormpoint were eclipsed by clouds. Saenia had arranged a storm for our newly arrived desert guests to whom, back home, storms had been a wondrous thing.

I passed her a plate of food and she stared as though she'd never seen such a thing. 'What's this?'

'Supper. You've had a shock.'

'And I suppose you haven't?' she asked gently. 'You, with your body hijacked, your loyal Silverhand dead, your queen under threat and a mad mage out for your blood?'

'Of course I have. I'm just not showing it yet.'

'Ah,' she said knowingly. 'If you want my professional opinion as a healer, then I'd say that that way lies catastrophe. You will fight Xavian, you will win. You will show no sign that it's affected you. You will break down all of a sudden, days, months, even years later. And for every hour you spend not repairing the damage of a shock to the system, you'll spend a day suffering from the effects.'

'You're a great reassurance, sister.'

She was serious, though. Sometimes I wonder if Saenia is really the same girl I grew up with. It's hard to imagine her as anything other than the adult she so obviously is.

'Give me the Key,' I said.

For a second she frowned, not sure how to respond. Then she shrugged, opened her palm, and held out the little sphere that controlled my kingdom. I took it wordlessly, pulling it into myself and feeling it settle as it returned with ease to its former owner. Standing up, I strode to the door and out, into the night.

It was cool outside, made colder still by the wind blowing in response to the promised storm. Saenia emerged behind me a few moments later and stood there, shivering in the cold. I looked over the kingdom of Stormpoint, its dark forests that might have seemed sinister but that I could trace every path and describe every tree. The distant mountains which I knew were just an illusion. The nearby dip where a river flowed. The cut-off horizon where reality met impossibility at the edge of the kingdom.

Saenia smiled, sensing my intent. Sometimes you have to let these things out. The difficult thing is doing it without hurting another.

I started gently, telling the storm of the fatigue in my bones and the disgust I had felt as not one, not two but three relatively innocent people fell beneath Xavian's scheming. Clouds thickened, darkened, covered the sky.

I told it of how uncomfortable I felt struggling to save Lisana's life. How easy it would have been just to turn round suddenly and declare, no. No, I wasn't going to play. She could do as she wished, I had done. Cold rain began to fall, hard, proper rain that soaked everything within seconds. There was no point in the light drizzle that makes a pleasant day depressing, and this rain was the thick opposite of that in all respects.

I told the storm of the uselessness of it all. Of Rylam's small-minded ambition, of Xavian's far greater madness, of Renna's quiet cunning and Miriam's stubborn defiance. In the distance, thunder rolled, echoed across the landscape, bounced off the land and resounded back and forth in the low rumble of a god clearing his throat.

I told the storm of my battles with Xavian, from the first moment when he'd taken Miriam under his wing to that last, terrifying second when creatures of his imagination struck down Rinset. I told the storm of my battle against him, of tearing through his shields only to be repulsed, of staggering back as the full extent of his power became apparent.

Lightning struck. Struck again, tore the sky open and spat electric fury at the ground.

Mostly, I told the storm of the anger. Anger at Xavian for forcing me to a place that had long ago been buried in the past. Anger at Renna for using me, anger at Miriam for refusing to see the truth, anger that, in their own strange ways, all of them were right. Even Xavian, in a way. There had been too much war.

As the lightning tore at the ground and made the sky glow, I tilted my head back to the storm and poured it all out. All that fear and hatred and anger that, in my little world of deceit and corruption, I hadn't dared show. The storm answered. The storm understood perfectly.

And abruptly it was over. The thunder was receding, the lightning dying and Saenia was wrapping her arms around me.

'Come inside. You've been working too hard for too long.'

'I have to find Xavian,' I murmured as she led me towards the tower. I felt empty, as drained of feeling as the sky was of thunder.

'No. Xavian thinks he's safe in Sunpoint. Xavian can't do anything. You're ahead of the game. Now you just need to sleep.'

And she was right. Dreams help me, she too was right.

So I slept. And in sleep, Renna came.

I wanted to ask her, 'What shall I do next? How can I take revenge for all those deaths?'

But she refused to give a straight answer.

'Xavian can't move against us. Oh, he can kill us, no problem, but it won't get him anywhere. He needed to take a big power base like Haven or Nightkeep legitimately, not by force. Sunpoint isn't large enough, and he's stuck with it now. Let him worry about you. You don't have to do anything yet.'

'I can't just hang around doing *nothing*.'

'Yes, you can.' Renna sighed, foreseeing what I'd say before I'd even opened my mouth. 'But you won't. You desire action. There's an unsolved problem and it's going to eat away at you.' She smiled, cocking her head like I'd seen her do so often, a seeming lifetime ago. 'You'll find something else to keep you busy.'

And she was gone, leaving behind an empty night.

'You should go to Silverpoint,' said Saenia. I had slept until noon, to wake to breakfast in bed and my sister's smile. 'Show people you're all right.'

'There's a lot I should do.'

'But not so urgently. You have Xavian trapped.'

'Have I?' I mused. 'It may be that he's trapped himself. Probably he won't leave Sunpoint, because only there has he power, a kingdom. But he could leave at any time and vanish in the crowd.'

'You'd find him,' she said with confidence.

There were things to do though, before I left Stormpoint. I gave Saenia my Key, for one. 'Just in case,' I said. 'We wouldn't want Xavian to have *two* Keys, would we?'

'That's not even slightly funny, Laenan.'

Then, I called T'omar.

<Kite! Bloody hell, where are you? What's happened? Why didn't you call? What's going on?>

<Calm down. Everything's fine.>

<Fine? How's it fine? Feilim's dead, Rylam's kicking up hell in Haven, threatening to tell the court about his less-than-perfect bloodline, Miriam hasn't woken up, Lisana's going mad, Xavian's got a kingdom all to himself . . .>

<Xavian's on the run. He took the kingdom by force, there might be an uprising at any moment. He was no fool – he knew that to be safe he has to get power by legal means. We've succeeded in beating him back to the point where he can't move.>

<Can't move?! He can jump from place to place like *that*!>

<He could, but he won't. He wants power, he's drunk on it. How would it benefit him, abandoning his hard-won kingdom? Besides, he knows I'll come after him no matter what. He wants the final battle to be fought on his own territory.>

<Where are you?>

<Stormpoint. I'll be in Silverpoint very soon – you'd better tell your guards not to kill me on sight, by the way. I'll be arriving by somewhat unorthodox means.>

<There's a lot to be done.>

<Yes, but not urgently.> I felt pleased at being able to lecture someone else. <Relax, T'omar. Everything's more or less under control.>

That left family.

Saenia and I left the tower together, and went first in search of Tierne. On the way downstairs I stopped at my workroom, emerging a few minutes later with a bag full of obscure objects that had been hanging around for years just waiting for some action. Saenia raised her eyebrows.

'You never know when these things might be handy,' was the only answer I'd give.

After a second's consultation with the Key, Saenia concluded that Tierne was by the river. 'I think he's taken with the idea of green grass everywhere. There's a lot of kids rushing around there. Even some of the old ones like it.'

We walked in silence towards the river, brother and sister matching and enhancing the other to create as magely an effect as ever I saw. Heads turned as we reached the bank

Once there, however, I pulled Saenia back into the shade of a willow. 'Let's not embarrass the kid. You know what it's like, standing out as different in a crowd of similars.'

We waited until a gaggle of children had rushed into the nearby forest to play hide-and-seek, pursued by the elven guardians Saenia had set to watch them. The children didn't yet know that the elves, being part of the kingdom, could sense their exact location, therefore giving them an unfair advantage in the game.

Tierne hung back, as we'd known he would. We'd done the same, when we were children. A collection of women were talking by the river, pleased just to be by such a grand source of water. Some distance off, a group of men were looking less happy with their situation.

Saenia glanced at me in doubt. 'They're farmers. Perhaps we should create something for them to farm?'

'If it'll keep them happy,' I said, trying to hide my disappointment that my family, *my* family, didn't appreciate *my* kingdom.

Tierne slid down to the river's edge and threw cold

water in his face, as though still weary from the night. Saenia tilted her chin, stood up taller and opened her mind.

<Tierne.>

His head snapped round like a snake.

<Tierne, I know you can hear me. We're under the willow.>

His eyes flitted to where we stood, half-hidden by the cool cloak of shade. He rose, staring at us dumbly.

<This is my sister,> I sent. <She's a very powerful mage. Do you want to meet her?>

Suspicious, now. No one had ever offered anything good in Sunpoint.

But then, this isn't Sunpoint, is it? This is a kingdom founded by the one who escaped.

Slowly, he advanced towards us.

'Hello, Tierne,' said Saenia as he passed into the shade of the tree.

'Magess,' he said, bowing clumsily as if that was what you did in dreams.

'No one bows to me,' said Saenia, slightly reproving. Already she'd acquired the air of a teacher. 'Do you know why I want to talk to you?'

He bowed his head, ashamed of what he was. 'Yes. I think so.'

She stepped forward, the kindly aunt now. 'But do you know what I want to offer you, if you're ready?'

He looked sharply up, and his eyes glowed. There was magic in his soul already. Now it could be something more. It is a pity that, in that second of childish joy at the thought of what was to come, I swiped an image from his mind. He had been in places in Sunpoint that I hadn't. And, though he had all the raw power of a mage, he didn't even notice Uncle Laenan slip into his mind and take the thought of the palace, the image of the palace.

Sometimes I think I'm turning into a cynical old man.

The colours darken, thicken, acquire form. Sound returns bit by bit, bringing with it feeling. Insubstantiality becomes dense, is pressed together and twists into reality.

Silverpoint. I had brought myself straight into T'omar's office, and the general was already on his feet as I arrived. Someone grabbed me from behind as my arms became solid, but T'omar had already opened his mouth to speak. 'It's not him! Let him go!'

A Key-bound statue, for such it was, nodded obediently, stopped scraping my bones together and released me. T'omar sat down again, smiling faintly at the look of consternation on my face.

'You aren't taking any chances, are you?' I asked in outrage.

'A message has been dispatched to all kingdoms. No one of any import is to go around without an escort. Anyone using dreamer's powers is a danger and is to be killed on arrival. Good job you warned me you were coming.'

'Thank you most kindly for laying off the security in my passage,' I retorted hotly, shoving a pile of folders off the chair opposite his and sitting down in a huff. 'Here I am, ready to fight, quote, for dreams and light and goodness, close quote, and you decide to knock ten years off my life by having a statue come to life on my arrival!'

'Oh, stop complaining. This is just the kind of measure you yourself would take.'

'Possibly,' I said, with a note of petulance. I felt ready to deliver a real rant. *I put myself out for you, get bashed and*

beaten almost to bits so that you can save your scrawny little
necks . . .

And I'm still in one piece and fighting, aren't I?

'So tell me, T'omar. What wonderful new calamities
must we overcome today?'

'Nothing you don't know about. And they all stem
back to Xavian. Our illustrious friend.'

'I'm working on it,' I said as reassuringly as possible.

'What exactly are you planning on doing?'

'Well, I was thinking along the lines of teleporting into
wherever Xavian is, hitting him round the head and
undoing the spells he's written over Miriam in the
process.'

'Uhuh. More specifically?' T'omar, as always, had
seen the truth.

'I have no idea,' I admitted. 'I know I'm stronger than
Xavian, at least in theory. His connection with Miriam is
all artifice, his magical techniques lack refinement and
were it not for the dreamer's powers he possesses I could
tear him apart in the blink of an eye. But I can't. Because
I'd kill her too.'

'Does Renna know how to undo the spells?'

'I don't know.'

'Perhaps you might want to take another look at
them?' That was as close to an order as T'omar was
going to get. Nor was he meeting my eye, which was
always a bad sign.

'Perhaps,' I replied, just to gall him.

'Well it's up to you, of course.' *Of course.* 'You're the
mage.'

'I'll have a look,' I promised. 'Where's Commander
Janyvir?'

'Ah.' He looked shame-faced. 'Well, you know what a well-placed recruit is worth . . .'

I gaped. 'You recruited the commander of the city watch?!'

'It's not that bad!'

'It's every bit as bad! He's the least discreet man alive!'

'No. He's just a little unpractised, that's all. Very like you, though.'

'He's not!' I said defensively.

'Now, now, I like the commander. He's a nice guy.'

Some of my ruffled feathers were smoothed by this, but not many. 'All right. Tell me what else you want done. As well as the Miriam thing. And cut the modest, "I'm so embarrassed" crap.'

'All right,' said T'omar, straight to the point. 'We need to talk Rylam out of spreading rumours around the court about Lisana. She's agreed that when Xavian's out of Sunpoint—'

'If.'

'If Xavian's out of Sunpoint,' he continued, not missing a beat, 'Rylam can have the place. But she does want reassurances. Certain advantages. She just needs to talk him round to a number of articles, that's all.'

'Thank you for the dirty work,' I muttered. 'Rylam's a hard case to talk to, you know? He looks on me like I'm the scum of the Void.'

Which in a sense I am. But show me one man who hasn't in his life done something even a little dirty for whatever reason and I'll crown him the naive king of the world. 'Still, there might be someone else I can press into service.'

'I'll leave it to your discretion, Kite.'

'You're so kind. And what are you going to be doing in the meantime?'

'Oh, this. That. I still haven't had the guts to tell everyone about Rinset.'

I couldn't meet his eyes. 'We were stupid,' I said. 'I was stupid. I thought I could get to Xavian before he took the Key and that everyone else would be able to look after themselves. I was a fool.'

'Don't hold yourself responsible. You need allies, company even, no matter what you pretend. You had every right to believe you could get to Xavian faster. It was your kingdom, you had warning of his actions, you had the power. You just didn't have the time, but then no one does. You're not superhuman, Kite. You're simply borrowing a few remarkable attributes.'

There was a silence, while T'omar drummed his fingers on the desk. Finally he asked, 'Will this be like the time we drove the forces of nightmare out of Haven?' The two of us, separated from our own armies, entering the city in secret through the sewers. 'Or should we do something else?'

I smiled, without much cheer. 'Something else. This time there's only one man to kill, and he's ten times more powerful than any army. This time I'm the only one who can do it.'

'So. You're gonna be heroic.'

'Oh please. I'll try what I always do. Sneak up behind the guy when he's not looking and hit him with anything I can.'

'Roughly what chance do you think you have?'

I considered. 'Do you want me to draw odds or simply give it in terms of cuts and bruises?'

'Odds.'

'Three to two in my favour.'

'You're lying,' he said calmly. 'You're not a good liar, you haven't had enough practice.'

'Hey! I was in the snake-pit of Haven for years! A courtier!'

'And look what happened. You ended up being tried for treason.'

'Well, yes . . .'

'What's going to happen, Kite? Talk me through this. You arrive in Sunpoint under cover of a scry-block. You find Xavian, you fight. You gain the upper hand, but you can't exploit it because Miriam's tied into Xavian. He gains the upper hand. He has a Key, magic, dreamer's power. You have only two of those and the disadvantage of being constrained against a clean, quick death-blow. What do you do?'

'Obviously,' I said, 'I don't let the battle take place in Sunpoint. That loses him at least one of those advantages. I bring him to my own territory.'

'How?'

'I don't know. But I'll think of something.'

'You're a great reassurance, Kite. You really know how to make watertight plans.'

I smiled faintly. 'Tell Commander Janyvir Reshin I send my regards. Tell him . . . he was invaluable.'

Haven. I brought myself right down outside the queen's study. As in Silverpoint, a hundred alarms went off and a dozen guards bore down on me.

'Hey!' I yelled as rifles were raised. 'I'm not him!'

There was a certain confusion as the guards established that yes, I was indeed Laenan Kite and yes, the queen wasn't out for my blood for any particular crime at the moment. It was finally resolved with the arrival of Lisana herself.

She didn't even smile on seeing me. 'You're alive, then,' she said, gesturing me into her study. 'Wait outside,' she told the guards.

'But your majesty . . .' one protested.

'Captain, this man is the most powerful mage in the Void. If Xavian does take it into his head to appear, I'm sure we'll have no problem.' She glanced at me. 'Will *you* have a problem?'

'Only that of a heavy conscience and heavier responsibility, your majesty.'

'"Only",' she said with derision. 'Your conscience will be your downfall, Kite. You've been alive long enough to know that here it can't be allowed.'

The study door closed behind us. She didn't even move to the desk but just stood before the door, looking me up and down.

'Where have you come from?'

'Directly from Silverpoint. And before that Stormpoint. And before that Sunpoint.'

'What took you so long?'

I met her eyes squarely. 'For some reason I decided that the lives of my family took priority over the queen of dreams, your majesty.'

Lisana is a strange, strange woman. What goes on behind her mask I do not know. But I'll swear that for a second I saw a smile, as quickly gone as it had come.

'You have family?'

'It would be too much to say they're mine, but yes, I . . . am part of a family.'

'Am I still in danger, Kite? Tell me – as my Silvereye –
will Xavian come after me again?'

'I don't know. I don't think so – we've pressed him into
a tight corner. But . . . your Key should perhaps be active
at all hours. Is there someone you trust to keep it while
you sleep?'

'Out of the court? Not really. I'd rather give it to you.'

I fell silent. So did she. In that moment a thousand
thoughts crossed my mind. The most noticeable one was,
Bloody hell. Surely she doesn't trust me?

'Isn't that a risk?' I asked finally.

'Why? You've had the Key to Haven before, however
briefly. At least I can rely on you to give it back.'

'You don't think I might get it into my head to play . . .
practical jokes?'

'Would you?' she asked sharply.

'I don't know.' *Bloody hell. She trusts me.*

There was an uncomfortable silence, the kind made by
two people simultaneously wondering where the dark,
wiggly path ahead could possibly be leading.

I said, 'I'm going to talk to Corinna, see if I can convince her to calm Rylam down. If not, I'll try my luck on
him in person.'

'And Miriam? I know you care for her, whether you
mean to or not. What will you do about her?'

I shrugged. 'I'll look again at the spells. There's
something about a comatose dreamer that I don't
understand. They can create whole universes inside
their heads, and that somehow affects the outer world
too. The affairs of dreamers are still far above me, I
mean, I could tell you stories . . .' I stopped dead. 'Oh
my.'

'Yes?'

'Oh my, my, my.'

'Stop indulging your ego and tell me what it is,' she barked. How accustomed I am to Lisana mingling authority with childish annoyance.

'They . . . create worlds in their heads, which control the outside . . . oh my. Oh my, my, my.'

'Kite!'

No response.

'Silvereye! Mage!'

I stirred at her call, but my mind was already walking other paths. 'Yes?'

'What are you babbling about?'

'What? Oh, nothing. Probably wouldn't work. At least, in a properly functioning scientific universe it definitely wouldn't . . .'

'Dare I say, this universe is not scientific and is close to not functioning! Tell me what you're talking about!'

I stared at her, suddenly realizing how pretty she looked by the bright sun of Haven, how steady her gaze and how set her jaw.

'I think I know how I can kill Xavian, without killing him.'

'And?'

'And . . . I don't know if it'll work. I need to think about it. I need to have a look at the spells around Miriam.'

She folded her arms, hugging herself almost, and now she looked very small and fragile. 'Kite,' she said in a little voice. 'Please don't say you have a plan.'

TWELVE

The Plan

This is it, I thought as I marched down the corridor towards Miriam's room. *I know it in my bones. And since Renna's in my bones anyway, that's doubly why it might be right.*

I reached the room, burst inside and nearly fell over at the sight of Miriam. She was pale as a ghost and, worse, growing insubstantial around the edges. A certain misty quality hung over her. She was losing touch with her dream.

'Has anyone moved her?' I demanded.

'No sir,' said a guard.

'Has anyone touched her?'

'No sir.'

'Has anything at all happened to her since I left?'

'No sir. She's just been getting steadily worse.'

'Damn.' I sat on the edge of the bed, and took her cold, icy-cold hand.

<Miriam?>

The answer came. Instantly I was inside the church, with her at my side. She looked dreadful.

'I thought you were going to leave me alone,' she whispered. Her voice was hoarse with the caress of death.

'You're dying! You think I'm just going to stand by and let that happen to you?'

'I die. You die. We all die eventually.'

'You don't *have* to! You're not like us, you're not of flesh and blood. You can be something more.'

She smiled faintly, and there was madness born of sheer fatigue now in that smile. Her life was being drained from her and all I could do was argue.

'I don't want to be.'

'For dreams' sake! You don't have to die!' I caught her round the shoulders, and then instantly let go, remembering what happened last time I'd wanted to shake reason into her. 'Help me. Please, that's all I ask. Just *help*, and when it's all over you can do what you will. Live, die, I don't care. But for now please don't be an idiot.'

'Do you do this a lot? Say something, mean something different, beg and crawl when you know you could just take?'

I tried a different tack. Dreams help me, I abandoned all reason. Reason wasn't getting me anywhere. I backed off, willing the tension out of muscles I hadn't noticed bunching, shook my head as though saddened by her uncooperation and spun back on her, suddenly all aggression. You cannot be rational with an irrational person.

'Perhaps I'm just lazy!' I said, in a steadily growing

voice. 'You think I'd waste valuable time and strength on forcing something from you, tearing it out bit by bit when I can simply ask? You really think I can be bothered to cast *my* spells over Xavian's? Drain yourself into me instead? You think I care that much?!'

'Oh, and now you've changed tack!' she spat, her aggression rising to meet my own. 'Now I see what you're really trying to achieve!'

She advanced, and there was real anger in there – not the irrationality of before, but genuine, over-the-top anger. 'You're pushing me this way, pulling me that. You're trying to spin me round and round and hope that when I stop I'm looking your way! You're a clever man, Kite, but I know where I stand!'

'Yes! As one of Xavian's conquests! As the means by which he kills Rinset, Corbe, his own apprentice! He's killed a servant of Feilim's, he's killed Feilim himself, he's come bloody close to killing me and I am tired of it! Five people are dead because you led me – the one person in the Void who cared for you – to a nightmare! You bear some of the responsibility **for their** deaths – *you*!'

'How dare you lectur**e me? How m**any people have you killed, Kite? How ma**ny useless li**ves wasted for your sake, for your battles?'

'Don't think saying that will make me back down, Miriam. I *know* who I've killed and, dreams help me, I see their faces every night. But I listen to them, I'm hurt by the worst of them dying at *my* hands. You,' – scorn and derision now, anger out of control – 'you can't even tell me who's dead. You don't see the blood on your own hands.'

'I see them all!' she yelled, wretched now.

'You see no further than your own nose!'

'No! I see them all because I see what he sees! We are one!'

There was a chance now, surely. Before, I'd just been running along blindly, but now I could see a way out of Miriam's self-imposed darkness. She was shaking, the tears starting to flow freely. My wrist itched, but there was no blood. Carefully, not sure what I did, I moved towards her. She stood there, sobbing like a baby. There is an embarrassed sympathy that people experience in these situations, where they want to do something but, like me at that moment, they don't know what. I reached out and gently touched her shoulder. If anything, her crying became more intense. Miriam, for all she had experienced and seen, was just a child.

'It's all right,' I murmured, holding her close now and wrapping my arms round her little frame, made smaller still by the wasting of Xavian's magic and the grief of her own conscience. 'Everything's going to be all right.'

She clung on, the fight all gone from her. 'I saw every one,' she whispered, the sound muffled by my clothes.

'I know. We're going to end it, don't worry about that. I know how I can separate you from Xavian.'

She raised her head, and there was light in her eyes. 'Without killing him?'

'I can't say that, you know I can't.'

She pulled away, suddenly cold again. 'Then I won't help you.'

'Miriam . . .' I tried to think. 'You know all my arguments. You know that I'm right. Not from any moral sense, I admit, because even one death is one too many. But in reason – no, not even in that . . .' I looked and felt pained by my own shortcomings. 'You know what I'm trying to say. You know it's right.'

She hung her head, and asked in a voice so soft I almost didn't hear it, 'What do you want?'

This was the point, so the Consortium taught, where you had to keep going no matter what. Once you saw even a glimmer of willingness you had to keep up your momentum, or else your best-laid plans would just crumble.

'Dreamers' minds control physical things,' I said. 'When you come here we affect your heads, we leave an impression that stays with you when you return to Earth. But in your case, unable to return, the role is reversed and you take an active part in manipulating the environment.

'So what happens when we go inside a dreamer's mind, and they start to affect our physical aspects? I am in your head now; if you scratch me I will bear real marks. The same happened when Renna used me.'

She saw where I was going. 'You want to use me. Against him!'

'Not with a dreamer already inside me.' She opened her mouth to protest but I got there first. 'Renna can create the unreal reality that I need. I just want a way to get Xavian in it. Once there, I think it will be possible . . . no, I *know* it's possible – that Xavian can be separated out from you. And it will all be over.'

'You make it sound so simple. So much like nothing.'

'Miriam, I'm going after Xavian with or without your permission. I'm going to find a way to get him inside that world and there I will kill him. But it would be better, for all our sakes, if I had your cooperation. It's too risky even

for my tastes to be linked to Xavian, but not knowing
how the dreamer who powers him will react to that link.
I need reassurances.'

'What reassurances?' she asked in a hushed voice.

'I want guarantees that when push comes to shove,
you'll have a place to hide from him.' I drew a knife from
my belt. 'Never go into battle without a fallback, I
always say.'

Nervously she took the blade, turning it over and
over and holding it as thought it might explode. 'You
want to link with me? You think I trust you that far?'

'I think that I'm going to find Xavian, and I may not
be able to separate you properly. If so, I want you to
have a place where you'll temporarily be safe.'

'It's a trick. You're trying to use me.'

I shrugged. 'Once we're joined you'll find out for
yourself that I'm not. I don't expect you to aid me. I just
don't want to risk your survival. For my sake, as much as
yours, do this.'

She turned the blade, poised over my open hand, hesitated. Shook her head. 'No. This will be my ultimate seal
of defection against Xavian. For all he's done, for all he
wants to be, I still love him.'

'You love your memory of him.'

'That's all that there is left! You can't get your own
way all the time, *great* mage.'

'Bloody hell, when was the last time that happened?
You know the one time I was really happy? That brief,
brief period when I was alone in nightmare. Everyone
else was gone, no one knew who I was, what I was
capable of. For just once I had control! And how did I
end up? A battered old mage trying to save the lives of

fools! And you – a child who thinks that, just because she's lived a brief little life in one world, she knows the ways and means of a whole universe! This is not Earth, Miriam. This is not real!'

'No! It's a dream! *You're* a dream, a nothing, a nobody, an insignificant insult! I'm real, Xavian and I! You're an illusion, a fake, a mockery, a twisting of reality into something evil and cruel and . . .'

'Made evil and cruel by you! By dreamers' twisted minds!' I lunged forward, grabbing her hard. My voice dropped to a growl. 'Listen to me. Your thoughts, as dreamer, shape the physical aspects of this world. Somewhere, someone thought of a mage with dark hair and blue eyes and lo, here I am. My home is the dream of storms, my queen is the incarnation of strength as imagined by some dreamer's mind.

'Now see it from my point of view. *This* is the real world. It's what we live with, so it must be the genuine article. We have no proof to say otherwise. Earth has no substance, *dreamers* are an illusion. If here they dream of Nightkeep or Chaospoint or Firepoint, when they wake they will reflect in some small way an aspect of that kingdom. The more you live in nightmare the more the nightmare becomes part of you.

'You dreamers can shape our lives, our DNA, our characters and our fates but we shape your thoughts! Who now the greater power holds? Who now is the illusion?'

She was sobbing again, limp in my grasp but, unrelenting, I went on. 'Xavian is a physical being, shaped by you. You, who remember a man you loved, had your dream betrayed by Xavian. This twisted dream was waiting for you, in his form, in Sunpoint, and you went to it obediently. Now he's twisting your mind. You can't tell illusion from reality, truth from lies or light from dark. He's bringing you closer to nightmare with every step, turning into nightmare, becoming *his* creation! And you presume to tell me that *I'm* the illusion? I, who do know what I regret and who I love?'

There was a flash of pain across my palm, lessened because I hadn't really noticed. The knife clattered to the floor and Miriam grasped my hand and pressed it against hers. As with Renna, she'd found her access point.

It was different from when Renna entered. For a start, Miriam held back. She didn't give her all and I didn't blame her. Nor was the link as smooth or efficient. But there was the same iciness. And the same darkness. And the same feeling of pressure all around and the roar of my body being crammed with yet another shard of yet another soul.

In the end, the darkness won.

Someone was shaking me. Hard. And yelling a name. After a while I realised it was my own.

Lisana, her face surprising with its look of worry, was standing over me. 'Kite! Kite, are you all right?'

'Concerned?' I asked weakly. I'd fallen across Miriam's legs. Our hands were still locked together. The cut had healed already.

Immediately Lisana drew back, regaining her regal detachment. 'You started bleeding. Then you just toppled like a tree.'

'I'm right sorry for it,' I replied, sitting up and staring at my whole hand. I felt no different, but then, Miriam was still separate from me. We'd opened a possible escape route for her, nothing more.

I am one large warehouse for frightened souls, including my own, I thought wearily. I looked up at Lisana. 'What's this, your majesty? Surely you didn't come running to see if your Silvereye was well?'

'Watch your tongue, Kite.'

Oooh. She's defensive. Rubbing my hand, still doubting the reality of what had happened, I stood up. 'I think . . . yes. I think it will work. In fact, I'm confident . . .'

The door burst open. 'Your majesty!' It was a captain of the guard, red-faced from running, his chest heaving.

Lisana and I exchanged a look. Out of all the degrees of exclamation, ranging from the calm retort up to a mad scream, this had bordered on the frantic.

'What's happened?' asked Lisana, all calm and reserve.

'In the scry room, your majesty!'

She didn't bother to hear the rest of the message. Her gaze went distant as her Key-bound senses swept over the palace and into the room in question.

Then her eyes widened. 'Kite. Come.'

'He says he'll speak to his grace Kite only, your majesty!' exclaimed the captain.

In that case why did you bother telling the queen?

'Why?'

'He wouldn't say, ma'am.'

'Kite?' she said, turning to me.

I raised my hand. 'Small question, maybe irrelevant. Who's this "he", to whom we're referring?'

The corridor outside the scry room was thronged with

guards by the time I arrived. Several mages were also crowded round the door, for all the world as if they could stop whatever was going to happen. Lisana took command instantly, telling everyone to keep back and ordering riflemen to fire if anyone came out of that room.

I went to the mages by the door. 'What is it?'

'A Key-bound construct, if you must know, sir,' said one, clearly unaware that I was inclined to turn people who took that tone into toads.

'A Key-bound construct, somehow given life and reality outside its specific kingdom,' agreed another who annoyed me even more. He had the smooth manner of a professional who can't believe anyone would be ignorant enough not to see that much.

'How did it get here?'

'Appeared out of nowhere. Made no move to attack but demanded to speak with Laenan Kite. Wherever he is right now.'

'It is, however, not a particularly fine example of a Key-bound construct existing outside its kingdom.'

'How so?'

'It's . . . unstable.'

'Is the room empty?'

'Yes.'

'Right.' To Lisana and the captain of the guard I said, 'I'll knock five times to come out. If you don't hear the knocks, shoot whatever emerges.' With that I barged straight into the room and slammed the door behind me.

It was peaceful inside. A few globes of magelight hovered over the central scrying pool, which was still and clear. There were no windows, but the air was cool and fresh nonetheless.

The creature, for no other higher term could be accorded it, was standing on the other side of the scrying pool. Its head snapped up as I entered. I could see that it was trying to be Xavian, or rather, what Xavian wished he were. It was slightly taller, the nose straighter, the eyes firmer, the fingers stronger. At least, that's how it would have been, but that parts of it were openly dissolving and re-building on the spot.

'Ugh,' I said on seeing this. 'Nice try, Xavian, but I don't think you've got the knack just yet of making unreal things real.'

There was a delay before the creature answered, which gave the impression of my words being relayed to another source. 'Merely a first attempt,' it growled in a guttural voice that a shark would have used, could it speak.

'What do you want, Xavian?'

'I felt you in Miriam.'

'How flattering that I could make such an impression. And?'

'You are more powerful and cunning than I thought. I believed when I met you that all legends are made ten times greater by those who tell of them.'

'That's true. But I didn't have to be a legend to see that you, yours and all tied to you were screwed.'

The creature shifted uneasily. 'I offer . . . a bargain.'

'Indeed? Of what kind?'

'I will no longer be a threat to you or to dreams. Indeed, I intend to turn my attentions to nightmare. You, in return, will trouble me no more.'

I thought about this for all of a second. 'You would continue to kill people in another kingdom, and expect us not to care?'

'You cannot stay awake all the time, Kite. You know that one day I'd come after you. This way, you can be sure of safety.'

'And Miriam?' I asked. 'What about her? I would be willing to negotiate, on condition that she's set free.'

The creature shook its head, the laborious movement of an old man. *Or a badly, badly made magical entity that's falling apart.* 'I am no fool.'

'I appreciate that. Indeed, your intelligence is probably your only endearing quality. And even that sucks.'

'Miriam stays mine. Sunpoint stays mine. You lose an enemy for nothing, and your other enemy becomes mine too.'

I leaned forwards on the edge of the pool, making the water tremble. 'I lose one enemy for the lives of five men and the enslavement of a dreamer's mind. And you know I'm capable of dealing with all my current enemies. Nightmare is no threat. Indeed, you'll probably be flattered when I say that right now you rank my number one adversary.'

It made a noise like air bubbling through oil, which I realised was a laugh. 'Defiant unto the last. You think I don't know that you're trying to save Miriam from me? She came to me willingly, Kite. And that has given me a sort of immunity, because to harm me is to harm her.'

'You know nothing. Remember – I move like a dreamer. I heal like a dreamer. I fight like a dreamer. And, when you get down to it, my dreamer is stronger than yours.'

'Ah yes. The mysterious entity that gives you strength and clouds your magic from my sight. Is it the bitch dreamer who tried to take Miriam from me in the first place?'

'Even she. And you can take it personally from me that she's really, really annoyed with you.'

'I'm quaking.'

'You're a mad thug.'

'That too. You know we're not that different, you and I.'

'Huh,' I said, because it was the only thing I could think of without being shamefully slow to answer. 'You're the thug. I'm the muggins who clears up after.'

'No. We both know what it's like to grow up in an unloving world. To possess true magical genius but have it rejected.'

'True magical genius.' Coming from anyone else, I might like the sound of that. Even my enemy had managed to give my ego a boost. Was I really that starved of things to feel proud of?

Xavian persisted. 'We both know the world – that to get things done you sometimes have to get your hands dirty. We're both fighting for similar causes – we both want peace and harmony. Your ideal only differs from mine in that you're too cowardly to extend it to its logical conclusion.'

'You mean, and kill all the kings?' I asked, almost smiling at his sincerity.

'Weak kings. Pathetic, warring kings who want nothing better than to steal their neighbour's land.'

'Let every man be judged by actions done, not actions wished on,' I said, half amazed at the sound of my own righteousness.

'We both know that sometimes, to get the right thing

done, someone has to do something bad. And we take responsibility for it, yes, even though society will shun us and throw up obstacles in our way.'

'Xavian,' I said, without any feeling whatsoever, 'if you believe that, you just haven't tried hard enough. Yes, there are some real bastards out there, but there's a balance of good people too. You just haven't been bothered to go looking for them. In the case of evil, I'm afraid that like attracts like.'

'You call it evil?'

'If you were half the man you claim to be, you wouldn't even ask that.'

'And can you see what you are, or do you live under some pleasant illusion?'

'Illusions come all sorts. The ones people believe. Those they live, even. If you can live the illusion, but still know your real self, that's not too far off from enlightenment.'

The misshapen creature managed to look grieved, a remarkable achievement by any book. 'So. You are determined to wage futile war? I respect you, Kite. I am sorry you cannot bring yourself to do the same for me.'

'Piss off, Xavian,' I said wearily. 'I don't know why you came.'

'I came to offer peace.'

'Well you should have done that before you even declared war. Go on, get out of this place. Can't you see you never were and never will be welcome? Little mage.'

His face bunched in anger for a second, then relaxed. I felt something on the edge of feeling, of a mind withdrawing from the area around. The figure became slack, faded into thin mist, and disappeared within a second, no longer supported by Xavian's powers.

I knocked on the door five times, pressed my ear against the wood to hear any sound (there was none) and carefully pushed the door open. A dozen rifles swung into my face.

'Hey, hey, hey! Get control over yourselves!'

Lisana was trying to look regal. After all, there were a lot of people watching. So, for her sake, I effected a bow and spoke in ridged, formal tones. 'Your majesty.'

'What did the mage want, Warden?' she asked in a soft but carrying voice.

'Peace. He keeps Miriam and Sunpoint, we leave him alone.'

'What did you say to him?'

'I said no, your majesty.'

Her lips thinned ever so slightly. 'Why?'

'Because Xavian wouldn't even know he was breaking a treaty when he killed you, your majesty.'

All that remained was a lure. And yes, I knew it would have to be me. I just about remembered how to tie the headdress of the desert, bringing it across the nose and mouth. I didn't put it past Xavian to throw up a sand-storm in my path. Lisana wanted me to wear armour, but I explained as patiently as possible that not only would I fall over from the weight but that I wanted to be able to run away as well as fight. The most important part of war is living after, and one of the best means of survival is a watertight escape plan – something that usually involves running places.

Then, out of a bottom drawer, I took a very dusty set of grey clothes. Grey, the colour of the neutral king-doms. I had always favoured it over white for practical reasons, and never quite brought myself to wear black. I had the feeling that if I even started looking like a necromancer, the temptation to become one would be overwhelming.

In these same clothes I had killed a king. It was a kind of reassurance, a lucky talisman, almost. Except for the fact that I was of the lonely, cynical kind who believes that a man makes his own luck, or if luck does befall it's at the cost of someone else.

'They tell me,' said a voice from the door – I hadn't even heard it open – 'that you're going in alone.'

'Not alone, Commander,' I said, trying to hide my smile at seeing him. 'With Renna and a well-charged staff.'

'Ah. The ever faithful Renna.' He wandered into the room and looked around. 'You know, it took murders galore and chaos to get me into the palace, and I'm only here because I snuck in through the trader's entrance.'

'Any particular reason?' I asked lightly.

'Not really,' he replied, equally aloof. 'Just happened to be passing, heard from my new friends that you were in town . . . you know about the new friends?'

'At Silverpoint? T'omar did mention it.'

'You know,' he said lightly, 'I thought I'd never have any stories to tell my grandchildren. Only how I was a watchman, drinking too much, sleeping too little. Then one day I've met a living legend, been dragged round the palace in quest of a mad mage, travelled to far-off lands in the blink of an eye and met the queen. Do you think my grandchildren will be interested?'

'They'd probably prefer to hear about things they know. Maybe horses and singing birds.'

'Really?' he asked, crestfallen. 'Ah well . . .' His eyes
had been sweeping the room all the time, the way a good
copper looks on automatic for clues even to an uncom-
mitted crime, and had fallen on the desert headdress.
'Bloody hell, what's that?'

'This,' I said proudly, picking it up, 'is what Brawn
would have worn if he wanted to make it utterly clear
that he was from Sunpoint.'

I placed it back on the table and continued pottering
around with little aim. At this stage of preparation there
was too much time for thinking.

'Are you frightened?' asked Janyvir finally.

'Yes.'

'And still going in to try something complicated and
dangerous?'

'Yes.'

'Do you want this, then?' he asked, holding out his
hand.

I stared at the thing he offered, taking it carefully and
turning it over and over in my palm. It was a little silver
flower, with four petals. The edges of each one had been
honed to razor sharpness. 'What's this?'

'I was given it by my father before he died. He was a
watchman too, but he never made commander. I don't
pretend it's magical or anything, but it is convenient in
certain situations. Most searchers overlook it. I mean, I
know you'll probably be fighting with magic and the like,
but I hate to hang around knowing someone might be
about to die and me utterly useless to them . . .'

'Thank you. I mean, yes. I'd be honoured to use it.
And if I don't bring it back I hope it gives Xavian at least
a cut finger.'

He smiled, a smile of thoughtfulness. 'I wonder what soldiers are like before they go into a battle.'

'Like this, I suppose.'

'I know you'll be fighting in places where only dreamers can go. But if thinking helps even slightly, then I'll be thinking for a whole army.'

'Thank you.'

His ever-inquisitive gaze had settled on the tall staff nestled in a corner, only recently infused with magic. 'You're not going to carry *that*, are you?'

'Yes, as a matter of fact I am.'

'So where's the pointy hat?'

'After due consideration,' I said, with a prickly pride, 'I think it'd be best if you kept your thoughts to yourself.'

Tell me before you go, Lisana had said.

As I wandered down the dark corridor to her apartments on that dark night, staff in hand, Janyvir's little talisman hanging round my neck, dagger in my belt, bag on my back and scarf flopping round my neck, I wondered what Lisana would be doing while I was fighting Xavian. Sitting in her study praying, probably. As would be T'omar, Janyvir, Saenia and all the rest with any inkling of what I was going after. Suddenly I wished I could take someone with me, at least so that I'd be less tempted to turn round and run down the passage yelling in fear. I wished I could divide Renna's protective powers between two Kites, not one. That way I'd have someone to talk to. There is a certain kind of fright you get when you know that the inevitable is heading towards you – but that behind the great veil of inevitability there lies in wait a whole uncharted universe of chances and disasters.

Look on the bright side. If everything goes wrong you won't have to worry about tomorrow.

When I knocked on Lisana's door, it was answered so fast that she must have felt me coming. She was wearing a pair of fluffy slippers underneath a ballgown, but I managed not to laugh. The room was illuminated by magelight, but she'd scattered it so that the place was quite gloomy. She was apt to complain that, when tired, bright light hurt her eyes.

'Kite,' she said quietly as I entered the room.

'Your majesty.'

There was an awkward silence.

'Everything about this feels wrong,' she said finally.

'How so?'

'You're going to go and fight for my crown and my throne. Again. What have either done for you?'

'Sod all, since you ask.'

She too wanted to know if I was really going alone.

'No,' I told her, mildly. 'I have Renna. In a small way, Miriam. And when I've got time to remember, I have everyone else I've ever met.'

'I want . . . no, that's overused. I want this, I want that – you must be sick of it by now. I *need* to know certain things.'

'Like what?'

'What are you fighting for?'

I considered long and hard. 'The first answer would be along the lines of love, laughter, goodness, grace, and the uniqueness of man. But we both know that'd be a lie.'

'And the next thing that comes to mind?' This was a Lisana few people knew. For once, she was sincere.

'Perhaps I'm fighting for a niche of certainty and

contentment which, no matter how small and insignificant, I'll defend to the last. Even great mages, radical
mages, are allowed to be afraid of change.'

'Tell me, Kite, are you ever fighting for you?'

'All the time. Haven't you noticed? Without me my life
just loses all purpose,' I said with a smile. 'Is that all, or
does her majesty wish to know my soul inside out, in case
a part of it really does consider putting frogs in her bed?'

'You're not fighting for me, then?'

I considered. 'No,' I said. 'Sorry. But . . .'

'But?' she prompted.

'I . . . think I'm fighting for Renna. I think there's a
chance I still love her.'

Her face didn't change, but there was something
behind her eyes that went out. 'Well,' she said finally, 'I
haven't had the pleasure of Renna's company as much as
you, but I'm sure she must be worth it.'

I smiled and nodded. 'I think so. Is there anything
else?'

She bit her lip. 'I need to know . . . if you can forgive
the king's mistress for making your life a misery, all those
years ago.' Her eyes were hopeful, her breathing shallow
and on edge.

'Forgive the king's mistress?' I asked. 'For all those
beatings and betrayals and taunts and rejections and
spectacles? No. I cannot, and I never will.'

Her face fell, then became icy hard as she began to
retreat into herself. The little shard of Lisana's soul that
I'd so briefly seen was fading behind a mask of office.

'However,' I said, and watched her head snap up, 'I
might find it in my heart to forgive the queen.'

She smiled, a rarely seen smile of pleasure of a kind I'd

forgotten long ago. It had all the life and sparkle that every one of her false smiles tried to echo, but this time it was *real*. And for all I hated the king's mistress of old, I could not find it in my heart to hate this woman.

There would be arguments. There would be anger, there would be conflict, there would be old memories brought to light and new outrages performed. But for now, we stood together.

THIRTEEN

Dreams and Memories

I came in under a scry-block on the edge of the town, and immediately saw that Xavian wanted his presence felt. The first clue was the roaring sandstorm which ran through the streets and turned my dark hair sand-coloured within a second. I struggled into the shelter of a doorway and pulled my scarf around my face as tightly as possible. The storm, I soon discovered after a quick probe through the kingdom, was merely a by-product of a huge magical wind centred around a walled compound in the centre of the city. If you weren't already inside the compound walls, you'd never get there through this storm.

Visibility was down to a few feet. Sound too was snatched away by the roar of the storm. But in the distance I could hear the occasional noise of many voices, from what source I knew not. Then I felt it. The distant flare of dreamer's magic that proved beyond all doubt that Xavian had set to work.

I didn't have an image on which to focus Renna's power, so I cast around with my mind, cowering in the doorway while I searched out threats and destinations.

Fear. A huge wellspring of fear. A lot of people were gathered in one place, and all were afraid. And behind the fear, a shadow of greed. These scared people were seeing, after their own terror, an opportunity, but for what I couldn't say. To sway the new leader? To exploit him?

Then I sensed stillness. Not mental stillness, because no mind is ever entirely silent, but a great mass of people standing in silence, listening to one voice. I tried to focus on that stillness, tried to will myself to be part of it, another face in the crowd of so many. The power was reluctant to respond – I hadn't given it a very clear image. I tried again, whispering of the things I had sensed, that unique combination of feelings and sensations that distinctly marked out the place where I wanted, *needed* to be.

It responded. The world dissolved and re-built itself in an eternal second. Renna's guiding hand was there, too – I came down right on the edge of the crowd, and now I could see what it was that held so many people enthralled.

I had appeared with my back pressed against a huge golden wall. A pair of golden gates were locked and all around the battlements huge golden warriors regarded the crowd with impassive faces. I was almost immediately pressed back harder against the wall by the shuffling masses, pressed shoulder to shoulder. A thousand, ten thousand men and women of the desert wearing robes and scarves were all turned to face a single point. I craned my neck back to stare.

Xavian was an extraordinarily vain man, I decided. And for one who employed necromantic magic, the golden crown and white robe trimmed with gold were especially out of place. I didn't approve of the golden staff either – it couldn't possibly have a practical purpose since gold of any kind is a poor conductor of magic. It was from pure vanity that Xavian possessed it.

He had also cast a clever, complicated series of glamours, using Miriam's power bound by his magic. The result was a web of light that made his less-than-handsome face shine out like a thing of beauty and surrounded him with a halo. The best mages would have been hard pressed to see exactly how he'd created that effect, but then not every mage shared his body with a dreamer.

Xavian was floating in mid-air, untouched as we all were by the sandstorm that raged everywhere except inside the compound walls. His voice was magically amplified, and he was gesturing extravagantly with his free hand as though mere words weren't enough for the wonderful things he wanted to say. It was crude stuff. And though his magic swept the whole gathering, bringing waves of contentment with it as he carefully doctored the minds of everyone present, I found my anger at his arrogance deepening with every passing second.

'Every one of you,' he was saying, 'was blind until this moment! I have given you sight, and I will give you so much more besides!'

Calmly, resolved now, I slung my bag from off my shoulder, and began to dig around in its depths. My hand closed over a sphere of glass, warm to the touch. I had many of these in Stormpoint, built out of magic and

thought during my long years of semi-exile. I brought
one out of the bag, and smiled to see it.

Beneath the glass, writhing magic curled, hammering
for a way out. No one seemed to have noticed what I
held. Xavian was keeping them enthralled. Turning the
sphere over, I checked the little daub of paint on the
back. Blue. That meant this was bottled frost. Kneeling
down, I discreetly dug a small hole for it in the sand, and
covered it. Then I began to push my way through the
crowd, keeping my back pressed against the wall at all
times and stopping at regular intervals to bury five more
globes.

*Don't look for danger, just look like you know what you're
doing. If you look as though you've got some purpose and it's
nothing to be ashamed of, no one will bother you. Be confident,
assured. This is a game, and you hold all the cards.*

Two bottled fireworks, one bottled river spell, one
bottled summoning, one bottled ivy. At the gate I put my
especial favourite – a bottled fist. This wasn't a sphere,
this was a cone, one of my proudest inventions. The cone
itself was not much larger than my hand, but it was
divided up into segments that would shatter one after the
other, releasing the spell in stages so that the final effect
was of several fists, not one. I buried it with the end of
the cone pointing straight at the gate. That done, I
began to press my way into the crowd.

'The decadence of Haven cannot be tolerated any
more!' Xavian yelled, gesturing madly. 'When we are finished, the whole Void will recognise us as the true
people! We have suffered centuries of hardship, and it
has made us strong!'

Uhuh. That's why you're who you are.

The trick was to act surprised when the spells started going off. I had several more bottled spells in my bag, but I didn't think they'd be noticed there in the rush. My scry-block was still raised, and Xavian would be so busy looking this way and that, he'd hardly be able to pick me out. Nevertheless, I kept my scarf drawn across my face and tried to move inconspicuously through the crowd.

When I was within only a few pressed and silent bodies of Xavian, I stopped, craning my neck hard to see him clearly as though I were, indeed, just another watcher.

'My people, I will bring you greatness!'

'My people.' You really are an idiot.

I extended my mind, felt my imprisoned magic answer within the glass spheres. Brushed them with the lightest thought, felt them crack.

There was a scream from one end of the compound. The river spell had gone off first, and sand was rippling in circles, heaving outward like waves and spreading across the whole compound. It was hard to keep your balance when the very ground you stood on moved, and there was a general panic-stricken crumpling round the area of the spell as people lost their footing. Xavian turned and, as happens when you don't understand what's happening, and have your own thoughts to dwell on, did nothing for a long moment. I could see him trying to fathom it out.

The ivy spell chose that moment to fire off. Sand came alive, curled round feet, yanked at them with savage force. It pulled and kept on pulling, extending claws of sand that sprouted leaves and curled like a vine to grapple with people's ankles.

Xavian raised his hands, silencing the ivy spell with horrible efficiency. Even as golden warriors began to appear in the crowd, he turned his attention to the river spell.

'Where is he?' he yelled. I had a feeling 'he' meant me, Laenan Kite. His mind raced across my scry-block, but he didn't even recognise its spell. I gave a grim smile of satisfaction and moved with the crowd as golden warriors began to spread out, pulling scarves from faces, searching for a familiar visage among the many. The sheer weight of people was my protection, and I knew it.

The frost spell went off. A large section of wall turned a cheerful white as frost began to crawl over it. There was a surge of people away from it – and at that moment the fist spell erupted. The gates shuddered under the impact of the spell, shook again, began to give as the third wall of force concussed them. Sprang open.

The final spells went off, simultaneously. These were the perilous ones, apt to inspire panic in a crowd. The dangers of playing with fire were the reason I'd got so close to Xavian, who would try to escape some of their effects. In defending himself, let him protect me, and so waste his strength on helping an enemy.

Two walls of fire shot skywards from the bottled fire-works at opposite ends of the compound. There was a gasp from the crowd, which turned fearful as the spells, at the height of their arc, exploded and rained large cinders, still flickering with fire. People began to panic. To avoid being crushed, I moved with the crowd as it swarmed to the gate. Xavian was yelling something, but it was lost under the general roar of shouts and cries.

Golden guards appeared at the gate and began to try and force the crowd back.

I felt the twisting of reality and a huge dome of power began to draw itself over the compound. Impotent now, my fear-inducing firework spells spattered and dissolved against its surface. But Xavian had still made a mistake. Just because nothing could get in from outside, that didn't mean things on the inside wouldn't shatter off the dome, with spectacular effect. I reached into my bag and extracted another sphere. It had a little lightning sign on the base, and I grinned. Yes, this one was a real panic-inspirer, and one of my better spells. As Warden of the dream of storms, I'd always been good with lightning. I lobbed the sphere up as hard as possible, guiding it with a wall of magic. It blasted Xavian's magic dome of power and shattered it, raining down glass. Golden guards began to converge on the place whence the sphere had risen, but the crowds around me were so dense that it was almost impossible to move.

The spell worked to hijack Xavian's own powers. Jagged white lightning filled the shield and within seconds had infested all his magic. With deadly accuracy it was arcing back towards the man who'd summoned the surface on which it now fed.

But I had made a mistake. I'd been too intent on the shield, and not enough on where I was going – and rammed almost straight into a golden guard. Empty gold eyes surveyed me, golden hands gloved in golden gauntlets ripped the scarf from my face. The warrior opened its mouth, but I was there faster, wrapping my scry-block around the creature even as I stopped its mouth with raw magic. It crumpled.

But not without drawing attention.

Xavian's mind was suddenly everywhere, searching desperately around me, striving at least to detect the scry-block that kept me so well hidden. If he did find it out, I could well be doomed. On the other hand, if possible I wanted to take the battle right out of his kingdom. So I lowered the scry-block, raised my staff and turned, sending a bolt of fire in his direction. He caught it on his shields and tried to tear the ground open around me.

But I was already moving, or rather I was letting the world move while I remained stationary. The ground gaped beneath my feet, fire rushed up to engulf me, but there was only a pale, insubstantial me to grasp.

I came down inside the palace itself – the image swiped from Tierne's mind had been perfect. Just this once I was grateful for the tradition that brought all boys of a certain age to be 'inspected'. The distant roar of the crowd and rush of the sandstorm were a long way off. The corridors were dark and empty, but I could see well enough. Hefting my staff and wiping my sweat-soaked face, I closed my ears to the sound of the frightened crowd and moved stealthily through the building, pushing doors open and checking the whereabouts of stairs. I was under my scry-block again, wrapping it round myself like a cloak, feeling safe now that the madness was distant.

I had never been in the palace of Sunpoint. Notwithstanding all the courts where I've been an honoured guest, or all the great kings I've fought for or against, my homeland was the only realm where I had not experienced something of another life, of that semi-life

where the peasant boy learns to talk big and bow to his
lords. Sunpoint was the only kingdom where I hadn't
been welcomed.

I pushed a door open, and nearly gasped at what I
saw. A little room, lined with shelves much as my own
workroom in Stormpoint. A small scrying mirror hung
on one wall. In the centre of the room, however, was a
man-sized altar. I could almost taste the death that surrounded this room, and the power.

I moved inside slowly, drawn by a sick fascination
with something I understood too well. The knife lay at
the head of the altar. For what reason I don't know, I
picked it up. And dropped it with a gasp. All those
lives, all that hate and all that power that had either
been lost or gained through this simple blade – the
shadows of it engulfed me, warning me to flee. Biting
my lip I took up the knife again, willing myself to listen
to everything it had to say even though it turned my
stomach.

All that power . . .

My wrist was burning, hotter than it had ever been
before. With a shudder I put the knife down again, but I
couldn't shut out that little thought that whispered its
seductive words in my ear.

All that power . . .

I ran for the door, suddenly overwhelmed by a desire
to get out of the room.

*Think what you could do. No more war, no more fighting. You
could finally be your own man, all you need do is take up the knife
again, perform the rites and feel the power that you've always
secretly craved. Your magic is strong, but only strong enough so
that you can sense the potential in the Void, only strong enough*

to show you glimpses of the power you could have, that tempting shadow that you know, have always known you could make real . . .

Shivering, I turned on the room, raised my hands, drew them apart so that a wall of golden lightning was arranged between my fingers, and hurled it at the room. A part of me cried out to cancel the spell but I closed my eyes and ran from that place, refusing to listen to the voice that demanded the room be saved, and that such a great base of power be used . . .

There was an explosion behind me. I kept on running, feeling the world dissolve around me even as Xavian's mind swept down on the source of the explosion. But with the roar of magic that transported me away once more, the voice inside me fell silent, leaving only the shame. And the anger. And the hatred, which threatened to overwhelm all restraint and rationality.

I had passed through the Void without even noticing, and emerged in the desert, once more sheltered by the scry-block. Here, there was no sandstorm, and the stars were bright over the peaceful courtyard with its little well. I pulled my scarf from around my face, and shook my head violently to get some of the sand out of my hair. Sand is remarkable stuff that manages to get into the most bizarre places. My shoes were also full of it, not just uncomfortable but making a crunching noise whenever I walked.

I looked around the dark courtyard. Shutters hung limply off the building where guards had smashed them. One half of the house was missing, dissolved to nothing. A lot of roof tiles had been blown off. Xavian had found the home of the Kites, if not the Kites themselves.

Seeing all this gave me a certain resolve. I felt the tide of anger retreat, to be replaced by emotionless determination. I was an executioner, ridding the world of a monster. Who cared what I was fighting for? What mattered was that the alternative was ten times, a thousand times, worse than what was in place. Miriam's warped memory, in the form of Xavian, hadn't been like nightmare after all. At least nightmare knew it was evil and accorded its enemies an undisguised, pure hatred. At least nightmare understood what it was.

But this force would destroy and corrupt and manipulate and not even notice what it did.

There was something out of place in the courtyard, too. A mound of earth before the well, above which someone had hammered in a sign. I peered closer, not caring to summon light.

Here lies the remains of a man who tried to defy your God and failed. Let no man dare such defiance again.

A grave in a ruined house. Rinset's grave. I didn't need to ask. I knew. The only consolation I could find was that, at the end, he'd achieved the death he always wanted, serving goodness. Kneeling before the mound, I unslung my bag and took out a series of spheres, examining each one in turn. I chose a firework, and laid it on his grave. Even in death, it seemed only appropriate that Rinset should have some of the glory of the hunt.

From a safe distance I was breaking the glass even as I willed the teleport to another part of the kingdom, just a little nearer the Void, just that much farther from Xavian. I would make him follow me, lure him on bit by bit.

The glass shattered. Xavian's mind was crowding round me, seeking his invisible enemy, but to no avail.

I staggered on my arrival, on the ground near the road and the Void beyond, and I quickly saw why. All around the edge of the kingdom Xavian had drawn a ring of fire, as much to stop people escaping as to prevent anyone getting in. I was teetering just a few inches Void-side of this. The heat was incredible.

Just one short step back from where I stood was the Void. I reached into my bag to call his attention once more, and found another bottled storm. Lowering my scry-block I hurled it over my head and through the fire. It shattered a hundred feet up and began to rain lightning down on the silent, unresponsive desert.

<Here I am, Xavian! Come and get me if you dare, little mage!>

<Watch me.> A voice trembling with fury.

I felt reality change, and sprang hastily out of his kingdom into the blessed cool of the Void. It was strange, watching from the silent, no-heat, no-cold surroundings of the Void a kingdom where fire and lightning played. Fanged monstrosities shimmered into existence where I'd stood and hissed poison at me, reaching out claws to tear me. I stood my ground, and watched their hands become insubstantial as shadow the second they reached beyond the confines of the kingdom.

As I'd planned long since, I undid my bandage. Stuffing it into a pocket, I sent a triumphant call in the direction of Sunpoint. <You'll have to do better than that!> Shrugging my bag to the ground and readying my staff, I felt prepared to meet anything he sent.

His response was hardly a second in coming. As I felt the shimmer behind me that suggested something coming into existence I was already turning with my staff low, ready to knock his legs out from under him.

Xavian swiftly backed off. He still wore his white robes, and his face was sheened with sweat from the rush of suppressing all my bottled spells. He carried that same golden staff, and his left hand still bore a cut much in the same way as my unbandaged wrist.

As my staff moved, he blocked. I spun away, grinning at the sight of him. 'You're very unfit, you know that? Both as a physical fighter and a necromancer. I mean, Serein. There was a good fighter. He was arrogant and stupid, I grant you, but he *knew* how to fight. You're just going on little fragments of inspired guesswork.'

'And you aren't?' he asked.

'Nope. I've got a *plan*.'

I advanced on him, but only half my attention was on the attack. All I had to do was keep going at a steady rhythm, to push us both to where our links with dreamers began to show their physical signs. When his hand bled and my wrist did too, then I could contemplate killing him.

It was a precarious battle this time. Before, we'd fought with the steady determination of people who knew the ground. Out in the Void, with the threat of an endless fall on either side and clawed shadows leering at us from behind, there was a fear in each of us to keep us going.

I was afraid, for several kinds of reason, not all of them irrational.

He was afraid of me, and for that at least I was pleased.

Did the fighting have no end? I was sick of it before I started. One endless, mindless quest for blood as thrust met counter-thrust and every lunge was batted to one side with barely enough time to swing the butt of the staff up and across to deflect . . .

My wrist was itching. Xavian was driving me back towards his kingdom. I held my ground, daring his whirling staff for all. What a pair of adversaries we made, through the endless blank of grim, determined survival. The man in white and gold striking out to unite the Void under one crown. The man in grey who looked more of a necromancer than his necromantic enemy, striking blow after blow to save the corrupt, feud-ridden system already in place.

I was aware of a warm wetness around my wrist. Xavian broke away and backed off, gasping for breath, golden staff weighing heavy in his hand. As he did so I turned over my wrist and stared at where the blood was now freely flowing. Moving like a madman – slowly and without looking at what I was doing – I drew my dagger and slipped it into my left hand. Xavian had no dagger. He took a firmer grip on his staff and I felt a tinge across the sixth sense as his shields rose. I matched his movements perfectly, pulling my shield tight around myself and charging my staff with even more magic than it already had to cut and tear a way through his defences.

The wood grew hot beneath my fingers. Sparks flashed from my hair and off the dagger point. Xavian took a deep breath, but didn't attack. I realized how tired he'd grown.

Bracing myself, I attacked, bringing the staff crashing towards his head. He brought his own staff up to deflect the blow and then pushed forward, trying to hit me on the reply. I sprang away from it, my staff retreating to shield my body even as my dagger hand shot out towards him. He knocked it away with his staff in a single movement and pain exploded across my wrist as it struck. But I had scored a thin line down one arm. Neither side had gained, both had lost something by the skirmish. Such is the way of war.

This time he tried an attack, wielding the staff with increasing force. I deflected it to one side and forced it down, pinning it to the ground with all my might. If I relaxed the pressure his staff would snap up and catch me a ringing, possibly fatal blow. If he relaxed his efforts I would be able to jerk his weapon from his hand. I held the staff in place, even though the dagger was still ignored in my left. Shuffling back a little, I raised my left hand. His staff sprang free, but my hand was already sailing towards his throat. His left hand moved in a blur and locked around my wrist.

Even as icy pain exploded inside my skull and the world began to darken, I grinned a grin of triumph. His eyes widened as he realized the fatal error he'd made. Our bloods mixed. Renna and Miriam mixed, and as icy power flooded through me I drew him into a link.

In the real world, our bodies crumpled lifeless to the road.

In the world that mattered now, our minds curled up into the other's embrace.

FOURTEEN

A Sprung Trap

I came to sprawled across an uncomfortable bed in a tent filled with white sunlight. My wrist was healed. In a corner of the room lay a sword. I was wearing a set of blue clothes that I had never before seen in my life. A blue banner hung limply in one corner of the tent. On it, a silver dove soared towards the sky. As I sat up, still groggy from whatever had transpired, I realized I was wearing a matching silver brooch that fastened a blue cloak.

The tent flap was opened and I was already reaching for the sword in the corner, but the man who came in wasn't Xavian. Indeed, he wore blue livery much like my own and saluted stiffly at seeing me. 'Good morning, sir. Are you ready to meet with the emissaries now?'

'Emissaries?' I echoed weakly.

'Of King Xavian.'

Something of order returned to my thoughts. 'King

Xavian? Has . . . dispatched emissaries to talk to King
Kite, possibly?'

'Exactly, sir,' he said, looking slightly bemused as
junior officers do when their respected commanders are
being particularly slow.

I rose, strapping the sword to my side. Of my staff I
could see no sign and I reasoned that in this madhouse
I'd probably need whatever weapon I could find.

Outside the tent was an army camp. White tents,
bored soldiers in blue, flapping pennants and, directly
ahead, a group of men in red. They bowed stiffly as I
approached, so I returned the formality. Their clothes
were cut in much the same style as my own, and behind
them flapped a red flag on which someone had embroi-
dered a golden crown. They all wore crown brooches.

A tall man whom I took to be their leader spoke. 'Are
you prepared to meet battle here, Warden?'

'Yep,' I said. 'If you tell me where "here" is.'

'This is the place created by minds meeting. This is
where every thought affects reality, insofar that reality
can be said to be real. Are your troops ready to meet
battle?'

This is the place created by minds meeting . . .

'So on one side, trying to affect this world you have
me, using Renna. On the other we have Xavian. Which
side is Miriam on?'

'Are your troops ready?' he repeated.

I looked at the men in blue around me, who nodded
confidently. I shrugged. 'I guess so.'

'Then let battle begin.'

Overhead, there was the sudden roar of cannon. I
looked up but saw nothing except a grey sky full of rain.

Looking back down, I found that the whole army camp had vanished, to be replaced by fields torn up by war until they were just a mess of brown hills. Rain tore down in waves, soaking me to the skin, but my clothes had somehow adjusted to this unpleasant change of circumstance. My sword was hidden beneath a waterproof cloak that some helpful nonentity had fastened about me.

There was a hail of gunfire, and the air around me was suddenly full of bullets. I dived for cover, slipping and scrambling down a muddy slope into a dip where a group of wet and muddy soldiers cowered.

'Whatever happens, sir!' yelled one as I buried my head from the battle above us, 'don't get caught in red's territory! Xavian's out to hunt you down!'

A thought occurred, and my hand flew to my throat. Yes, even through unreality and change, Janyvir's little amulet, or at least a convincing illusion of it, still hung about my neck.

'Where do I find Xavian?' I yelled.

'Everywhere! You and he and Miriam and Renna are one! All you've got to do is disentangle the mess!'

'What side is Miriam on?'

The soldier shrugged, just as a nearby explosion showered us with more mud. I squeezed my eyes shut, and felt something race across my foot. It was a squirrel.

I was standing alone in a pleasant forest. Covered in mud and dripping wet, but otherwise unscathed. I turned in slow circles, dreading that another change might come. This was a world made of four minds, assuming Renna and Miriam were indeed taking an active part in the proceedings rather than just prompting them. With every passing second a part of someone else's mind was seizing control and I was just a leaf being carried along by this tide of thought.

The sooner I find Xavian and end this all, the better. I'm not sure I can cope if a baking summer turns to snowstorm. I wonder how he's managing?

I had no idea of direction, nor of how to find Xavian, so I struck out at random through the forest. Tall pines diluted the light down to a mixture of stray gold and blanket green; in the distance I could hear the sound of a river. *Déjà vu.*

Still alone, I trudged warily through the trees, ready to throw fire at a moment's notice. It felt strange that, in an unreal landscape formed for the purpose of war, such a peaceful scene should have arisen as this sunlit paradise. Birdsong and the buzz of insects were accompanied once or twice by the light thud of hooves from a passing deer, and though I strained my ears for any sound of fighting, I heard none.

Something bit me, a fly of some kind. More annoyed at this irritation than at anything else so far, I turned my hand over and stared at where it had been bitten. Then I rolled my sleeve up. Across my wrist there was still a thin red line, but now it had a twin across my palm. I wouldn't have been at all surprised if Xavian had discovered roughly the same marks singling him out. Doubly reassured now that the link was working and that we were indeed inside each other's head, I picked up my pace again with a lighter heart.

The trees thinned abruptly. I stopped, still in their shadows. Here was the river that I'd heard from farther off; I recognised the sparkling water and the two figures standing by it on the other side. This was part of Miriam's mind, this image.

And there she was. Standing by Xavian's side, her eyes empty, her skin pale and soaked with sweat. I've never seen a real zombie, for the practical reason that they're almost impossible to conjure, but she was the closest I'd come. Xavian was dressed identically to me, save that his clothes were red rather than blue. He grinned triumphantly and pressed a sword into Miriam's unresisting hand.

'You made a mistake, Kite!' he called. 'You tried to turn her against me. But she's still mine!'

Cautiously I waded into the river, sword bared in my hand, ignoring the cold water that rushed round my ankles. Halfway across I stopped.

'There's no way out of here, Xavian. Not for you – you don't know how to escape. I do. I made this place.'

He scowled, and I knew he'd been trying in vain to find a way out of this semi-reality. 'You will tell me,' he warned. 'Have no doubt about that.'

To my surprise, and no doubt his, I actually smiled at the threat. 'Even if I did tell you, it'd avail you nothing. Because if I go down, I take you with me. And if you go down, then it's because of me. And I know how to take you down without harming another soul.' My eyes flickered to Miriam at that – I couldn't help it.

'You're lying!' he spat. 'The only way out of here for either of us is if the other dies!'

I raised my arms. 'Come on then! Let's end it.'

He shook his head, backing off. 'No. I'm not an idiot.'

'So you keep saying.'

'You're the stronger mage – your dreamer, the one

inside you, making you strong, is more powerful than mine. But you – like all your feeble kind – you have a fatal weakness.'

He gestured. Miriam, her face empty, came towards me, lifting her feet high above the water. I watched her, unable to do anything more. Xavian turned on his heel and ran. I began to follow, ready to end his life forever, but Miriam was in the way. I made to move round her, but her sword lashed out towards me in a vicious side-swipe. I yelped and sprang back.

Like a machine she struck again, and I parried clumsily. The parry nearly cost me my wrist – dreams above, she was *strong*.

'Miriam, you mustn't help him! He's evil!'

A child's simplistic version of Xavian, but then she was little more than a child. A slow blink, snakelike. Then she attacked again. The move was clumsy, slow and about as devastating as a tonne of marble falling on a passing pigeon. I parried and the repercussions made me feel wobbly at the knees.

'Miriam! Listen to me. You've got to fight his spells! He's inside you, using you, but you're the stronger! You and I mustn't fight, not now!'

'Miriam.' A calm, cool voice from the riverbank.

Miriam turned slowly. Her face, worse than simple emptiness, now bore the shadow of what had once gone before.

Renna stood on the bank, holding out her hands in entreaty. 'Come with me. Fight the spells. You have no need to die. Not now, not ever.'

Miriam, confused, was turning between Renna and me as though uncertain whom to attack first. Unfortunately

I was nearer. I fell back, literally, my feet slipping on the algae-covered pebbles as I crashed into the riverbed, swiping her blade aside with all my strength.

Renna hadn't moved. *She can't do anything. She's all in me, this is just a projection of her. I can't hurt Miriam, I can't . . .*

'Miriam! Remember your escape route!' Renna called. 'When Xavian leaves you to die, as he eventually will, you have to escape through Kite. How can you escape if you kill your only way out?'

Miriam was shaking. Soaked through, I scrambled to my feet and backed away through the river. She raised the sword into guard position, her teeth gritted.

'Run,' she whispered, ever so softly. 'I can't control it.' The sword drew up and round for the swing. 'Run,' she repeated.

I looked to Renna for counsel, and found the thought formed in my head. <This is a world made of minds. Therefore make it!>

Renna was part of me, yet Renna was a dreamer. This was the false world made in dreamers' heads, controlled by the conflicting interests of Miriam, Xavian, Renna and, in a very small way, me.

As the blade swung, I ducked below, bringing my sword up instinctively to where I expected the blow to form, and dived face-first into the river. It was ankle height when I'd last checked, a thing of clear, cold melt-water.

So I couldn't necessarily expect to find my head covered by warm, blue depths, nor feel my feet pulled down an unknown distance, my heavy, heavy sword weighing in my arms as the water pulled and pushed at me. I struggled, kicking mightily as I found myself submerged and sinking. From above, a sword tip cleaved the water, but even as it did so it faded.

I broke surface at last, spurting water from my nose and mouth. My fingers released the sword as a dead weight, to be dragged spinning into an unknown darkness. I began frantically to tread water, revolving as I did so to see where I was. Of the other three players in my game, there was no sign.

Reeds waved in a gentle breeze. In all the flatland around, there was scarcely the sound of a creature stirring, except for the buzz of insects and the occasional alarm call from some marsh bird forced skyward by a predator swooping on the reeds.

I knew this place, having visited it many a time. The empty marshlands of Northpoint, where a recluse Warden had hit on the perfect scheme for making a safe profit. Have no people in your kingdom, unless allowed in by special permit to harvest the crop of fruits and reeds that grew in no other kingdom. Or if that other person in the kingdom is another Warden, searching for a little company. Yes, I knew this place. This was out of my own mind.

Swimming to the bank I pulled myself out of the water, through reeds which scratched angrily at my hands, arms, knees and face. I coughed up more water, feeling as though half of my internal organs came out as well, and started to feel a bit better.

Thereafter I simply fell back on the bank, staring at the ominous sky, and thanked whatever powers were above for a little peace. Suddenly I didn't feel like fighting for whatever it was I was championing. Miriam was a foolish girl and Renna a manipulating creature who thought that it was all right to use her best friend, and if Xavian wanted to wage futile war he was signing his own death warrant, not mine.

Immediately the obvious objection was there. *Morally.* Morally speaking, Miriam was an innocent caught up in games too big for her. And Renna was right to try and help her, by whatever means she had. And besides! – without Renna's powers inside me I would long ago have been another chalk outline. Morally speaking . . . well, Xavian might have thought he had justification but I, with all my high morals, could see through *that*, couldn't I?

Of course I could. I felt disgusted at myself, unclean.

I'd always believed, deep down in a place which I never let show, that I fought for goodness. But now that I was being lived through by people with their own 'morals', what did I find? That the very principles for which I so fondly claimed to fight were forged of necessity.

My entire life was made of other people's agendas. Other people's morals or lack of them. What little control I pretended to have was nothing more than a knack at bringing the plans of *others* to completion without losing my neck in the process. That was why I'd been dumped in this unreal world. That was why my wrist burned. That was why I was soaking wet, freezing cold, shivering and afraid that, at any world now, this illusion might darken and death would call my name for not the first, but definitely the last, time. Because I had fought for others, without even seeing what I did.

Of all the emotions to have felt at that time, anger was the most potent. It was taught that a mage who gave way to anger would achieve an attack beyond anything, but at the price of fighting while blind to the little needle which slips through his defences and pricks the life from him. I had always avoided achieving strength while being so exposed, because I had seen good mages grow angry, fight, and die in anger.

But now the anger welled up inside me like never before and sparks flew around me as the wind answered my anger and shook the reeds.

'Where are you, Xavian?!' I yelled. 'Where are you?!'

You fool, whispered a voice in my mind. At first I thought it was Renna. But on closer inspection I heard nothing but my own thoughts clicking away with a precision that astounded me. *You are a fool if you think you're just a puppet. You know perfectly well, Laenan Kite, that you could have backed out at any moment. Could have spent your life as a hermit in Stormpoint, could have closed your roads and sealed your borders and been troubled no more. You could have thrown your books away and never touched magic again, growing less and less a mage. You could have been whatever you wanted and you chose –* you *chose, not someone else – you chose to be what you are today. And now you've gotta live with it, Laenan Kite, and feeling sorry for yourself doesn't justify anything.*

The voice was undeniably my own. *Irritating thing*. But I couldn't feel angry any more. I wasn't sure if this made me more angry, but without the heat of the emotion itself to give satisfaction. It's never pleasant when your conscious mind is lectured by your subconscious, and it's even worse when your subconscious is right.

A sound to my right distracted me, and I turned. A

flight of birds erupted out of the reeds a few yards off,
and this would have been all right, were it not that these
particular birds, with their lavish tail feathers and deep
alarm call, were the bright red of a chaotic rainforest.

The same unreal red of Xavian's unreal army.
Suddenly my anger was gone and I was crouching back
in the reeds, and wondering what else I'd disturbed
besides a flock of tropical birds. I didn't understand the
rules of this world, but I wasn't prepared to take risks
either. On hands and knees I began crawling through the
reeds, glancing over their tops to see if anyone else
stirred. The magical wind of my anger was gone and I
was already feeling ashamed of myself, but there was still
a gentle rustling of reeds that was caused by more than
just what little breeze remained.

Then I heard voices.

Five men carrying scythes and deadly three-pronged
pitchforks were wading through the reeds in a line,
sweeping around them in wide arcs to disturb whatever
might be hiding there. At first I thought they were just
another part of this world, almost a piece of scenery, but
then I spotted the red scarf round each one's neck.

Glancing round wildly I made out three more groups
sweeping the reeds. With one of them stood Miriam,
empty-eyed and leaning on her sword. She was wearing
red, but it was a deeper, darker red, almost verging on
purple as though some mad tailor had half dipped it in
blue and then thought better of it. As I watched, it
seemed to oscillate, sometimes darkening to pure purple,
then even a little towards blue, but rapidly returning to
red; lightening, then darkening again.

No sign of Xavian.

I began to crawl deeper into the reeds, hardly daring to breathe. Another flock of birds went skywards, blue this time. The red-scarfed men turned towards them, startled. Blue was my colour. Blue meant help was at hand.

I heard Miriam. 'Keep looking! Ignore them! You find him and they won't be able to fight!'

It wasn't her normal voice. It was deeper, and growled like that of the half-melted construct Xavian had used to convey his messages to me in Haven when he'd realized how tight his situation was. I wondered what would have really happened if I'd agreed to his terms, but immediately stopped myself. The last thing I needed was to start thinking 'what if?'.

One group was almost on top of me. Hell, they were almost all about to flush me out. The nearest were was ten yards away and closing. I braced myself for magic, not sure of the results but determined to try anything.

There was a sudden roar from behind the nearest group. Fifteen men or so – I couldn't tell fast enough – wearing blue scarves sprang up from the reeds and charged, waving their pitchforks and scythes. They showed all the skill of schoolboys on a camping holiday, made up for only slightly by their eagerness to fight.

Immediately all red groups began to rush towards the blue, who were quickly outnumbered. Miriam joined in the fray, wielding her sword with the brutal mindlessness I'd encountered a few minutes before. As the last group of reds rushed past I made a move which, in retrospect, I deny as my own. I'm a practical man, so I cannot tell why, instead of using magic, I suddenly lashed out to trip a passing red before springing onto his back and hammering his head against the ground as hard as I could.

At this, three reds turned towards me. I brought my hands together and then forced them sharply apart again, palms towards my attackers. The men were flung back off their feet, colliding with the fighting mass. I was reassured to find that my favourite weapon was still under my command.

Miriam had turned. The gap left by her was filled by a red. Near her another man went down – what colour, I couldn't tell. I had eyes for nothing but Miriam.

She advanced on me. As she did, so the screams of the dying and the yells of combat faded out to nothing but the beating of my heart. I brought my empty hands up, fire glowing round them. I could turn her to a living flame. I could stop her heart. I could throw her across the marsh at a gesture, breaking her neck. I could summon lightning from the sky, I could . . .

Do none of it. Though she advanced still and though I was ready to repel her, I could not raise my hands against her. There was no bind on me save my own, but that was enough.

'Miriam,' I begged, backing through the reeds, aware that I couldn't back far in this dangerous place. Her red clothes darkened to purple and went back to red in succession, and I knew it was no trick of the light.

'Miriam, I won't fight you.'

I'd come up against the edge of one of the pools, and could go no further. I raised my hands, willing the fire that roared for blood to be extinguished.

'I won't fight you,' I repeated, for this seemed to have

some effect on her, and the purple deepened still further towards blue.

She was within a sword's reach of me, but made no move to kill. Moving with agonising slowness she raised the tip of the blade to the level of my throat, but went no further. Her face was twisted in a bizarre mockery of indecision. My eyes were on the red clothes that garbed her. They were rising almost to a very, very dark blue . . .

With a sudden cry she lunged forwards. So surprised was I by this that I didn't even move. She reversed the sword, bringing the butt crashing into my gut so that I curled up like a rag doll around it and sagged, winded, to my knees. Suddenly I was blind, but the madness of this was discounted when I felt her hands pressed over my eyes.

'Run, damn you,' she hissed. 'Please run, I don't want to kill you . . .'

The darkness was total. Her voice had fallen silent. I still felt the warmth of her hands over my eyes, but also over my chin and hands. With a gasp I shook myself free, and in my struggle nearly knocked over a huge pile of stacked crates which teetered menacingly.

The only thing I had struggled against was a blanket. I ached all over and every nerve was on fire. The only consolation I could find in this was that whatever I was going through, Xavian was probably suffering the same.

'Get up.'

Renna, leaning over me. We were in a dark warehouse which, but for the crates I'd almost knocked over, was entirely empty. Through the rectangular windows that pierced the very top of the walls, flickering orange light shone, as though of a fire outside. There was no other light, but I could see clearly the long metal walkways and staircases that ran around the ceiling and down to the floor.

Painfully I sat up. 'You're judicious about when you turn up.'

'I'm just a projection,' she retorted. 'You know I am. Miriam is only slightly more than a projection, but there's enough of her still independent of Xavian to make her dangerous. I hadn't thought he'd use her as a puppet instead of a source of power to do his dirty work.'

'It's gone wrong, hasn't it?' I asked, sitting up and rubbing my head. 'I got Xavian into this link so that I could separate him from Miriam, but it's gone too far. He's separated out from Miriam as planned, but he's still got enough power over her to use her.' She nodded.

'What must I do?' I asked wearily.

'Kill Xavian. There's no change in that.'

'Even if it means going through Miriam?'

'You can disable her, surely?'

I gave her a corner-of-the-eye look. A father telling his ignorant son that no, money doesn't grow on trees, or something like. 'To think you're the one who's always been out to save Miriam.'

She shrugged. 'I . . . feel not entirely satisfied with the way I've used you, put it like that. Now that we're here, I find the part of me that was human cares for a mortal more than for one of my kind.' She laughed, suddenly unable to meet my eye. 'When I was human, I did love you. I only realized when I lost humanity.'

'This is probably the wrong time to ask this,' I said quietly, 'but is it worth it, being whatever you are?'

She smiled, and there was joy in it. 'Oh yes. In a thousand ways that I can't describe, it is worth it.'

Something thudded in the distance of the warehouse. Our heads snapped round simultaneously. When I looked again, Renna had gone. *Damn*. Even a projection was better than the crushing loneliness of not being certain where you were going or to what end.

There was the faintest pad of a foot falling on hard metal. I pressed myself into a corner, behind a pile of crates and peered upwards. Miriam was there, apparently alone, looking round the warehouse with bright red eyes. Her clothes were blood red, not a hint of blue to be seen. One side of her face was bruised. Had Xavian punished her for letting me go, or did I imagine it? With my thoughts my only companion, even they were so loud, I could almost have been whispering them. She hadn't seen me, but how long was that likely to last?

'Kite,' she called suddenly, and it was distinctly Miriam's voice. I felt like rising and calling out to her, overjoyed at this sign of normality. But the instincts kicked in whose development had taken years of the living daylights being beaten out of me by everyone and anyone. *Don't trust her – she wears red, don't trust her. She is with the enemy.*

'Kite, it's all right,' she called. 'I've fought his spells off. I'm ready to fight with you.'

I began to edge further back into the shadows, my previous joy now suppressed beneath a wave of revulsion. Miriam, the real Miriam, would never fight Xavian, even at the last. I knew that all too well.

'Please, come out,' she begged. 'I want to help you.'

No. I *want to help* you. *You want to discuss life and death at the end of a red-hot poker.*

'I know you're here.' Menace now in her voice – she was aware that her 'cured' ploy had failed, and the growl was returning to her tones. 'You can't hide for ever. Not from me. I'm in you, you're in me, we're all one. This world is made from our minds, and they're jumbled together. I just have to look for you, and there you'll be. Scattered across my own mind.'

She began to descend a flight of metal stairs, the sound ringing across the warehouse and echoing back to where I cowered. I tried to close my eyes, tried to will myself to be in another place. Nothing happened and the pessimist in me wasn't remotely surprised.

She'd reached the bottom. Her voice was now unmistakably Xavian's. Not in sound, but in its words. He was speaking, in some way I didn't understand, through her.

'If you end this now, break the link, Xavian will let your family go,' she was saying. 'Surely you want that? Your precious family, for whom you risked life and limb? Surely you don't want to see them all murdered, every child, every proud father and every weeping mother? Even you wouldn't sacrifice them for your own, false beliefs.'

I said nothing, clenching my fists at my side and trusting in the cover of the crates and darkness, closing my ears to her – his – words.

I will win. Then *there'll be no question of what happens to my family.*

'But of course, they're not even false beliefs. You don't believe anything, do you, Kite?'

Sudden brilliance, and I shied away from it. Xavian was standing on one of the high metal walkways, magelight glowing round his fingers.

'Come out, Kite!' he yelled. 'There's nothing you can

do! You tried your best, forced the game to switch to a dreamer's world but, as you see, I control the dreamer!'

The anger was back. That same rage that gave strength to an attack but made you so blind to your own self that if someone dug a dagger in your gut you'd hardly notice. I could see Xavian clearly, in the mage-light. He looked a mess – where I'd spent a lot of time being soaked to the skin, scorched fragments of clothing suggested that he'd gone through fire. I wondered if time worked in this place, or if that was some illusion that we mere mortals brought with us.

'We're not that different, you and I.' Xavian's voice again. I could feel him probing for me, and blocked his questing mind quickly. He felt my deflection, and smiled.

'Ah,' he breathed. 'So you are there.' His eyes roamed the warehouse and settled on the pile of crates behind which I cowered. I felt the build up of magic and was already running by the time his fireball smashed into them. Debris rained down around me but I had shields up and was moving fast. Miriam turned, raising her sword but for all that she was strong, she was still a puppet of Xavian. Every action of hers was delayed, every reflex just a little slower. I dodged past her and accelerated straight towards Xavian. Fire was already building around my fingers.

'You made a mistake too!' I yelled. 'You've separated yourself from the dreamer so that she can do your dirty work! Now there's nothing to protect you from me!'

My first fireball impacted off his shields and I saw him stagger back, white and shaken with the realization that yes, I meant every word. Xavian was weakened, while I was as strong as before. He began to run, slipping and scrambling on the walkway. I reached a flight of stairs and rushed up it two at a time, throwing magic as I went, sometimes fire, sometimes ice, sometimes those nice invisible spells that latch onto the other's shields, sometimes subtle spells that attack the very blood of the target. Always varying. Never relenting.

Miriam's hand grabbed my ankle as I took another step, and I fell hard. The shock made sparks flash across my eyes, but I was too far gone in a torrent of hatred to notice the pain as my whole body vibrated to the same frequency as the metal. I yanked my ankle free, not caring how strong her grip was. Xavian was getting away, and I was going to follow.

While Miriam lashed out to seize me again I raised my hands, tilting my head back so I could clearly see the walkway above. Magic flared as I tried to pull the walkway towards me. It was a fine balance to achieve – the difference between exerting enough magic to break the walkway or enough magic to bring my own body to the walkway. But my reflexes were refined by Renna, and I got it perfectly. My feet lifted off the stairs and I literally flew the last few metres to the walkway, leaving Miriam below me howling like an animal as her prey got away.

Xavian was at the end of the walkway, having found nowhere else to go. He spun round, and there was fear in his eyes.

How does it feel now, you utter bastard? I thought savagely. Snapping my hand across the edge of the stairway, I summoned a wall of force that Miriam ungracefully walked straight into, to recoil mewing like a kitten. I advanced on Xavian, still keeping one hand behind me to sustain the shield.

'How does it feel?' I hissed. 'To have nowhere to run? How does it feel to be alone? *You bastard.*'

He tried to throw a spell, but I batted it aside without even noticing its nature or formation. 'You arrogant bastard,' I repeated, drawing strength from the sureness of my feelings.

'You can't kill me,' he whimpered. 'We're the same person, you and I. It's just that you chose one path, and I chose the other. We're the same! We walk parallel paths down the same river to the same destination! You can't kill me!'

'I don't care! I'm not you! I could have been – I could have been ten times what you are! But I'm not!' I threw a salvo of spells, which thickened and darkened as they flew through the air, shattering off his shields, forcing him back a step with every impact, at every strike driving a little more light from the bubble of magic that protected him.

'I could have been the greatest necromancer, the most powerful king, the most feared tyrant. I could have had anything I wanted, but no! And now *you* . . .' – another halo of magic, tearing through his shields, slashing and scratching at his weakening defences – '*you* think you can take what I left behind me, that gaping space that just cried out for a real bastard to fill it?'

His lips shaped a word, but no sound came out. At length, I realized what it was. 'Please.'

A combination of facts came to mind at this point. Firstly, I had never imagined seeing Xavian say that. Secondly, there was a light in his eye, and the almost convincing passion of an actor pushing a performance just a little too far. Thirdly, perhaps because of the other two thoughts, I found myself wondering just how far across the walkway I'd extended the shield.

I spun, one hand raised. Miriam's sword froze inches from where it had been about to bury itself in my back. It hummed past the air as she fought to thrust it through the wall of magic I'd thrown in its path.

It was now that Xavian chose this opportunity to pull himself over the railings. Impossible to stop him – I couldn't throw spells at him and keep Miriam's sword away at the same time. He sprang off the edge of the walkway and into the darkness of the warehouse.

I didn't hear his body hit. Which probably meant it hadn't.

Now there was only Miriam to contend with. Bringing both my hands in front of me I shoved with all my magic, sending her staggering back. She snarled and charged. I ducked beneath her stroke and caught her wrist in both of my hands, trying to squeeze and wrench at the same time. She released one hand from her sword, but my sense of triumph at this was short-lived, when she pressed the free hand across my nose and mouth, squeezing the breath from my lungs by sheer physical strength. For such situations I usually summoned a halo of fire, but not now. Though every instinct cried out that I must, Laenan Kite, cowardly Laenan Kite, did not.

By this point I was running painfully short of air and it was taking nearly all the strength of both my hands just holding off her sword arm. Freeing my right hand I dug the elbow hard into her gut, repaying an old debt. She made a little noise and curled up, her grip temporarily relaxing. I freed myself, and rushed to the end of the walkway, springing as quickly as I dared over the railing to balance precariously on the edge.

Miriam had already recovered herself and was barrelling towards me.

'Don't you ever give up?!' I yelled.

She made no answer, which spoke volumes. Closing my eyes, I tried not to look down, prayed to every deity I'd ever neglected, and let go.

I was definitely falling, but after a brief space of what felt more like eternity I was pretty sure that inside the warehouse I should have hit something. Bits of my life had been flashing before my eyes, yes – and, partnered with an overall impression that it hadn't been worth it, there came the realization that we'd gone a fairish way through the story of my life without said existence being terminated.

So I opened my eyes. As if this were a cue for reality to reassert itself, I hit something. I was shaken to the core and my head rang. But at least it wasn't the bone-shattering concussion I'd anticipated. Nor was it the impact of my soul, having said goodbye to my body, hitting the bottom of hell. For one thing I was pretty sure my soul wouldn't have felt this physically battered and exhausted.

Sitting up stiffly, I realized I was bleeding. My knees, from when they'd hit the stairs as Miriam caught me, my head from this latest thump, and my wrist and hand from old wounds. Only trickles, but enough to make my stomach turn and other squeamish parts recoil in shock. I'd be half tempted to say it was my feminine side but that womankind are, as a general rule, a lot better than men at coping with blood.

Blearily, for bleariness was all I could manage by now, I looked around me, expecting another festering nightmare.

The first thing that struck me was the silence. I think I must have been giving my eyes the day off, because the place was in total, unbroken darkness. Nevertheless the most striking feature was the silence. Never had I heard anything as complete, as resounding, as loud. This was the silence of the Void, that threatened to drive sane men mad and where madmen kept their court.

I summoned magelight, wondering if I really had hit something, or if I was still falling and simply hadn't noticed. My senses had already started playing tricks on me, and I imagined I heard the scuttle of crab's claws on marble and saw the leer of a skull from the darkness which, when focused on, turned out to be nothing. Pure and unbroken nothing.

The light fell on a platform, and I felt grateful for at least this small proof that something was real. With light, the illusions of my mind were banished, presenting me with a far, far greater illusion to justify as reality.

Illusion is what I would have called it, for I could think of nothing better. Illuminated by the small circle of light around me, but stretching on further than my little sphere of magic could penetrate, were endless gears. Cogs. Levers. Silent chains wound from one axle to another, driving some unseen motor. The nearest round, toothy cog was at least five times my size, and this was just one of the smaller ones. All around were endless whirring black cogs, ticking away a silent count to eternity.

The sudden, ludicrous urge to yell overtook me, but

when I mustered the guts to deliver a weak, 'hello?' the sound was almost immediately snatched away, leaving me wondering if I'd actually spoken, or if it was just another twisting of my imagination.

And whose mind does this come from? A fruitless question – I already knew the answer. *Renna. This huge, silent machine is the woman I loved. She is what she is because I made her that way. She is a shadow of a human, and so much more besides. And what I call love is some tiny, tiny concept to her, something just about remembered from her childhood life. This love is all that's left of what I can understand.*

I felt safe here, in a way. Exposed to the past, yes, but shielded from whatever the future might hold. Renna would protect me from that uncertainty.

I leaned against the platform, and closed my eyes. Here I could be at rest. Here I could heal, ready for the fight still left unfinished.

How long I stayed in that world, eyes shut benignly and aware of nothing, I do not know. But my awakening was sudden, to say the least.

A cat was mewing at my feet. Black, needless to say. I smiled at the sight of it, once I'd recovered a little of my self-confidence.

'So soon?' I asked. 'Back to just another battle? Just another death? Yes, I suppose that's what must happen. It's . . . *morally* demanded.' I said the word with all the conviction of a fish who's just been told by his leader to swim up that there waterfall, soldier, and be quick about it.

Rising to my feet I looked around the room. It was Sunpoint. I knew it from the heat, from the huge windows facing north, from the sandy dunes rolling away for miles, from the four mud walls around me and the long tapestries that draped the room. And I knew that this was my mind. This was an image from my memory of childhood. I could even hear the children playing in the street.

I was smiling, knowing every inch of this house, knowing where to find what, knowing every grain of sand that pressed against the doorway and every half-hearted brown leaf that struggled for supremacy in the courtyard.

I went into the kitchen. Without question I took up the sling and pouch of small stones that lay on the table. In youth, this had been one of my favourite weapons. Saenia's also. We used to cheat, often without realizing it, but even with the aid of magic we were regarded as good slingers. It was an outdated way of fighting, considering the onset of rifles and the power of mages, but in Sunpoint, here, now, it felt right.

My family didn't even notice me, and I was grateful. Young Brernt was doing what he always did – showing off to his younger brothers in a corner by demonstrating how well he cocked and loaded the family's prize possession – its first rifle.

I ignored him as the simple memory he was, and looked for signs of red and blue. A woman at a sink had a blue bead necklace around her neck. A child wore a blue ribbon in her hair. A man was pulling off his blue head-scarf after a hard day in the fields. Lighter of heart, on my own territory at last, I walked to the door, taking a floppy hat from its hook by the door and pulling it over my head to shield me from the sun, and walked outside. I immediately began to steam – the water from my adventures in the marshes had been drying of its own accord, but now it evaporated fast. Leaving the courtyard, I stepped out into the village where I'd grown up. Watching the sand blow down the street in the so-familiar patterns, I wondered where Xavian was in all of this.

Someone came rushing round a corner. He was wearing blue.

'Xavian's coming!' he yelled. 'The reds are coming!'

I felt a strange gratification in the thought that my family were on my side, even in this unreal world. The response from the village was universal. First came cries of alarm, then the yelling of men and women combined as they rushed to and fro, taking up rifles, slings, forks, swords, spears, then pouring into the street where I stood. Even some of the bolder children joined the gathering ranks of scruffy blues, wielding their pathetic little weapons and trying to stand as tall as their fathers.

I looked at the assembling blues and realized that, in a way, this was not just my memory. This was my fear of what might have happened. A desperate stand by my family against Xavian. My rag-tag, disordered family, maybe even the whole village, against Xavian's might. This was what my mind had created. Only now did I begin to realize how easy memories were to twist, and felt a little better inclined towards Miriam.

I began to act on automatic, striding to the end of the column to begin yelling instructions. They obeyed as if programmed, everyone falling silent to hear what I had to say. Into the houses. Lock the doors. Open the shutters. You can't hope to win by staying in the middle of the street. Hide. Take them by surprise.

And dreams help me, win this war. This is my memory, this is my territory. If Xavian has come for the final reckoning then he's going to find the full force of my past as well as my present predicament, and let's face it, my past is one large predicament, ready to stand in his way.

The blues departed in a heave of bodies, silent and obeying. Doors clicked shut. Windows were flung open but no faces appeared, even though I could feel a hundred watching eyes on me. I heard the jingle of harness, and loaded my sling even as I jogged to a stony outcrop where I'd often played with Saenia. It was just the base of a path that led up a high, red cliff to the plateau where we'd often pretended to be kings of the world. If I remembered rightly the climb was extremely difficult, and at the top you commanded a view over just about everywhere.

The jingling was louder. Even before the first red horse turned the corner I had started to revolve the sling, thumb pressed to forefinger to release one end of it at the perfect moment.

A soldier in red came first. I released the sling and the stone struck him right in the arm. He yelled – those small stones could be remarkably efficient. Ten more guards in red appeared, then Xavian and Miriam themselves. Xavian, not surprisingly, was right at the back of the column, while Miriam galloped straight to the front.

'Don't shoot at Miriam!' I yelled at the empty street. Then, to Xavian, 'This is *my* memory! Here, we play by my games!'

'Get him!' roared Xavian. The guards broke into a gallop, Miriam leading. I turned on my heel and ran, reaching as I had when a boy for all the familiar handholds as I scrambled like an animal up the steep, red path. My feet slipped in the dust and I pulled myself from handhold to handhold in the hill by fingertips alone, but it wasn't as hard as I remembered. Of course, I'd grown a lot since I'd last climbed this. Every hold was ingrained on my mind but, instead of having to stretch and heave as I had in the past, I found it easier now.

Below me, I heard the gunfire begin. *Get Xavian. Kill Xavian*, I thought grimly. This is a world of dangers, and you're on my territory now.

Behind I heard the yell of Miriam as her horse went down, but didn't dare look back to see if I was being followed. There was a whoomph of magical fire and more screams as something exploded, but I was intent on the climb. I was going to get Xavian, that was all I knew. By whatever means necessary, I was going to get him.

There was definitely someone behind me. I could tell by the occasional rushes of breath and the odd clatter of falling stones below me. Already the gunfire seemed distant, but I could hear Xavian yelling, 'Don't waste your time on them! Get Kite!'

This is my territory. How dare you intrude into my mind!

I was at the top, scrambling to my feet, covered with red dust but on the bumpy summit of the cliff. I glanced below me. Miriam was bravely attempting the ascent, but she was a first-time climber. She didn't know where to reach, and kept on slipping as far back as she climbed. I ignored her.

From the edge of the cliff I could see Xavian cowering behind a long wall that separated one field from another while his reds engaged the blues hand-to-hand. He was all alone.

I gave him no warning but raised my shields, drew my hands back and threw everything I had down at him.

He wasn't expecting the attack, his attention occupied with other things. The spell sent him crawling back on his hands and knees, retching from the impact. Nothing stirred in me to see his suffering. I was the executioner, I felt nothing, cared nothing for this monster.

'Join Rinset!' I yelled, hurling more and more spells down from my advantaged position, so fast he didn't have time to retaliate. His face twisted in pain as a frost spell wormed through his almost ruined shields, clinging to his skin and turning it white. Somehow he managed to shake it off, trying to crawl away on his belly from my onslaught.

And I rained down spell after spell. To save dreams, to save nightmare, to save the balance that had been drawn up between the two. To save what others believed in, others who I believed in, for that was the only kind of belief I had left. To save myself. To save Miriam. To kill a monster. To kill the part of Kite that had revelled at the touch of a monster's power when he held Xavian's knife and felt the power in death.

Xavian collapsed, breathing shallowly, his shields a bare flicker. I drew on reserves of power deep within for that final spell – and someone knocked my knees out from beneath me.

Miriam, her clothes now bleached white, neither a hint of red or blue on her, struck. Her fist caught me across the side of my face, sent screams of agony across my back, through my arms. I slipped to the hot rock, hat falling from my face so that I was briefly blinded by the sun.

'Don't hurt him!' she screamed.

No side but her own, now. No appeal.

'Don't hurt him, don't hurt him!' she screamed. She'd raised her sword and it smashed into the dirt next to me, but I'd already rolled. A weak roll, painful and clumsy, but enough to save my life. She brought the sword across but I'd raised my hands. As before, her sword was caught in a fist of power and she could neither release it nor move it. Blood was running down my face, I could hardly breathe and what air I did get in was full of dust. I coughed it up again, my magic faltering ever so slightly at the action, but not giving. We'd reached stalemate. Neither of us could move, not me to retaliate against her, nor her to strike me.

I decided there wasn't any more point. I couldn't move. When had I ever been able to move? Nor could I choose what action I took next, but had to wait on someone else to move. So it had always been. So it would always remain.

I opened my fingers, feeling the magic slip through them like water. Miriam's sword jerked suddenly as the force holding it vanished, and I let my head fall back, expecting at any second to fall asleep forever.

If I ever make any choice, let it be this, I thought. *I just don't care any more.*

But the death-stroke didn't come. Miriam stood over me, trembling, sword pricking my skin, but going no deeper. In the end, having lived my life by other people's choices, it seemed someone else was incapable of making the most important one for me.

I heard a scrambling on stone. Someone very out of breath, coughing. Out of the corner of my eye I glimpsed

Xavian, making the top of the cliff. Below, there was no sound of shooting any more. Nor any cry of victory. Just the still silence of the desert.

Xavian was in a state. I realized with a shock that for torn clothes, bloodied faces, weary eyes and shattered magics he and I were almost identical. Two kings who'd lost the swords that crowned them, entirely dependent now on two fair queens to maintain their thrones. I doubted if Xavian could have lit a match, I'd done such damage to his magic.

'Kill him,' Xavian whispered in a hoarse voice that sounded like it had been rubbed with sandpaper.

'No.'

Renna, standing directly opposite Xavian. 'Kite has done you no harm,' she declared.

'Kill him,' repeated Xavian. 'He is our enemy.'

Our, I thought. There was no feeling in my thought, but flat recognition of a word that, at any other time, would have amused or disgusted me.

Miriam didn't move.

'Kite,' said Renna, desperately. 'You are not defeated. I'm in you. You can keep going, *must*. It's not over.' *When I was human, I did love you. I only realized when I lost humanity.* 'Don't give up on me! Laenan!'

I turned my head ever so slightly, though the edge of the sword grated against my skin and I felt as if my brain would pour out of my ears at the least disturbance.

Renna was standing as I'd always remembered her – alone and brave. One hand rose to her throat, and very gently she pulled something out for my inspection on a piece of string. It was a four-sided silver flower. With razor-sharp edges.

Turning my head back I stared at Miriam. She was crying silently.

You know. You know what I must do and you don't even care. You know.

'Kill him.' Xavian's voice was barely a whisper.

I felt the magic inside me. Felt Renna's power. Felt it flow through me like coldfire, felt a warm stickiness round my burning wrist. Felt the magic mass to a point.

I rolled. Miriam's sword followed the movement but I was already in the heat of a spell. As I rolled I rose, so that my entire body was already several feet above the ground by the time I stopped rolling. As Miriam tried to bring the sword up and round to counter this I sprang, calling Janyvir's little amulet to my hand, feeling it strain at my neck and the chain snap as it flew into my grasp. Felt its razor-sharp edges slice my fingertips, turned one edge outward. Impacted.

Miriam was already a dead weight in my grasp by the time she began to slip to the ground. The blood was everywhere. Who would have thought that such a small weapon could produce so much blood?

I lowered her to the ground even as Xavian screamed his futile rage. He began running towards me, ready to try and strangle the life from his hated enemy. But already I was seeing him for what he was as Miriam lay bleeding, pulling her life back into herself by the act of death.

I was turning. My hands rose up, there was fire in my eyes, fire in my blood, fire in my fingers. I caught him in a grip of fire and held, even though he writhed and screamed in my grasp.

'This is of your making!' I screamed at him. 'You've forced me to become you, and look what I am!'

The fire rose all around him, became one with him. I shoved him with all my might towards the edge of the cliff, willing him with thunder and with flame to be gone from this world, gone from every world.

He fell from my sight, carried over the edge by the force of my magic.

I slipped to my knees next to Miriam, empty and drained.

'This isn't real,' I whispered to her, not even bothering to look back. 'In this place, whatever we believe is real.'

I was healing. Warmth was racing through me, sharp pains retreating to leave only dull aches. I looked down at my wrist, finding it impossible now to tell whose blood was whose. A white mist was wrapped round my fingers. Somewhere in the back of my mind a cat mewed. A clock struck. A silent machine counted the seconds to doomsday.

The darkness was beckoning. Whether the darkness of death or sleep or guilt or loss I couldn't tell. But I welcomed it, whatever it was.

Epilogue

There were eight of us in the bedroom in Haven that morning. Among us, Lisana, all expressionless majesty and folded arms. Janyvir, all weary comprehension of things he didn't want to understand. T'omar. Renna. Saenia. Me.

I will dwell firstly on me, since that's something I can describe with accuracy. On the outside, I was healed. Healed of every bruise, every cut, every shadow under the eye. No sand in my hair, no blood-stained clothes, no hands stained with a murderer's dye. And inside, I was me once more. No marks on my wrist, nor on my hands. I was as complete as the day I was born.

But still little more than a cracked pot smashed on an enemy's head in the night.

Secondly, I will touch on Renna. She wore no expression, and had one arm protectively flung across the shoulders of the third person of interest. Miriam. And it was Miriam who gazed at the silent, sleeping figure in the bed, one hand pink where it had been slashed by a knife, but otherwise intact. Xavian, a body if not a mind, was breathing peacefully, eyes shut.

In this place, whatever we believe is real.

'Tell me.' Janyvir.

'There's not much to tell.'

'Try.'

I glance at Saenia, being the room's only other occupant. Renna and Miriam are gone. Lisana and T'omar are 'discussing things' as they always do whenever there's been a catastrophe or near equivalent and they want someone to blame. Officials who didn't notice this, guards who didn't see that, ways and means by which the whole thing could have spiralled out of control. Saenia nods.

'The place where Miriam died,' I explain as patiently as possible.

'Yes?'

'It's not real. It's an illusion, the whole thing. The blood on her hands, the pain of the attack, the weakness. It's what she believed was supposed to happen when she was stabbed.

'But Miriam's body wasn't hurt, was it? Especially not there. So how could it be real? How could she die that way, unless she believed she was going to die?'

'But she was hurt. She couldn't fight.' Saenia pointed out.

'She thought she was going to die. Once Xavian was gone, Renna left me, broke the link, and showed her otherwise.'

'And Xavian?' asks Janyvir, intently. To him, this kind

of thing is important. Anything to do with justice is significant in his trade.

'Xavian didn't have Renna to assure him of the illusion of the world. Xavian had a body, and he knew it. Therefore when I turned Xavian into a living flame, he believed he was one. And his mind shut down.'

I want to add: *It was the only way to break the spells. Xavian was right – if he died Miriam died. They were too closely tied up. But if Xavian's controlling mind died, leaving the body that sustained the spells intact, then Miriam would survive. Xavian's mind is dead. But consciousness is, after all, just a spark. The machinery still keeps on running.*

But I don't say it all. I've had enough death for one lifetime.

'You know what this means?' Saenia asks as we wander through the gardens of the palace, alone at last. At her side I have to remember not to hobble. Even though I'm unhurt, I still feel a million aches from where I had imagined pain. Lisana is trying her best to say sorry without speaking the hated words. Bottled lightnings have been strung from one end of the garden to the other, and when the sun goes down they'll provide as much white light as the sun gave golden. She's made an attempt at summoning crystal flowers, and I don't have the heart to tell her they aren't really to my taste – sometimes, dear dreamer, dreams can be a little too chic. Even the kite, watching us beadily from the top of a willow tree, was supposed to be for us, although I think it fell a long way short of wit.

'What, big sister?' I feel safe with her, safer than I have for a long time. At long last I feel almost ready to take her on at word games, even though part of me will forever shrink at any play of minds.

'You weren't that heroic, after all. You knew that even if Miriam swung the blade to take your head from the rest of you, you'd survive. The only reason your wrist ever bled was because it was Renna's entrance point, the connection between two worlds. All that stuff about dreamers affecting the physical side of things was bullshit.'

'No, not really. Dreamers create a world that feels real. How much more physical can you get? Physical is what we perceive. If we happen to believe something else, then yippee! But belief is part of the mind.'

'And dreamers affect the physical, but we affect the mental?' she asks softly, quoting a younger Kite from a much younger time.

'Who now the greater power holds?' I murmur, finishing her sentence for her. 'But thank you, I'm not sure that even with all my knowledge and wit and skill I would have been able to cope with the thought of decapitation. It was certainly scary at the time.'

She considers what I've said, and more importantly what I haven't. Finally she reaches a conclusion. 'Nah. You were bluffing. Kite never gives up.'

We walk in silence for a little longer. Without noticing, we've done a circuit of the garden, but now we're going to do another. Finally she speaks. 'Tierne's a good pupil. He'll go far.'

'So long as he goes far in the right direction,' I reply, recalling the necromancer's knife, and the lure of the power, as I had remembered them through every waking moment.

'And Brernt's taking the family back to Sunpoint, now that the Father's dead.'

'Are they burying him there?'

'No. In the Void.'

'How . . . did he die?'

'Peacefully. In his sleep.'

We turn a corner, saying nothing as we start our third circuit arm in arm. There's nothing more that needs to be said.

Rylam returned to Sunpoint. I don't pretend I was pleased with this, since I still regarded him as, if not a madman, then certainly a twat in shiny armour. But Corinna returned with him too, so I guess there's hope. Janyvir was offered a job in the palace, but declined it on the grounds of an allergy to backstabbing loons. (His words, not mine.) Lisana didn't say thank you or offer me any prospect of love, affection, money or holidays. But my hopes hadn't been high anyway.

And me? I gathered up my stuff and headed back to Stormpoint for the three weeks before I would next be summoned back to Haven, to pick up my old job exactly where I'd left off, as if nothing had happened. Miriam and Renna vanished in the night, but sometimes I let my imagination get ahead of itself and they are still there. Sometimes.

Wearily, I went home.